sammy keyes

AND THE night OF skulls

Also by Wendelin Van Draanen

Sammy Keyes and the Hotel Thief
Sammy Keyes and the Skeleton Man
Sammy Keyes and the Sisters of Mercy
Sammy Keyes and the Runaway Elf
Sammy Keyes and the Curse of Moustache Mary
Sammy Keyes and the Hollywood Mummy
Sammy Keyes and the Search for Snake Eyes
Sammy Keyes and the Art of Deception
Sammy Keyes and the Psycho Kitty Queen
Sammy Keyes and the Dead Giveaway
Sammy Keyes and the Wild Things
Sammy Keyes and the Cold Hard Cash
Sammy Keyes and the Wedding Crasher

◆ ◆ ◆

Shredderman: Secret Identity
Shredderman: Attack of the Tagger
Shredderman: Meet the Gecko
Shredderman: Enemy Spy

◆ ◆ ◆

The Gecko & Sticky: Villain's Lair
The Gecko & Sticky: The Greatest Power
The Gecko & Sticky: Sinister Substitute
The Gecko & Sticky: The Power Potion

◆ ◆ ◆

How I Survived Being a Girl
Flipped
Swear to Howdy
Runaway
Confessions of a Serial Kisser
The Running Dream

sammy keyes
AND THE night OF skulls

WENDELIN VAN DRAANEN

ALFRED A. KNOPF
New York

THIS IS A BORZOI BOOK PUBLISHED BY ALFRED A. KNOPF

All rights reserved. Published in the United States by Alfred A. Knopf, an imprint of Random House Children's Books, a division of Random House, Inc., New York.

Knopf, Borzoi Books, and the colophon are registered trademarks of Random House, Inc.

Visit us on the Web! www.randomhouse.com/kids

Educators and librarians, for a variety of teaching tools, visit us at www.randomhouse.com/teachers

Library of Congress Cataloging-in-Publication Data is available upon request.
ISBN 978-0-375-86108-6 (trade)
ISBN 978-0-375-96108-3 (lib. bdg.)
ISBN 978-0-375-89735-1 (ebook)

The text of this book is set in 12-point Galliard.

Printed in the United States of America
October 2011
10 9 8 7 6 5 4 3 2
First Edition

For the dead

Special thanks to Melissa and Bryon Tomlinson at
Marshall-Spoo Sunset Funeral Chapel for answering
my many questions with humor and grace,
and to Michael Marsalek and his crew of merry men
for helping me feel peace among the tombstones.

sammy keyes
AND THE night OF skulls

PROLOGUE

I love Halloween.

And I'm sorry, but trick-or-treating is *not* just for little kids. It's for anyone who likes to dress wacky and tear through neighborhoods in search of free candy.

Which definitely includes me and my friends.

And since last year was sort of a disaster because my friends and I wound up going into the scariest house in town to put out a *fire* and discovered a guy inside all bound and gagged and conked over the *head*, and since we had to deal with police and perpetrators and all of *that*, I swore that this year we were just going to have a fun, carefree Halloween, where the worst thing that would happen was we'd eat too much candy.

But then Billy wanted to cut through the graveyard.

And I made the mistake of going along.

ONE

Hudson Graham may be seventy-three, but he's the coolest old guy you'd ever want to meet. I mean, how many "seniors" will offer up their house to a bunch of teenagers to use as their Halloween headquarters? Most old people zip up their homes, shut off their lights, and hide in a back room until Halloween is over. They don't even hand out candy, let alone lend you stuff to help transform you into scar-faced zombies.

Dressing up as a zombie was new for me. I usually go as the Marsh Monster, with ratty green hair and marshy-looking clothes, but this year Casey and Billy were going trick-or-treating with Marissa and Holly and me, and they wanted to use super creepy makeup and blood capsules and fake scars and stuff, so just painting myself green seemed pretty lame in comparison. And after I jumped on the scar-faced zombie wagon, Marissa and Holly got on board, too.

Our friend Dot didn't want anything to do with our little death brigade. She said she was going to "reprise" her bumblebee costume from last year and take her little sisters trick-or-treating instead, but I think she just didn't want to risk another Halloween like last year.

Anyway, Holly, Marissa, Billy, Casey, and I all met at Hudson's house and had a blast painting and spraying and plastering scars onto each other. It got uuuuuugly! And even uglier when we put in our fake rotten teeth!

"You look hideous, darling!" Billy says to Marissa in a Count Dracula accent.

"And you're revolting!" Marissa says back with a laugh.

Then Hudson comes in with some old, worn flannels and a pair of scissors. "Seems you could use some tatters to go with those faces."

"Are you serious?" Casey asks him.

"Rip away," he says with a laugh.

So we put on the shirts, then we tear and tatter and, you know, *destroy* them, which really does a lot to complete our zombie look.

"Very gruesome," Hudson says as he lets us out. "You look like you're straight from the grave."

Billy hunches over like Quasimodo as we go down the porch steps, then makes a horrifying sound in his throat and says, "Let's go, my pretties!"

So off we go, racing from house to house, collecting candy in our pillowcases, and it doesn't take long for Billy to really start hamming it up.

"Aaaaah," he'd gurgle when someone answered the door. "I think I'm . . . dyyyyyyyying!" Then he'd grab his throat and stagger around, finally collapsing onto the porch. "Caaaaaaandy!" he'd gasp, holding up his sack. "Save me!"

The person who answered the door would always

laugh, then give all of us two or three pieces instead of just one.

"You're the master at this," Casey tells him after about the sixth performance.

"And you, my pretty, are my slave!"

Casey laughs, "Dude, there's no way I'm your pretty."

"My pretty ugly, then!" Billy rasps. "But still my slave."

So we're all laughing and chasing after Billy as he scurries back onto the sidewalk, but we quit laughing quick when we find ourselves doing a domino-style bump-up into a *cop*.

It's pretty shadowy right there, so it takes a second for me to realize that it's not a real cop—it's just a guy in costume. And *then* it hits me that this fake cop is none other than Danny Urbanski.

Now, let's just say that Danny Urbanski doesn't need to dress up for Halloween. Anyone with two eyes can see that he's a snake. Trouble is, Marissa's two eyes don't focus where Danny's concerned. She's had a crush on him *forever*, and even though she knows he's a slithering sneak, she still can't seem to shake him.

"Dude!" Billy says to him. "A cop?"

Danny laughs. "Best way to stay out of trouble, man." He checks us all over. "You, on the other hand, are dead meat!" Then he laughs really hard at his own joke.

I hate the way Danny laughs. It's one of those forced, kind of hacking laughs that sounds like a lawn mower that won't start.

Ha-ha-ha. Ha-ha-ha.

Like he needs a new spark plug.

Anyway, Danny and Casey used to be really good friends, but not anymore. And I think Danny knows that Holly and I aren't exactly his biggest fans, so it was kinda awkward standing there in the middle of the sidewalk. Especially since Marissa was mortified to be looking so drop-dead ugly.

"Hide me!" she whimpers, then slouches behind me and Holly.

But Danny knows that Marissa and I are usually together, so he sort of leans around and says, "Marissa?"

Marissa spits her nasty yellow teeth into her hand and smiles at him. But all those white teeth flashing through warts and scars and peeling skin looks weird.

Like, *extra* creepy.

Danny laughs again. "Hey, beautiful. Wanna be my *ghoul*friend?"

Now, he says this all, you know, *suave*-like, but there's also a hint of sarcasm to it and it's hard to tell—is he making fun of her? Or is he actually saying, You want to hang out with me tonight?

Or maybe this is his snarky way of apologizing for sucking face with that nasty Heather Acosta and flirting with every hot girl who walks by.

With Danny you just can't tell.

Anyway, Marissa obviously doesn't know what to say because she just *stares* until Casey comes to the rescue, asking him, "So who you hangin' with tonight?"

"I'm meeting up with Nick and some of the guys at the haunted house on Feere Street." Then he kinda throws a smirk at the rest of us and says to Casey, "I can't believe you're trick-or-treating, man."

What's totally implied in this is, I can't believe you're hanging out with these *babies*. See, even though we went to the same junior high, Danny and Casey are both freshmen in high school now. Billy would be, too, only he got held back a year, so he's stuck in eighth grade with us.

And I'm sure Casey's at least a *little* embarrassed by Danny's comment, but he doesn't show it. Instead he moves past Danny saying, "Hey, if I'm ever too cool for free candy, I really will be a walking dead man."

Danny lets out another one of his stupid fake laughs, then says, "Whatever, man. I'm heading over to the haunted house," and he takes a few steps before calling over his shoulder, "There'll be people from *high* school there."

So he went one way and we went the other. And even though we tried to act like Officer Urbanski had never crossed our path, he had definitely put a damper on our fun. Oh, Billy did the whole die-on-the-doorstep thing a few more times, but his performance went from great to lame pretty quick, and before you know it we were back to straight trick-or-treating.

And then we got caught in the Invasion of Little People. I don't know if it was the neighborhood or what, but little Luke Skywalkers and ghosts and teddy bears were suddenly everywhere, scampering up and down the walkways, blasting past us or squealing at the sight of five big zombies in their way.

So finally I say what I know everyone else is thinking. "Why don't we go check out the haunted house?"

Everyone's quiet until Holly shrugs and says, "I've heard it's pretty cool."

Marissa nods. "Me too."

Casey shakes his head. "Yeah, but I really *don't* want to go, you know that?"

I grab his arm and give him a deathly smile. "Yes, you do."

Somehow this pushes the reset on Billy's mood. He grabs Casey's other arm and says, "Yes, my pretty ugly, you do!"

So we duck out of that neighborhood and head for Feere Street, and pretty soon we find ourselves on the corner of Stowell and Nightingale waiting for the light to turn green.

"Perfect!" Billy says, pointing across the street. "Bonesville!"

Casey gives him a grin. "The old side, too!"

Now, the Santa Martina Cemetery is big, and is basically divided into two sections—the old and the new. And the whole thing's separated from the rest of the world by a stone wall that's topped with wrought-iron fencing. So it's not like you're actually *next* to graves as you go by, but still, there's no ignoring that there are people buried on the other side of the wall—especially when you're going past the old part. It's hilly and has big gnarled trees, and there's everything from life-sized angels on huge podiums to marble grave markers that look like tall skinny pyramids to the Sunset Crypt—a full-blown mausoleum with Roman pillars and flower urns and a shiny black threshold that says DISTURB NOT THE SLEEP OF DEATH.

The *new* part, on the other hand, was leveled before they started burying people and has only flat grave markers with built-in holes for flowers. Nothing sticks up so a riding mower can drive right over the graves.

When I first found out about the riding mower, it really bothered me. But now I try to think of it as a sort of gentle massage for dead people. I mean, they're six feet under and in a box, right? So they probably barely feel the big ol' lawn mower rumbling around above them. And if they *do,* it's gotta be a pretty quiet, soothing vibration, right?

Anyway, when the light turns green we start to cross Stowell, but jump back quick when a silver minivan looks like it's going to barrel right through the light. It nose-dives to a halt at the last second, and as we cross in front of it Holly says, "Another idiot breaking the law."

At first I don't know what she's talking about, but she's looking at the driver, so I do, too, and what I see is a woman with ruby red hair talking on her cell phone.

"Everybody does that," I tell her.

"Which is why there are so many crazy drivers!"

So we cross the street, and as we walk away from the traffic on Stowell Road and down the cemetery side of Nightingale Lane, we pass by a crooked old gate. It's just a single-person gate and it's got a chain and lock around it, but I know from experience that it's definitely not kid-proof.

Now, I'm not about to mention this little fact, but Billy figures it out for himself. "What are we *thinking?*" he cries. "We're zombies! We need to join our brethren!" and in a flash he's squeezing through the gate.

"No!" Marissa cries. "I do *not* want to go into the graveyard!"

"Uh, why?" Casey asks as he follows Billy. "Are you afraid you'll scare the ghosts?"

"I . . . I just don't!"

"It's a shortcut," Billy singsongs. "It'll save us at least ten minutes."

"Will not!"

Holly steps forward, following Casey and Billy. "Come on, Marissa. It's Halloween. It'll be fun." Then she adds, "You don't believe in ghosts, do you?"

"No, but . . . !" Marissa looks to me for help, and the truth is, I'm kinda torn. I mean, I'm not crazy about the idea, but it *is* Halloween, and we *are* dressed up like zombies, and something about doing it sounds fun.

In a heart-in-your-throat kind of way, but still.

"You're kidding me!" Marissa says, watching me think. "You're going to abandon me? What kind of friend are you? Why are you always dragging me places I don't want to go? Do you remember the last time we took a shortcut? Do you *remember*?"

"Yeah. Through the mall. Nice cool air . . ."

"No! The time before that!"

"Uh, let's see . . . I remember the last time we took a *long* cut. . . ."

"No!" she says, pointing a finger at me. "Don't you *even* bring that up!"

"Bring what up?" Holly asks through the gate. Then she says, "Oh. That you go by—"

"No!" Marissa cries, because there's no way in the

world she wants Casey and Billy to know that she's so obsessed with Danny Urbanski that she takes the long way home from school, just so she can walk past his house.

And she's so desperate to shut us up that she grabs my wrist and before you know it, we're squeezing through the graveyard gate.

TWO

The last time I snuck into the graveyard I got busted by the groundskeeper—a small, dusty guy who hobbled around with a hoe. In my head I'd called him Dusty but his name was really Mike. And when he'd found out that I was looking for a little girl named Elyssa who kept running away, he'd been nice and very helpful. And after I figured out why Elyssa kept coming to the graveyard, I sorta promised him I wouldn't be sneaking through his side gate anymore.

But here I am, sneaking through that same gate, and I'm telling myself that Dusty Mike will never know, but then I see his hoe leaning up against the wall.

I know it's Dusty Mike's, too. It's ancient, with a graceful curve in the neck and a sharp, shiny blade. The handle is also shaped nicely—like a long hickory bat—and is stained almost black in places from being used so much.

I try to blink it away, but it just stands there like a big, wagging finger, telling me, Ah-ah-ah! Sammy, you promised. Now turn back!

I don't turn back, though. Instead I turn away and follow the others into the graveyard.

Now, near the street there's enough light to see where we're going. But the deeper into the graveyard we go, the darker it gets. Plus, the old part of the graveyard is not exactly laid out in a grid. Besides being hilly, there are walkways that wind around, dead-end, or just vanish. One minute you're going along on a strip of ancient cement, the next it's covered in dirt, and then *poof*—it's gone and you're following some little dirt path that leads you to a big, crooked tombstone.

So it's pretty slow going and not feeling like much of a shortcut, and everyone's kinda quiet until Marissa says, "Why would anyone want to be buried, anyway? The whole idea's just gross."

"So you'd rather be cremated?" Holly asks.

"Sizzleleeeeean!" Billy says. "Bad choice, though, 'cause you couldn't come back and bwa-ha-haunt the rest of us!"

I shake my head. "Isn't your soul supposed to leave your body after you die? And it's your soul that haunts, right? So it shouldn't matter if you get buried or cremated."

Marissa shudders. "I don't want to bwa-ha-haunt anybody! I don't want to di-i-ie!"

Holly snorts. "Well, good luck there."

"I'm serious. I hate thinking about death. I hate thinking about . . . all of it! And, as if being gone forever isn't bad enough, I have to decide if I want to get eaten by maggots or turned into ash."

Over his shoulder Casey calls, "So you don't believe in heaven? God? The glorious ever-after?"

"Do *you*?" I ask him, because Casey and I may have

discussed a lot of things, but not God or any glorious ever-after.

"I'd like to," he says, taking a path between two graves. "It sure would beat getting eaten by maggots or turned into ash."

I hurry to catch up to him. "But that happens to you anyway, even if there is a heaven."

Holly says, "Some people think your body goes with you to heaven."

Billy looks back at her. "Then what are all these bodies doing in the graveyard?"

So *I* add, "My grams thinks there's a purgatory. It's someplace you go after you die to pay for your sins."

Holly nods. "Right. It's like hell, only your relatives can pray you out of it and into heaven."

"Whatever," Marissa grumbles. "The point is the thought of death freaks me out and you guys are dragging me through a graveyard full of maggot-infested bodies!"

"They are not maggot-infested," Holly says.

"Yes they are," Marissa snaps. "You just don't want to think about it, that's all."

"Hey, you can get an airtight coffin, did you know that?" I tell her. "No maggots allowed."

Casey leads us around a giant tombstone. "*Or* you can be embalmed and then no bugs'll want to touch you!"

Billy holds up a hand and hops up and down. "Pickle *me*. Pickle *me*."

"Ewww!" Marissa cries.

Casey shrugs. "Well, it keeps you from decomposing. At least for a while."

"So there you go," I say to Marissa. "Get embalmed and get an airtight coffin."

"But I have claustrophobia!"

Holly laughs. "Well, then, I guess burial of any kind is out. No mausoleum for you, either." She points to the Sunset Crypt sort of glowing in the moonlight at the top of the rise ahead of us. "That thing is big!"

Marissa shivers. "Can we *please* change the subject? I know I'm dressed as a walking dead thing, but this is really, *really* creeping me out." She points toward the right. "And if this is supposedly a shortcut, shouldn't we be going that way?"

Casey changes direction a little. "How about a *funny* dead-guy story?"

"Sure," Marissa grumbles. "Anything."

"Let me start by saying it's a *true* funny dead-guy story. And it takes place in the Wild West. In Oklahoma."

"Oklahoma wasn't the Wild West, was it?" Holly asks. "It's in the middle of the country."

Casey glances back. "Yeah, but at one point it was as far west as they'd gotten, and from what I've read it was pretty wild." We follow him single file between two tall, skinny grave monuments as he goes on with the story. "So there was this guy named Elmer McCurdy who turned to a life of crime at the ripe old age of fifteen when he found out that his mother was really his aunt, and his aunt was really his mother."

"Oh, nice," I grumble, because let's just say I have deep-seated parental issues involving secrecy and unknown identities.

15

Casey goes on with the story. "But as fate would have it, Elmer McCurdy was not cut out to be an outlaw. He tried to be feared and he tried to be fearless, but he was neither. He'd jump a train to rob it, but it would be the wrong train. He'd blow up a safe with nitroglycerin, but he'd use too much and melt everything inside it. He was embarrassingly lame at being a criminal."

"The Unlucky Outlaw!" Billy cries, and I add, "The Bumbling Bandit!"

Casey laughs. "Exactly. So of course when there was finally a showdown, he was the one who got killed."

We're following Casey through an area where the trees are extra big, and it's really dark and very creepy, but I'm actually not scared. For one thing, I'm with four other people, but what's really helping all of us forget that we're walking through a spooky old graveyard is the story.

"That's it?" Holly asks. "Boom, he's dead, end of story?"

"Actually, no," Casey says. "This is where it starts getting interesting. It turned out that nobody wanted to pay for Elmer McCurdy's burial."

"Or burning?" Billy asks.

Casey thinks a minute. "I'm not sure they even had cremations in the Wild West. I think everyone got buried."

Marissa edges ahead so she can hear better. "Why not just dig a grave and be done with it?"

"Because it's a lot of work to dig out six feet of dirt."

I kind of half-trip on a tree root, then catch myself. "So what'd they do?"

"They pumped him full of arsenic—"

"Arsenic!?" the rest of us cry.

Casey laughs. "Well, yeah, arsenic will kill you, but he was already dead, right? Arsenic is what they used to embalm him. And the undertaker must've thought it would take a while for a relative to claim him because he used a *lot* of arsenic. Like, hundreds of times more than usual. Then he left him on a marble slab and waited for someone to come get him."

"And did they?" Holly asks.

"Nope. And after a while the undertaker got sick of him hogging up the marble slab, so he stood him in a corner."

Billy dodges around a big white cross. "He could stand by himself because he was all stiff from rigor mortis?"

"Exactly. And pretty soon word got around that for a nickel you could see Outlaw McCurdy in his shoot-out clothes. He stood in that corner for five years."

All of us go, "Five years!" and Billy adds, "Beats my time-out record." Then he laughs, "But barely!"

We're walking behind the cemetery's Garden of Repose now, which is just a little plaza with benches and a small pond that is surrounded by willow trees. Nobody's in the mood to "repose" though. We're just following Casey like he's the graveyard's very own Pied Piper as he goes on with his outlaw story.

"Then one day two relatives of Elmer's showed up saying they wanted to give their uncle a proper burial. So they paid for him and took him away, only they weren't actually relatives. They were carnival owners."

Billy laughs. "They wanted the Unlucky Outlaw as a sideshow?"

"Exactly. And for the next who-knows-how-many years, Elmer McCurdy traveled from town to town, until eventually they had to coat his body with wax to keep him from falling apart."

Marissa is so into this story that she's grabbing onto tombstones to steady herself as she tries to close in on Casey. "So . . . he became a waxed-over corpse in a traveling freak show? For how long?"

"For years and years and years. *Decades.* He finally wound up as part of a sideshow in an amusement park in California, but at that point people had forgotten where he'd come from—they all thought he was just a wax figure. But then a television studio rented him to use in a TV show, and while they were filming, his *arm* broke off."

Marissa gasps. "It just broke off?"

"Yup. And in one whiff they knew there was a corpse inside."

"So . . . what did they do with him?" Holly asks.

"That Wild West town in Oklahoma decided they wanted him back, and finally buried him." Casey laughs. "Being a celebrity has its rewards, I guess. Before he was just a bumbling bandit. Now they give tours of his gravesite."

"Well, that's ironic," Holly says. "First nobody wanted him, and now total strangers go visit him."

"That's another thing about graveyards," Marissa says. "If you're not some notorious outlaw or a celebrity or something, who visits you? When the people who knew you are gone, who comes to see you? Nobody! You're just stuck in the ground until the end of time, alone."

"Wow," I tell her, "that's a cheerful thought."

"We're in a *graveyard*! There are *dead* people all . . . all *under* us. What do you expect!"

Billy leapfrogs over a headstone. "Good thing we showed up then, huh? Doing our civic duty for all the lonely bones."

"They're not just lonely!" Marissa cries. "They're *forgotten*."

She's getting herself all worked up again, so I put a hand on her shoulder and say, "Hey, it's okay, don't freak out."

"I really, really hate death," she whimpers.

I grin at her. "So why'd you drag me in here?"

"What?"

Our little argument gets cut short because just then Casey stops dead in his tracks.

"Whoa," Billy says, pulling up right beside him.

So the rest of us stop, too, and that's when I see something running across graves in the new section.

"Is that a *person*?" Holly whispers.

Billy's voice comes out all hoarse when he says, "That's no person. That's a *beast*."

In the clouded moonlight it *looks* like a beast, too. It has weird wings that are half-flapping at its side and, even though it's moving fast, it's sort of hunched over and hobbling, like one leg is longer than the other.

Then Marissa chokes out, "Oh my God!" because the Beast has turned and there's no doubt about it—it's coming our way.

"Hide!" Casey says. So we all take cover behind different tombstones.

"I don't want to die," Marissa whimpers.

"Shh!" I tell her. "You're not gonna die."

"And I really, really, *really* don't want to die in a grave-yard! It would be so wrong to die in a graveyard."

"Shhh!"

"I mean it!" she whispers. "It's like showing up early for your own death!"

I peek around the tombstone and that's when I see that the Beast is being chased by a man.

A *big* man.

One who's wearing a ball cap and carrying a shovel.

So everyone peeks around their tombstone, watching the Beast as it runs out of the new section toward the old.

"That thing is coming to get us," Billy says.

"Shh!" I tell him, but it's too late—Marissa's totally freaking out. "Ohmygod, ohmygod, ohmygod!" she pants like she's about to die.

We watch the Beast get closer.

And closer.

My heart is beating like crazy and my whole body feels tense and twitchy. Like it's a fuse sparking and sputtering toward a bomb. And since the Beast is coming straight for us, we finally quit looking and cower behind our tomb-stones and hold our breath.

The footsteps get louder.

Then there's heavy breathing.

And all at once there it is.

Right above us.

The Beast.

THREE

Out of reflex I sort of jump and I go, "Aaagh!" And I guess Casey thought I was trying to scare the Beast off because he does the same thing, only on purpose.

And then Holly does it, too.

Since our eyes are already bugged out and we look like death in our makeup and tatters, the Beast must have thought we'd just risen from the graves we were on, because he backpedals like mad to get away from us.

And then he stumbles over Billy.

"Aaaah!" he cries, and when Billy lunges at him, he stumbles again, and this time the woven sack he's carrying flies out of his hand and drops in Billy's lap.

That's when I finally realize that the Beast is not a beast at all. It's a guy wearing a zarape—you know, one of those Mexican poncho-type things?

So, ding-dong!

Trick-or-treat!

I feel like such an idiot. Why hadn't I thought of that before?

But El Zarape doesn't seem to get that *we're* trick-or-treaters, and when he realizes that there are *five* of us ugly, warty creatures hanging out on graves and hears the guy who's been chasing him call, "I know you're in there, punk!" he does what any sensible trick-or-treater who's been chased through a graveyard into a pack of zombies would do.

He abandons his candy sack and takes off running.

Now, it's pretty obvious that it would be bad news if Shovel Man found *us*. I mean, what kind of man chases a trick-or-treater through a graveyard with a *shovel*?

So we hide behind our tombstones holding our breath, and when Shovel Man doesn't show up after a few minutes, we finally get brave and peek.

"There he is," Casey whispers, and we can see him skirting the edge of the old section, searching for El Zarape as he moves farther and farther away.

"It looks like he's afraid to come into this part," I whisper back.

"Smart guy," Marissa says, and her teeth are chattering so bad she can barely talk. "Can we *please* get out of here?"

So we get up and start moving along the border of the old section, staying far enough back so we can duck behind gravestones again if we have to hide. I keep looking over my shoulder for signs of Shovel Man or El Zarape, and finally I ask, "What do you think El Zarape did?"

Everyone turns and looks at me. "El Zarape?"

"You know, the guy in costume? The one who lost his candy bag?"

Billy holds the woven bag up. "If I see him, I'll give it back."

Casey snorts. "*Sure* you will."

"Dude, I'm serious. I'm no sugar-lootin' ghoul. I'm a good ghoul!"

Casey chuckles, and then he starts singing,

"He's a good ghoul, loves his mama . . ."

And Billy chimes in louder with,

"Yeah, I'm free! Free fallin'!"

"Are you guys crazy?" Marissa says. "Do you *want* that guy with the shovel to hear you?"

"He won't hear us," Billy says. "He's long gone."

"What song was that?" I ask, because it was pretty obvious they weren't just making it up.

Holly turns to me. "'Free Fallin',' Tom Petty."

Casey nods. "Also covered by both John Mayer and The Almost."

Marissa and I give each other a never-heard-of-it shrug, but very quietly Holly says, "My mom used to sing it."

So now Marissa and I look at each other like, *Oh, maaaaan,* because to make a long, sad story short, Holly's real mom is dead and Holly has no idea if she's buried, or cremated, or what happened to her because Holly and her mom were homeless and her mom was a junkie, and when Holly was, like, ten, she found her mother dead from an overdose. And since Holly was just a kid with no relatives and no money, she wound up in foster care.

Anyway, the point is, I know it really bothers Holly that

she doesn't know what happened to her mom's body, and all of a sudden I'm feeling awful for Holly. I mean, maybe nobody visits these graves we're walking by anymore, but at least at one point someone cared enough to bury them and put up a grave marker, right?

Thankfully Holly seems to be thinking nice thoughts about her mother because she gives a little smile and says, "But when my mom sang it, it wasn't 'ghouls' in the lyrics. It was 'girl.'"

Now I'm hoping Billy won't say anything that's meant to be funny but winds up being hurtful because I don't know how much he knows about Holly and her mom and their awful past. But before he can say anything at all, Marissa changes the subject: "How are we going to get out of here, anyway?"

Casey points across the new section. "I'm thinking we'll make a break for it and climb the fence."

Marissa looks at him, horrified. "You're serious?"

"Sure, why not?"

Now, I knew it wasn't the "make a break for it" part that was the problem. And I knew climbing the wall section of the fence wasn't the problem, either. It was the wrought-iron posts on *top* of the wall section that were the problem.

Specifically the pointy spears at the tippy top of each post.

See, Marissa has a history of getting stuck on fences that *don't* have spears, so I didn't even want to picture what might happen on one that did.

"Trust me," I tell Casey. "You do not want Marissa to climb the fence."

"Is there another gate?" Holly asks. "You know, like the one we came through?"

"There's a bigger one on Battles Road," I tell her, "but it's newer and you probably can't squeeze through it. And it's got those spears on top, too."

"So then what was the plan?" Holly asks Billy. "I figured you knew an actual shortcut."

Billy shrugs. "My plan was to commune with my brethren," he says with a goofy grin.

Just then Marissa does a double take over her shoulder and points to the new section. "Is that a car?"

We stop and look, and sure enough, there's an old sedan driving through the graveyard.

Now, another difference between the old section and the new is that the new part has skinny little asphalt roads. There's the main one that hearses use when they come through the big gate on College Street. It winds past the cemetery office, then goes out to another drive-through gate on Battles Road. But off that main road are skinnier asphalt paths that weave in and out and all around the new section.

Maybe for drive-by visits to the dearly departed?

Don't ask me.

Anyway, we watch as the car moves along. It seems to be in a hurry and its headlights are shining straight at the Battles Road gate.

"It's going to go out that gate!" Marissa cries. "Come on!"

I chase after her. "Wait! What if the person driving the car is Shovel Man?"

They all look at me. "Shovel Man?"

"You know! The mad guy with the shovel!"

Billy shoots a fist into the air and goes, "Shovel Man to the rescue!"

Casey throws Billy a grin. "You will dig him, man."

"He will unearth even the deepest plots . . ."

"The dirtiest deeds . . ."

"He will *bury . . . filthy . . . fiends!*"

They slap five on each other and laugh, and we just shake our heads. Then Holly says, "Well, if it's Shovel Man in that car, why was he chasing El Zarape on foot? Why didn't he drive his car?"

Marissa's like a caged animal. "Right! And since there's a gate about to open over *there*"— she points ahead of us— "and there's an angry guy with a shovel and a freaked-out trick-or-treater somewhere over *there*"—she points behind us—"I say we make a break for it!"

The gate the car is heading for matches the fencing on top of the stone wall—black iron posts with pointy spears on top—but the cross braces of the gate would make it pretty easy to climb over. So I say, "How about we just wait for him to drive through and *then* climb the gate?"

Marissa blinks at me. "Like, after it's *closed*?"

"Yeah. The cross braces are—"

"No way!" she snaps. "I would get stuck. I *always* get stuck." She looks at me in disbelief. "You *know* I always get stuck!"

I sigh because she's right—cross braces or not, I could just see her up on top of the gate, stuck. "Fine," I grumble. "We'll make a break for it."

So we all wait and watch as the car stops in front of the gate and a thin man with kinda long black hair gets out.

"See?" Marissa whispers. "It's a different guy!"

We hold still for a minute as the guy walks toward the gate, and when we're sure he's going to open it, Casey says, "Let's go!"

And with that, we *charge*.

FOUR

Casey leads the charge into the new section, with Billy behind him, then me, Holly, and Marissa. We have to dodge fake flowers and little flags sticking out of the built-in vases and also not get tripped up by the empty ones, but it's still way easier than moving through the old section.

So we're flying along when all of a sudden we hit some wooden planks that are just lying in the middle of our path. There are four of them side by side, and they sort of bounce and sag as I run over them, which is bad enough, but then I hear *grrrrr-ruff-ruff-ruff, grrrrr-ruff-ruff-ruff* in the distance, like a pack of dogs is after us, which makes me practically jump out of my skin.

I look over my shoulder toward the old section, but all I can see is darkness. "Hurry!" I call to Marissa 'cause she's fallen behind. "I heard dogs!"

"Dogs?" she and Holly both gasp, then sprint to catch up.

Now, I guess we're so busy making a break for it that we forget how we're dressed. I mean, at that point we're pretty much used to each other being all gnarly and ugly and shredded, but when the guy opening the gate sees us coming at him, he panics. First he jumps back, then real fast he starts closing the gate again, with him on the outside and his car still on the inside.

"Wait!" Casey calls.

But the guy doesn't wait. He leans into the gate like his life depends on it. And since the car is blocking our way out, and since the gate is going to be totally closed in no time, I shout, "Come on!" to the others, then jump on the car's trunk, catapult onto the roof, slide down the windshield onto the hood, and jump to freedom.

Holly's right behind me, then Casey, then Billy with his two sacks, and finally Marissa. Only when Marissa slides down the windshield, her clothes get stuck on a windshield wiper.

"Help!" she cries, so I race back. She's *really* stuck, though, and I wind up bending the wiper to get her loose.

I want to tell the guy Sorry! but the look on his face is scary—somewhere between mad and *savage*. And I can't exactly offer to pay for the damage because what would I pay with?

Candy?

Holly's already taken off, so Casey grabs my hand and Billy grabs Marissa's and we ditch it up the street as fast as we can.

We find Holly waiting for us behind a car about half a block away, and then we tear up to a side street together and hang a right.

Once we round the corner we slow down a little, because at this point we could scatter and escape pretty easily. But then I see that across the street from us, parked near the corner, is that same silver van that almost ran us over when we were crossing Stowell. I know it's the same van because right there in the driver's seat with a phone up to her ear is the ruby-haired lady.

And there's no doubt about it—she's watching us.

I look back at the cemetery gate and realize that she probably saw the whole thing and that she's most likely speed-dialing the cops.

Casey sees her, too, and knows exactly what I'm thinking. "Come on!" he calls to the others and we take off running, zigzagging blocks, going down smaller streets that are away from the main traffic routes.

"We're okay!" I finally pant. And after we're sure we're not being followed, we hang out between some parked cars and a hedge for a while catching our breath.

Billy puts El Zarape's sack inside his pillowcase and says, "I think I dented his roof."

I nod. "And I definitely bent his windshield wiper!"

Marissa pants, "It was old and ugly to begin with. I can't believe *anyone* would *ever* have wanted to buy a deli-mustard car!"

We were rationalizing, of course, but the car *was* ugly. It had a big, flat hood and a big, flat trunk and Marissa was right about the color. Plus it had worn, rusty spots on the hood and the trunk.

"Look," Casey says, "I don't know why we're acting so guilty. It's not like we really did anything wrong."

Marissa drills him with a look. "Ever heard of *trespassing*?"

I sling my arm around her and raise an eyebrow at Casey. "Yeah, man. Ever heard of *trespassing*?" Then I add, "And you know ol' Ruby Red was calling the cops on us. Why would she do that if we weren't doing anything wrong?"

"Ruby Red?" they all say, but they know exactly who I'm talking about.

Holly shakes her head. "Why was she parked there, anyway?"

Casey eyes her. "Probably waiting for her busload of kids to come back from trick-or-treating."

"My mom hates people who do that," Billy says. "Once the vans start dropping off kids in our neighborhood, she just closes up shop."

"Well, whatever," Marissa says. "I'm just glad to be out of that stupid graveyard!" She levels an angry look at Billy. "That was the worst shortcut *ever*."

I laugh. "And that's saying something!"

Billy gives her his best puppy dog face—which looks totally ridiculous on a zombie. "Sorryyyyy," he says, then adds, "At least nobody will recognize us if we run into them after tonight."

"Well, *I'm* sure not going to forget *them*," Holly mutters, "especially that guy at the gate."

"I know, huh?" I say.

Billy cocks his head a little. "What do you mean?"

I look at Holly. "His skin?"

She nods. "And those *teeth*."

Marissa looks back and forth between us. "What do

you mean? I was so freaked out from getting stuck on the wiper that I didn't even look at him."

"His skin was really pale," I tell her.

Holly nods. "*Really* pale."

"And his teeth were kind of . . ." I move my fingers around in front of my mouth, then look to Holly for help.

"Pointy here, and pushed in there," she says, moving her fingers around, too.

"Pointy?" Marissa asks. "Like vampire teeth?"

Holly and I look at each other. Then we both pull a face and say, "Kind of."

"Oh my God!" Marissa gasps. "He was a *vampire*? Oh my *God*."

I roll my eyes. "Oh, Marissa, please. He wasn't a vampire! There's no such thing as vampires!"

"Oh, yeah? Then who was he? And what was he doing there?" She stares at us, her eyes all bugged out. "Seriously! Why else would he be driving around a graveyard in the middle of the night? He's a vampire!"

Casey just shakes his head like he can't believe what he's hearing. "Vampires don't cruise through graveyards in cars. And if they did, they sure wouldn't do it in a rust bucket."

"That's *exactly* what they'd cruise a graveyard in!"

I'm trying not to laugh at her, but it's hard. "You don't think they'd use a hearse?"

"No! A hearse would totally give them away!" She blinks at me like I'm the dumbest person on the planet. "Besides, bodies in hearses are dead, right? What good would that do him?"

"How's that work, anyway?" Holly asks. "Isn't blood blood? Why does it matter if the person's alive?"

I shrug. "They like it warm?"

Holly's still trying to make sense of it. "Well, what if the person has *just* died? It's still warm, right?"

I throw my hands in the air. "If vampires were real, it would all make sense. But they're *not*." I turn to Marissa. "Everything's fine. There's nothing to worry about. He wasn't a vampire. He was just . . . Well, I don't know what he was doing there, but he wasn't a vampire."

Holly nods. "She's right, Marissa. He was probably just an undertaker or something."

I look at Holly. "What *is* an undertaker, anyway? Is that the guy who does the burying?"

Casey shakes his head. "I think the undertaker's the guy who arranges everything. Like at a mortuary?"

"Then what's a mortician?" I ask.

Casey shrugs. "I think it's the same as the undertaker?"

"Okay . . . so maybe the guy with the car was setting up for a burial?"

Marissa squints at me. *"In the middle of the night?"*

I shrug. "Maybe he's a gravedigger? Maybe it's one of those sensitive activities. You know—maybe people don't like to *see* graves being dug? I mean, have *you* ever seen a grave being dug?"

"No! But . . . but . . ." She sputters for a minute, then crosses her arms and practically stomps a foot. "I can't believe you guys dragged me through a graveyard with vampires in it!"

Now, while the rest of us have been trying to talk Marissa

33

down, Billy's been slyly maneuvering behind her. He lifts his arms way high, cranks his eyelids wide, and then zooms in with a big, wide chomp to Marissa's neck.

Marissa's not shy about screaming. Marissa's *never* been shy about screaming. But coming face to face with dangling spiders, or bloodied men in monster masks, or snarling, drooling, snapping dogs, or killer gang guys . . . none of that has *ever* made her scream like Billy's little chomp on the neck.

"AAAAAAAAaaaaaaaaaaaaaaaaaaaaah!" she screamed, and then she saw it was Billy and started *pounding* on him. "Don't you ever, ever, ever, ever, ever, ever, ever, ever, EVER do that again!"

Billy was laughing and hiding behind his arms and his dangling candy sack, but Marissa got in some really solid slugs.

"That was just so *mean*," she says with a pout.

Billy Pratt's a hugger. He hugs everybody. Guys, girls, teachers, dogs . . . That's just the way he is. So when he says, "Billy was a bad, bad boy," and opens his arms for a hug, of course Marissa lets him hug her.

Only as soon as he gets in close, he attacks her neck again, making loud slurping noises, going, "Aaaah! Blood at last, blood at last" in a Transylvanian accent.

Marissa swats him away, but this time she can't help laughing.

At this point we've pretty much relaxed about the Vampire and are back in Halloween mode. So when Holly says, "So are we going over to that haunted house, or what?" everyone else goes, Oh, yeah—*that's* where we were headed, and off we go in search of the haunted house.

Now, when it comes to people in Santa Martina decorating their houses, Halloween is like Christmas. You've got the neighborhoods that get way into it with everybody trying to outdo the guy next door, and then you've got the neighborhoods where it's completely dark—nobody does anything.

People at school had been talking about the haunted house on the end of Feere Street for weeks, but since it was quite a ways from Hudson's, I'd told myself that it was probably not worth going to—that if the goal was to get free candy, we'd be better off racing through neighborhoods where the houses were close together and not too big.

But as we reached the Feere Street cul-de-sac, I changed my mind. For one thing, the road was blocked off and there were big wooden signs on posts with black brushstroke letters reading BEWARE, DEAD END, ENTER AT YOUR OWN RISK, and FEAR STREET, so right away you got the feeling that you weren't just walking down another street. You were *entering* something.

What was sort of messing with the mood, though, was this middle-aged guy standing across the street, shouting into a microphone, his voice blaring through a little speaker. "Jesus said, 'Have ye not read that which was spoken to you by God, saying, I am the God of Abraham, and the God of Isaac, and the God of Jacob? God is not the God of the dead, but of the living.' Turn away! The God of the Bible is the God of the living, not the God of the dead! Do not celebrate rites dedicated to the dead! Serve the true God of Abraham, Isaac, and Jacob, not he who has blinded them!"

"Man, that's annoying," Holly says.

Marissa stares across the street at him. "I can't believe people still think dressing up for Halloween is serving the devil."

"Yeah, whatever," I grumble, and instead of "turning away," we escape the sermon by going down Feere Street.

Right away I notice that there are no cars anywhere— not in the driveways or parked on the curb—not one. What there *are* lots of are skeletons and tombstones and witches and ghosts.

Purple lights and orange lights and *black* lights.

Dry ice smoking away behind bushes and in cauldrons!

Jack-o'-lanterns and hissing cats and red-eyed mummies!

And spiderwebs.

Spiderwebs *everywhere*.

The farther we go, the darker and creepier it gets. There's a soundtrack for the whole neighborhood, with eerie creaking and cackling noises and random, heart-stopping screeches. I can't tell where it's coming from, because it's just . . . everywhere, and getting louder and louder the deeper into the neighborhood we get.

"This is *awesome*," Marissa whispers, but I notice that she's latching onto Billy's arm.

The whole thing *is* awesome. I feel like a stupid tourist

with my jaw dangling and my eyes sweeping around, taking it all in. "It's even spookier than the real graveyard!"

Marissa shoots me a look. "Not!"

Just then a lightning bolt streaks through the sky in front of us as a loud *crack* shakes the neighborhood.

"Wow!" I gasp, because even though I know it's a light and sound show, it lights up the house at the end of the street.

The haunted house.

"Did you *see* that?" Billy squeals. "Come on!"

So we don't even bother to do any trick-or-treating. We just hurry straight down to the end of the cul-de-sac.

Straight to the haunted house.

And, it turns out, straight into another scary heap of trouble.

FIVE

First I smell the cigarette.

Then I recognize her.

"Oh, brother," I grumble, which is kinda ironic because I happen to be holding hands *with* her brother.

"What's wrong?" Casey asks.

When I get nervous, my hands sweat. I hate it, but that's what they do. And of course seeing Heather always puts me on red alert.

Red alert. Yeah, right. That would be a pretty good pun because that backstabbing, two-faced, conniving witch *has* red hair, but at the moment it isn't showing. At the moment it's buried under the layers of a long black wig.

Unlike the rest of her, which isn't covered by much, let me tell you. She's wearing shiny black boy shorts over black fishnet stockings, and high-heeled black boots. The shirt—if you can call it that—is low cut *and* high cut, ending above her belly button, and has long black bell-shaped sleeves and a pointy red stand-up collar.

So yeah, she's trying to be some sort of she-vampire, but really, she looks like she should be dancing on a pole somewhere.

She's with her wannabe friends, Tenille and Monet, who are trying way too hard to look cool in their vampire capes and three-inch eyelashes, and she's flirting with two older guys dressed up as rockers—silver chains, boots, spiked hair—you know the type.

Anyway, seeing Heather makes me break out in a cold sweat because, even though she's had it in for me for over a year, she's become especially insane toward me since her brother and I got together. And it's bad enough to have sweaty hands on your own, but when you're holding hands with someone else?

That's just *embarrassing*.

So when Casey asks, "What's wrong?" I slip—or more like *slurp*—my hand out of his and wipe it on my tattered shirt. "Your sister's here."

He looks around. "Heather is? Where?"

"Right over there," I whisper, because she's only about twenty feet away, standing off to the side of the dirt drive-way that leads up to the haunted house.

"Where?"

Just then Marissa and Holly grab me and whisper, "Is that *Heather*?"

"*Where?*" Casey asks again, so I nod at the bloodsucker convention and say, "Right *there*. In the fishnets."

Heather turns her head to blow out cigarette smoke, and when she sees us staring and realizes who we are, she freezes. Then Tenille and Monet see us and their faces immediately go, Uh-oh.

For a second it's like time stands still. Then, without flinching a muscle, Heather drops her cigarette.

It's sly.

Controlled.

Like, cigarette? What cigarette?

She doesn't even bother to grind it out with her boot.

Without moving my lips, I ask Casey, "She doesn't know you know she smokes?"

"I *didn't* know."

I want to say, You didn't? Where have you been? but then he says, "And she sure didn't look like that when she left the house."

I kinda shrug. "Uh, neither did you?"

"Yeah, but she was dressed as Red Riding Hood."

"*Heather* was?" Then under my breath I say, "She's more like the Big Bad Wolf."

"And she told Mom she was going to a party at Tenille's house."

Now, I may not believe in vampires, but all of a sudden there's another streak of lightning and crack of thunder, and if eyes could flash red, Heather's did. She marches over and gets right in Casey's face. "If you narc, you are so dead, you hear me?"

Billy laughs. "He's already dead, can't you see that?"

Heather ignores him and tries to stare Casey down, but Casey just shakes his head and holds her gaze. "You're an embarrassment."

"No, *you're* an embarrassment. You're a dweeb and you hang out with dweeby losers."

Their eyes stay locked for another few seconds, and then Casey steps around her and heads over to Heather's little pack of friends.

"Hey!" she calls. "Where are you going?"

But Casey just keeps on walking, and when he gets to her group, he tells the rocker guys, "She's thirteen. You got that? Thirteen."

Their eyelinered eyes bug out and they look at each other like, Whoa. Then one of them says, "Thanks, man," and they both glance at Heather like, We are so out of here, and take off.

"I hate you!" Heather screams in Casey's face. "Stay out of my business! Stay out of my life!"

"I'd like to," he tells her, "but when you see a toxic spill, it's kind of your duty to try and contain it."

"What?" she screeches at him.

"You're toxic, Heather. You need, like, caution tape all around you."

"Yeah? Well you need caution tape all over your mouth!"

Casey just rolls his eyes and walks away.

She grabs him and says, "I'm serious. If you narc, I will kill you!"

Casey stops and turns to face her. And real calmly he says, "You'll kill me. Really."

Heather goes a little shifty-eyed, then snarls, "Narc and find out."

He stares at her a minute, then walks away.

"Do you want to leave?" I whisper, because I don't know if he's mad, or shocked, or embarrassed, or maybe a combination of all of those, but I can tell he's pretty upset.

He shakes his head. "No. Come on. Let's go."

So we start toward the haunted house, and as we're

walking along, Billy says, "It must totally *bite* to have her as a sister," and does his best vampire look.

Casey snorts and says, "Well, it definitely sucks."

Billy laughs. "Dude, we need to get you some garlic."

"And some holy water," Marissa adds, and then Holly says, "And a silver dagger," and I throw in, "And a blowtorch."

"A blowtorch?" Marissa asks me.

"Aren't vampires supposed to be afraid of fire?"

"Oh, yeah," she says like she can't quite believe she forgot this valuable piece of vampire-repelling information. She turns to Casey. "Sammy's right. No little candle is going to keep her back. You need a blowtorch."

"Or maybe just a lock on your door?" I say.

He laughs. "Now *that's* a good idea."

So we head up the driveway and the more distance we put between us and Heather, the better things get—which must be a law of physics or something, because no matter where on earth you are, it's always true.

Plus, there's now lots of decorations to distract us. The dirt driveway we're walking on is horseshoe-shaped—it curves up to the house, then curves back down to the street—and the yard that's on the inside of the horseshoe has awesome decorations. There are classic, arched-top tombstones, full-sized coffins, and giant spiders dangling in massive webs from the branches of a tree.

Between the driveway and the yard there's a white picket fence. It's not a tidy little white picket fence like you're used to thinking of. It's haphazard, with boards nailed on crooked and sideways and upside down. And the KEEP OUT

OR DIE signs inside the fence make it pretty clear you're not supposed to cross the barrier of haphazardness.

Besides coffins and tombstones and giant dangling spiders, there are also tall metal stakes with skulls wobbling on top of them. They're like a little army of laughing heads, and something about them is very creepy. I know it's all fake, but what's making everything seem *alive* is that the air is filled with the sounds of torture. Shrieking and creaking and moaning and groaning and demented laughing.

A shiver goes through me and I mutter, "Why do skulls always look like they're laughing?"

"They do, don't they?" Casey says.

"Yeah. It's like it takes dying to finally get the joke." I look at him. "Which is a weird thought."

I didn't have a chance to think about that weird thought too long, though, because all of a sudden Marissa grabs me. "Did you see that? It moved!"

"What moved?"

She points to one of the coffins. "There!"

Sure enough the lid is creaking back, and after it's open about six inches, a puff of smoke comes out before the lid settles back down. Then a big R.I.P. tombstone a few feet away from the coffin seems to shiver and the section of ground in front of it starts moving. Like something is pushing, pushing, pushing from underground, trying to escape.

"Do you see that?" Marissa gasps, squeezing my arm.

A bone-chilling scream fills the air as a corpse in a noose drops down right in front of us. So of course Marissa lets out a bone-chilling scream of her own, which seems to scare the corpse clear out of its mind because it goes shooting back up, disappearing inside the branches of the tree.

So there we are, trying to recover from all of *that,* when an eerie voice behind us says, "Tarry here and you too will DIE!"

Marissa screams again because the voice is *right* behind us, breathing down our necks. But when we whip around, we see that it's just Billy, and he is totally busting up.

"You brat!" Marissa cries, backhanding him.

He laughs. "You are so jumpy! Even in a *fake* graveyard!"

And yeah, the stuff may be fake, but it's *awesome* fake, and as we walk along I say, "I can't believe someone would do all this and not charge admission."

"They don't charge, *and* they give out candy," Billy says. "I heard last year they gave full-sized Snickers."

A black cat jumps off the lap of an overstuffed mummy that's slouched on a chair on the driveway side of the white picket fence. The mummy's obviously fake, but the cat?

"Is that real?" Holly asks as we watch it run across our path and disappear around the house.

I don't know why, but a little chill runs through me. "It *must* be."

"Great," Marissa mutters. "A black cat just crossed our path."

There's another flash of lightning and crack of thunder, and the light kind of catches in the mummy's eyes. I stop walking and look at it a little better. "Wow," I say, leaning forward. "Those eyes are so—"

"GHAAAAAAAHHHH!" the mummy cries, jolting at me.

"AAAAAAAHHHH!" I cry, jumping back.

The mummy smiles at me. "Gotcha."

I try to swallow my heart and act all cool, but the mummy's right—it got me.

Got me *good*.

Everyone else thinks it's hilarious, of course, and Billy slaps five on the mummy. "Dude, that was classic! She's really hard to get, too!"

Other kids are blasting past us, so the mummy gets back in position and we hurry toward the front porch, which is totally decked out with jack-o'-lanterns and spiderwebs and more laughing skulls. The person handing out candy is a classic-looking old witch with a honkin' nose, warts galore, and long stringy black and gray hair. She holds out a steaming cauldron to us. "Candy, dearie?"

So Billy sticks in his hand, but immediately yanks it out.

"You have to pass through me *eyeballs* for the sweets, dearie," the witch cackles.

Billy gives her the biggest smile. "You guys are awesome!" Then he jabs his hand in and comes up with a full-sized Snickers. "Yes!"

The rest of us do the same, and even though I know they couldn't be real, passing through the layer of gooshy "eyeballs" *is* very creepy—so much so that Marissa almost can't do it.

When we all have our monster bars of candy, we tell the witch, "Thank you!" and follow the painted wooden arrows that say, ESCAPE THIS WAY and FLEE THEE! and THE ONLY WAY OUT!

"That was incredible," Holly says when we're back on

45

Feere Street. But while the rest of us are going on and on about how cool it was, I notice that Casey's quiet and kind of looking around.

"Hey," I tell him, slipping my hand into his. "There's nothing you can do about her."

He just shakes his head and pulls a face like, Whatever. But as we're trick-or-treating our way up Feere Street and back to the barricades, I can tell he's still looking for her.

That it really bothers him.

"So what are you going to do?" I finally ask him.

He shrugs. "Nothing."

"You're not going to tell your mom?"

"Are you kidding? She's probably where Heather gets her cigarettes."

I bite back *And sense of style* and instead say, "Your mom smokes?"

Casey scowls. "Oh, yeah. And you're right—there's nothing I can do about it."

But even though he's acting like he's disgusted and blowing the whole thing off, I can tell he's worried. We're almost to the barricades when he frowns and says, "She is headed for some serious trouble."

And then, like an omen coming true, we see that there are two police cars parked across the street, and that there's a cop talking to a girl in shiny black shorts, fishnet stockings, and long black hair.

"Oh, no!" Casey says, then drops my hand and takes off running.

SIX

It made sense that Casey thought the cop cars had something to do with Heather because a cop *was* talking to her, but by the time Casey gets up to her, the cop has moved on to someone else.

I hang back, but I can still hear Casey ask her, "What happened?"

"Someone shut up the Preacher Man," Heather says, like she's in a little bit of shock.

There's a small mob of trick-or-treaters gathered, and we can see another cop kneeling beside someone lying on the ground. But all we can really see is the back of the cop and the legs of the body.

"Someone *killed* him?" Casey asks.

She shakes her head. "Beat him up." And then it's like the Evil Switch goes *click* inside her brain. She looks at Casey like she's just remembered she hates his guts. "See what happens when you try and tell other people how to run their lives?" She turns to Monet and Tenille. "Let's get out of here."

So they take off, and Casey goes, "Whatever," and we

all move in so we can check out what's going on with the Preacher Man.

Now, from his, uh, *girth,* I should probably have recognized the cop who was stooped down by the Preacher Man. But it's not until an ambulance turns onto the street and the cop stands up that I realize that it's the Ace of Mace.

The Bruiser with a Cruiser.

The Miranda Commanda!

Yup. It's the one and only Officer Borsch.

Actually, he got promoted, so it should be *Sergeant* Borsch, but I don't think I'll ever be able to make the transition.

And apparently I'm not the only one having transition problems, because Officer Borsch looks right at me as he starts commanding everyone, "Back up! All of you! Back up!" but he doesn't seem to recognize me.

"Hey!" I say to him. "What happened?"

"What *needs* to happen," he says, "is that you back up!" *Then* he finally recognizes me. *"Sammy?"* And before I can tell him, Duh, he says, "You look horrible!" Then he adds, "Did *you* see what happened?"

"Why would I be asking you what happened if I saw what happened?"

He stares at me a minute. "Right." The he rolls his eyes and shakes his head. "This has been some night." He snorts. "I hate Halloween."

I look over at the Preacher Man, who's sitting on the curb trying to put his broken glasses back together. "Do you have any idea who beat him up?"

Officer Borsch makes a sucking noise, like he's trying to vacuum some popcorn ball out of a tooth. "He claims a cop clubbed him with a nightstick and stole his P.A. system."

"A *cop* did?"

"Yeah. He couldn't tell me height, weight, age . . . couldn't tell me much of anything."

I eye my friends as I say, "Do you think it might have been someone in, you know, a cop costume?"

Officer Borsch vacuums some more. "He also keeps spouting off about the devil, so he may just be a nutcase."

"But someone obviously beat him up, right?"

Officer Borsch sighs. "Maybe he fell? It's hard to know what to take seriously with someone like this."

So he goes back to shooing away trick-or-treaters, and I exchange looks with Casey and Marissa. And I know we're all thinking the same thing—we have to be. But I'm pretty sure we're on opposite sides of the what-to-do fence, and I'm feeling trapped in very weird territory.

Still. I can't shake the feeling that Danny had something to do with this, so when Holly looks at me, like, I wouldn't be surprised if it was him, I give her a shrug back, like, I know what you mean.

Marissa is watching us and pops off with, "I can't believe you guys are even thinking it was Danny. There's no way he would do something like that!"

I raise a zombie eyebrow at her. "Who said anything about Danny?"

Billy's just tuning in to what was until right now a silent conversation. "You think it was Danny?"

I shrug. "Well, apparently Marissa does."

"I do not!"

"Well *I* wouldn't be surprised," Holly says.

Marissa gives her a hard look. "What did he ever do to you?"

Holly stares right back. "Totally mess with my friend's head."

"And her heart," I grumble.

"That doesn't mean he beat someone up!" Marissa snaps.

Casey nods. "She's right. It doesn't."

So fine. I drop it and so does Holly. And we hang around for a few more minutes, not saying much of anything while the paramedics check out the Preacher Man and clean up some blood on his cheek.

Finally Marissa asks, "Has anyone else had enough?"

Holly nods. "What time is it, anyway?"

"Almost ten," Casey says, looking at his phone.

"You're kidding!" I turn his hand and look at the display. "Wow." And since we were supposed to be back at Hudson's no later than ten, we hurry out of there, and believe me, none of us says, "Hey, let's take a shortcut through the graveyard!"

When we get to Hudson's house, there are two jack-o'-lanterns still lit up, and my favorite old guy is sitting on his porch.

"How was it?" he asks as we pound up the steps.

We all go, "Great!" because what else are we going to say? Uh, we cut through the graveyard and had to pretend like we were coming out of graves because an El Zarape trick-or-treater was being chased by Shovel Man, and we had to escape by catapulting over the Vampire's car and then ran into *Heather*—who was in a real bloodsucking mood—before discovering the Preacher Man had been clubbed by a cop who we think might be Danny Urbanski?

Much easier to just say "Great!"

Anyway, Hudson blows out the jack-o'-lanterns, then holds open the door for us, and after Holly and I call home and get extensions on our curfews, Hudson asks, "Would you like a snack and something to drink? Or are you sick from candy?"

"We haven't even *had* any," I laugh.

Hudson laughs, too. "What kind of teenagers are you?"

"Hungry ones!" Holly says, and she's right. All of a sudden I'm starving.

"Time to loot the loot!" Billy cries. "I'm *gobblin'* mine up!"

"Don't eat too fast," Casey says, "or you might start *coffin*."

They bump fists and the rest of us groan, then we head for the front room and get down to business.

Now, I don't know about you, but the way I check out my Halloween loot is I empty my pillowcase onto the floor. It's *way* better than pawing through a sack or a bag to see what you've got.

But before I dump it, I always take a second to stick my face in the sack and take a long, deep whiff. Maybe sour candy mixed with chocolate mixed with peanut butter mixed with bubblegum creates some kind of magic aroma, I don't know, but nothing in the world smells like a sack full of trick-or-treat candy.

Nothing.

And even though none of us *say* this to the others, we all do the same thing—we sit down on Hudson's living room floor, take a deep whiff of our sacks, then dump the candy onto the floor in front of us.

And while I'm tearing into a Reese's peanut butter cup, I see Billy's pile. "Oh, right! You got double loot!" I say, pointing at El Zarape's sack in the middle of his regular candy. I laugh. "You still going to return it?"

"I would if I could," Billy says with a grin.

Casey smirks. "Yeah, right."

Now, the El Zarape sack may be quite a bit smaller than a pillowcase, but it's pretty obvious that ol' El Zarape had a busy night trick-or-treating because the bag is stuffed.

"You're gonna share, right?" Casey asks.

Billy picks up the sack and starts talking like a pirate. "I may have a scrap or two fer ya, matey! Get yer chum buckets ready!"

Then he dumps over the bag.

But what comes rolling out is definitely not candy.

SEVEN

What came out of the El Zarape sack were two skulls wrapped in worn blue bandannas. They kinda thump-bumped onto the floor, then rolled right out of their head wraps and just lay there, grinning at us.

"Whoa!" Billy says with a great big Billy Pratt smile on his face.

The rest of us just stare until finally Marissa chokes out, "Are those *real*?"

"Real?" Billy laughs. "No way!"

"Are you sure?" Marissa says. "Look at those *teeth*."

They do have teeth.

Long yellow and brown teeth.

A lot are missing, but still. A lot *aren't*.

"Are you kidding me?" Billy says, picking them up. "They look just like those skulls at the haunted house."

"Did those have teeth?" I ask, because I sure didn't remember teeth. Not like these teeth, anyway.

"Sure they did!" Billy says, and then Casey nods like, Yeah, there were teeth.

"So . . . maybe this explains why that guy was chasing

him?" Holly says. "Maybe El Zarape stole those skulls from the haunted house?"

I shake my head. "Those do not look like the skulls we saw at the haunted house." What's also weird about them is that one of them is ashy white and the other is almost brown.

Casey takes the white one from Billy and raps it with his knuckles. "Does that sound real?"

"How should we know?" Marissa snaps. "Personally, I've never knocked on a skull before!"

"Well, here," Billy says, practically sticking his head in her lap. "Knock away!"

"You're a knucklehead, all right," Marissa says, pushing him back. "But I'm serious. What if those are real?"

"Aw, come on. They can't be," Holly says. "And I do think they look like the ones at the haunted house."

"But that's a long way to chase someone for a couple of fake skulls," I tell her. "And why would that guy be chasing him all that way with a *shovel*?"

Billy gives me a perky look. "Because he's Shovel Man!"

I grin and roll my eyes. "Oh, right. I forgot."

"Wait," Holly says to me. "Are you thinking he *dug* them up? *Tonight*?"

But before I can answer, Billy says, "If he dug them up, they'd be full of dirt! Or, uh"—he eyes Marissa—"crypt composting creatures."

I squint at him. "Crypt composting creatures?"

"I'm trying to be sensitive here . . . ," he whispers through gritted teeth. Then he cups a hand on the side of his mouth and leans my way. "You know . . . maggots?"

54

But Marissa hears him anyway. "Eeeeeew!" she squeaks.

"Well, they would be," Billy says. "And these bad boys are clean as a"—he blows down into one of the eye sockets like he's playing a flute—"whistle!"

Holly shrugs. "Billy's right. If they'd just been dug up, they'd be dirty. Besides, who digs up a grave in the middle of the night?"

"That's exactly when you'd dig up a grave! You wouldn't do it in broad daylight!"

"*Two* graves," Casey says.

"But on Halloween?" Holly asks. "When people are notorious for cutting through graveyards?"

But something else isn't making sense to me. "If a body's in a casket, would there even be dirt? I mean, what's the casket for? To keep the dirt and bugs out, right?"

Holly shakes her head. "Then how does the body decompose?"

"Can we *please* change the subject?" Marissa begs.

Casey turns the skull he's holding over and back, and says, "Sure. 'Cause you know what? If you saw this in a store you'd say, Cool skull! It's because they got handed off in a graveyard that we're talking about it."

"Yeah," Billy says, reaching for the skull Casey's holding. "So quit messin' with my head."

Marissa throws him a scowl, but it's not serious. "Very funny."

"Thank you," Billy says proudly as he puts the skulls down in front of him. "Now let's name 'em!"

"Name the *skulls*?" Holly asks.

"That's right! You know, Heckle and Jeckle? Tom and Jerry? Bert and Ernie?"

Casey adds, "Beavis and Butt-Head?" and then everybody starts throwing in names. "Batman and Robin!" "Bonnie and Clyde!" "Calvin and Hobbes!" "Lewis and Clark!"

Then Holly says, "How about Adam and Eve?" and Billy cries, "Scooby and Shaggy!" and Marissa throws in, "Edward and Bella?"

"Ew," Holly and I say, squinting at Marissa.

"Yeah, you're right," she says, looking embarrassed.

I mutter, "How about Grim and Reaper?"

"That's genius!" Billy cries. "Grim and Reaper!"

The darker skull is turned a little sideways in front of Billy and it feels like it's looking at me.

Laughing at me.

I try to ignore the eerie vibe I'm getting from it, but I can't seem to shake it. It's like the skull is letting out an invisible vapor.

Surrounding us.

Absorbing us.

Watching us.

Then all of a sudden there's a *honk, honk* outside and the invisible vapor goes *poof.*

Marissa sighs and says, "That's my mom," which makes me look at the clock and go, "Wow. I've got to go, too!"

So we all start scooping our candy back into our pillowcases, and that's when we hear Hudson's footsteps coming. Real quick Billy puts Grim and Reaper back into the El Zarape sack.

"Did Michael trick-or-treat tonight?" Hudson asks

Marissa because Marissa and her little brother, Mikey, have been living with Hudson on and off for months while their parents try to get out of crisis mode—something that's apparently hard to do when there's a gambling problem involved.

Marissa says, "Yeah. He went with a couple of friends from school."

"Really?" I ask, because until recently Mikey McKenze had no friends.

Marissa grins at me. "He went as Spy Guy."

The rest of us have our candy all put away, but since Billy had to tuck away Grim and Reaper he's still working on packing up. So I lean forward and fling the bandannas toward him. "That one feels *wet*," I tell him after I toss the second one.

Billy doesn't care. He just shoves them both in his sack while Hudson says, "I was really hoping Michael would come by."

Well, just like a wish being granted, Mikey comes busting through the front door, wearing a yellow cape, a black mask, and a black shirt with a big yellow SG on the chest.

"No bad guy too big, no crime too small!" he announces as he punches his fists onto his sides. "Spy Guy can do it all!"

I just bust up, because really, if you knew Mikey, you'd know how unbelievable his recent transformation from whiner to imaginary superhero has been.

Mikey sees Hudson and drops the act long enough to run up and give him a hug, but when Billy says, "Dude! I want that cape!" Mikey's instantly back in character. He flicks the cape back off his shoulder and takes on a deep voice. "Sorry, sir. It's mine." Then he looks at Billy sternly and says, "And if you steal it, I *will* catch you!"

I bust up again, only the fun's cut short because Mrs. McKenze hits the horn again. Marissa grumbles, "If I ever go out with a guy who honks from the curb, my parents had better not gripe about it."

So she and Mikey take off, and pretty soon the rest of us are leaving, too, telling Hudson thanks a million and promising to come by soon.

The four of us had about three blocks to walk together before we had to split up, and we pretty much just goofed around and ate candy. And at one point Billy's going on about Grim and Reaper being alien skulls from Planet Dirt when I interrupt him with, "I saw how fast you put them away when you heard Hudson coming."

"Yeah? Well, that's because I'm the Wise Keeper of Skulls."

"The Wise *Keeper* or Wise *Cracker*?"

"Ha-ha, Sammy-keyesta." Then he adds, "Would *you* want to explain how we got them?"

I think about this a minute. "Uh, no."

"See?"

"So it's not because you think that maybe they *are* real skulls?"

"Would I be naming skulls if I thought they were real? They would already have names!" He pouts a little. "I have great sensitivity for the dead, you know."

I punch him in the arm. "Shut *up*."

"Well, I do!"

I just shake my head and laugh like, Whatever, and drop it.

Now, Casey and I may be "an item," but since nobody else in our group is and we don't want our friends to feel weird around us, we try to act, you know, normal. So when the four of us get to the intersection where the guys have to go one way and we're going another, Casey and I just give each other a hug and a ghoulish smile and say, "See ya!" and off we go.

Well, okay, we throw in a few more waves and stuff as we're crossing the streets, but nothing, you know, *revolting*.

And I guess I'm still in a little bit of a Casey daze, because when Holly says, "You know where Danny lives, right?" I'm like, "Uh-huh," not really paying attention.

"How far off Broadway is it?"

"Five blocks? Maybe more 'cause you have to go—" I stop and look at her. "Why are you asking?"

"I think we ought to go by."

"Go by? Go by and do what?"

She eyes me. "I'd bet you anything he's the one who beat up that preacher guy and stole his stuff. And if I know Danny, he's messing around with it right now, pretending he's some rock star or something."

"You really don't like him, do you."

"Do *you*?"

"No."

"So?"

"So I promised Grams I'd be home before eleven and it's already ten forty-five!"

"And I promised Meg and Vera the same thing. But if we hurry, we can make it."

"There's no way."

"Come on, Sammy. How many times have I gone someplace with you when I really should have gone home?"

I moan, "Oh, man!" Then I frown at her and say, "You sound like Marissa, you know that?"

She grins at me and says, "See what a dangerous influence you are on people?"

I shake my head, because she's right—this is exactly the kind of stuff I always do to her.

"All right, all right! But we've got to *run*."

And that's what we do, all the way to Danny's house.

"This is it?" Holly pants as we get out of the streetlight and work at making ourselves invisible next to the trash cans near the sidewalk.

"Yup."

It's a pretty generic tract house, and every time I've gone past it I've thought that the place looks thirsty. Like the lawn would love to suck up some water, and the walls are dying to soak in some paint.

Still, even though it's a worn, brown paper sack of a house, compared to the one-bedroom apartment I share with Grams and the place above the Pup Parlor where Holly lives with her guardians, it's a sprawling mansion.

There's a car parked in the driveway, and after we've stayed still by the trash cans for a minute, I point past them to the wedge of light that's coming from around the swing-up garage door and whisper, "You want to sneak a peek inside? If there's anyone in there, they won't be able to see us 'cause it's light in there and dark out here."

She nods, so we scurry up alongside the car, hunching low so we're as concealed as possible from anyone going in or out of Danny's front door.

Turns out the front door's not our problem.

The garage door is.

We're about halfway up the driveway when it swings up. And all of a sudden, clear as day, there's Danny and Nick and two other guys we don't know, ducking underneath it as they yak away.

We freeze, and really, I don't know what to do. They may be blind to us right now, but if we turn around and run they'll see us. Especially under the streetlight. And if we stay crouched by the car, their eyes'll adjust and one of them's bound to spot us.

So I look around quick and then do the only thing I can think of.

Dive under the car!

Holly's right behind me, only her candy sack makes a sharp *thwack* as she hits the ground and suddenly the voices stop.

"What was that?" It's Danny's voice, and Holly and I hold our breath as we watch four sets of feet walking by and around the car.

Finally one of the other guys says, "There's nothing out here," and someone else says, "Probably just a cat messin' in your trash."

Then Nick's voice goes, "A cat? Dude, that was God getting ready to wrath on you, man. He knows you're possessed by the devil."

"Shut up," Danny says, but he's laughing.

"Yeah, dude," one of the other guys says. "The wrath of the Lord will befall you and ye shall perish among the sinners and enter into eternal damnation."

Holly and I look at each other like, Can you say stupid? but the guys all think it's hilarious.

And then Danny says, "Who believes that, anyway. What an idiot."

"So where you gonna pawn the mic? And how does that work?"

"There's a dive on Main. You go in, they lowball you, you haggle a little, and you walk out with cash. I'll probably get twenty bucks. No big deal. I do it all the time."

Holly and I look at each other like, Bingo! because we definitely have our answer.

The question now is, what are we going to do about it?

EIGHT

Lucky for us, Danny's friends left pretty quickly after that. And when Danny ducked back inside the garage and closed the door, we gave it a good minute before creeping from underneath the car and hightailing it out of there.

We were careful, keeping quiet and watching for Nick and the other two guys, but we were also in a hurry because of course we were *late*. And since it's hard to whisper *and* run *and* keep an eye out for people, we didn't exactly discuss what we were going to do about Danny.

And the truth is, I didn't know what I wanted to do. Not that I didn't want Danny to be caught or pay for what he'd done—I did. I was just feeling really queasy about being the one to report him. I mean, what was Casey going to think if he found out I'd ratted on someone who used to be his best friend? And what was Marissa going to think?

I needed time to figure out what to do, so when Holly had to turn left at the intersection of Broadway and Main, my plan was to keep on trucking. But Holly stopped me. "Hey, wait! Are you going to call Officer Borsch?"

"Uh, yeah, I guess so."

"Well, when?"

"Probably when Grams can't hear?"

"Why don't you just come over and use the phone downstairs?"

"But I'm already late and I promised—"

"So call your grandmother first." She pulls me along. "Come on. I'll keep Meg and Vera occupied upstairs."

Holly's plan *did* make sense. So I let her drag me to the Pup Parlor, and while she heads upstairs to the apartment to let Meg and Vera know she's home, I go over to the Pup Parlor phone and dial Grams.

"Oh, thank heavens!" she says when she picks up the phone. "I was so worried!"

"Grams, I'm not even that late—"

"But with everything that's been going on?"

I hesitate. "What do you mean? What's been going on?"

"Another person has disappeared! They think it may be a serial killer! And if that weren't frightening enough, an evangelist was beaten and robbed tonight, and there were two gang-related stabbings right near the mall! I called Hudson and he said you left half an hour ago! And I know you go right by the mall! Where there were stabbings!"

I pinch my eyes closed. "Grams, *why* do you watch the news?"

"Because I want to know what's going on in my community!"

I sigh. "Grams, I'm fine. Holly's fine. Everyone's fine. What's *really* going on in your community is that a gazillion kids had an amazing time getting free candy, okay?"

"That evangelist who was beaten up would not agree

with you." She lets out a weary sigh. "What's this world coming to? Who would do such a thing?"

Well, I don't want to get into *that,* so I just say, "Look, I'm going to be at Holly's for a few more minutes and then I'll be home, okay? Nothing to worry about. Everything's fine."

She takes a deep breath. "Okay. I'm glad you're safe. Thank you very much for calling, Samantha. I really appreciate it."

So I click off and then just stare at the phone for a minute.

I know I should call Officer Borsch.

I know it's the right thing to do.

So even though I'm not sure what it's going to wind up costing me, I take a deep breath and dial his cell.

He picks up on the first ring. "Borsch here."

"Uh, I'm calling with an anonymous tip, so don't even say my name, got it?"

He hesitates, then says, "Go on."

"The Preacher Man's stuff is going to be taken to a pawn shop on Main Street tomorrow."

"Which one?"

That throws me. "There's more than one?"

"Make that three."

I think a minute. "Well, east? West? Where?"

"Two near Blosser, one in the five hundred block. West."

"Uh, I'd guess that one."

"The one in the five hundred block?"

"Yeah."

There's a minute of silence and then he says, "That's it? That's all I'm getting?"

"Uh . . ." I scratch my head. "That's not enough?"

Officer Borsch is always gruff. Even when he's being nice, he *sounds* gruff. But when he says, "You're in a tough spot here, aren't you?" he sounds almost gentle.

I let out a little snort. "That's an understatement."

"Well, it may help your conscience to know that Reverend Pritchard has two fractured ribs and a concussion."

"The Preacher Man does?"

"That's right." Then he adds, "It's against the law to attack a man for expressing his beliefs, even if we don't like the way he does it. It's also against the law to rob him. But besides that, it's just *wrong* to do those things."

I want to tell him everything. I'm actually dying to. But there's that whole Casey-and-Marissa thing. So I'm quiet.

Just quiet.

Then over the phone comes, "I understand. You're in a rough spot."

Maybe it's the gentleness of his voice. Maybe it's my conscience. I don't know, but I finally just blurt out Danny's name and address and tell him, "You'll recognize him. He used to be part of our group."

"That's all I need. And don't worry. I have no idea who you are."

I hang up and hold my face in my hands. I feel all tied up in knots. Like I've just done something I'm really going to regret.

"You did the right thing," Holly says.

Her voice is quiet, but I still totally jump. "I didn't

know you were there." I shake my head. "I don't know why I feel like this."

She shrugs. "You don't want Casey to think you're a rat."

"But Danny's a full-on *criminal*. He talks like he's a pro at hocking stolen property, and he gave the Preacher Man two fractured ribs and a concussion."

"Wow."

I shake my head again. "I shouldn't feel like this."

"So don't."

I sigh and say, "I've got to go," then grab my candy sack and head for the door. And as she's letting me out, I ask, "You didn't tell Meg and Vera anything, did you?"

Holly shakes her head. "Vera's asleep and Meg's been waiting up, watching TV in bed. She doesn't even know you're here."

"Okay." Then I step outside and say, "I'll talk to you tomorrow."

She holds the door open and kind of stands half in and half out. "How could you *not* have called, huh?"

"I just feel like I have this secret from Casey now. And Marissa."

"It's the Casey part."

I sigh. "I know."

"It doesn't have to be a secret. You can just tell him."

"But they used to be like *brothers*. What if he thinks I should have told him and given him the chance to have Danny . . . confess, or whatever." I look right at her. "Holly, I called the *cops*."

Now, I'm pretty wrapped up in our conversation, so it's

not like I'm paying attention to the cars going by on Broadway. I mean, there are always cars going up and down Broadway. And even though it's late and traffic's pretty light, it's not like I'd interrupt talking to Holly to watch someone cruising up Broadway.

But out of the corner of my eye I see a car that makes me do a double take.

It's mustard colored.

Deli mustard colored.

And it's got a big, flat hood and a big, flat trunk.

And rust spots.

And the guy driving it has really pale skin.

And kinda long black hair.

I gasp, which makes Holly look, too. And my instinct is to grab her and dive back inside the Pup Parlor, but it's too late.

The Vampire has already seen us.

NINE

Instead of diving back inside the Pup Parlor, I grab Holly by the sleeve and say, "Act like we're trick-or-treating."

"At eleven at night?" Holly chokes out. "This is bad. This is very bad."

"Don't look!" I tell her as we hurry down the sidewalk toward the Heavenly Hotel.

But she looks anyway. "He's doing a U-turn!"

"Is he close enough to see us?"

"Yes!"

"Good," I tell her, then yank open the Heavenly's door.

The Heavenly Hotel always seems to be open. Maybe that's because André, the guy who runs the place, got tired of letting his low-life clients in and out all night. Plus, besides being old and run-down, the Heavenly's not exactly the kind of place to have a buzzer system.

That'd be much too sophisticated.

Not to mention high-tech.

"Hey," André growls when he sees us. "This is a hotel, not a candy shop. Scram!"

"Then why's the light on?" I ask, walking up to the counter.

"Huh?" He clamps his cigar stub between his front teeth and peels his lips back like an angry camel. "Sammy?"

"Hi, André."

"And that's Holly?" he says, bugging his eyes at her a little.

Holly nods. "Hi, André."

He laughs. "You two sure aren't playin' up your good looks tonight."

"Hey, it's the night of the dead," I tell him. "We're keeping with tradition."

André pulls some mint candies from behind the counter. "This is the best I can do, sorry."

"Actually," I tell him as I take a mint, "we're being followed by a creepy-looking guy in an old deli-mustard car—"

"What's a deli-mustard car?" he says, standing up.

"I mean the color."

He starts coming around from behind the counter with a baseball bat, and for a guy who always keeps things to a low growl, he's moving fast.

"Wait!" I call after him, because it looks like he's about to go beat in some windows. "We just want to ditch him. Can we go out the back way? And if he happens to come in looking for us, could you maybe tell him we were just trick-or-treating and went out *that* way?" I say, pointing to a side door.

He stops in his tracks and eyes me suspiciously. "Why would he be comin' in here?"

"I'm not saying he *will*. I'm just saying if he *does*."

An eyebrow arches way up as he lowers the bat. "What have you gotten yourselves into this time?"

I cringe. "Nothing?"

"Yeah, right," he grunts as he goes back behind the counter.

"We're not exactly sure what," Holly says.

I nod. "We were just out trick-or-treating and happened to cut through the graveyard—"

"Just happened to, huh?" André says, rolling his eyes.

"—and we wound up using that guy's car as an escape ramp out of there."

He eyes me. "Because of course that was the only way out, right?"

"It was!" I cringe again. "But we might've dented his roof." I cringe a little harder. "And we definitely bent one of his wipers."

André's back to clamping the cigar between his teeth. "So maybe I should turn you over to him?" But then all of a sudden he says, "Get down!"

His voice is like a shotgun cocking, and believe me, we do what he says, diving for cover behind a display rack of brochures and free papers. We hold our breath and bug our eyes through the rack as the Heavenly's door opens.

A man walks in, but it's not the Vampire.

It's a big man.

Wearing a ball cap.

"Can I help you?" André calls, because the guy's just standing there scoping out the lobby.

"I'm looking for my girls. They're late comin' home. Someone said they saw them trick-or-treating down here. Dressed up as a couple of zombies?"

Now, there are a lot of big men in ball caps in this world,

but the instant we hear his voice Holly and I look at each other like big-eyed mice in a cougar cage. There's no doubt about it—it's Shovel Man.

"Sure," André says. "They were just here. Went out that way. Probably at Maynard's Market by now."

"Thanks, sir."

"No problem."

He's already leaving when André says, "You want to leave a number in case you miss them and I see them walkin' around?"

"Nah. I'm sure I'll find them."

The minute he's gone, André says, "Stay low," then goes across the lobby and does a real sly check of Broadway. After a minute he saunters back to the counter, saying, "Deli mustard is a good description." He crouches beside us. "I get the feelin' that fella's bent about more than his wiper. I don't know what you two did, and I don't want to know. Just get home quick and stay there."

"Can we go out the back?" I ask him. "I know it's fenced in, but I've climbed it before."

"Why am I not surprised." He snorts. "Have at it." And as we scurry out the back door he says, "Good thing you don't look like yourselves or I'd be pretty worried about him trackin' you down. Once you're cleaned up you should be okay."

"For the record," I tell him as we're going outside, "all we did was cut through the graveyard and climb over a car to get out."

He rolls the cigar to the side of his mouth. "Then why's Big Boy there so interested in trackin' you down?"

"I have no idea." Then I turn and tell him, "Thanks, okay? And oh—if you see a guy with black hair and really pale skin—"

"And crazy weird teeth," Holly throws in.

"Right. Don't tell him anything!"

André squints at Holly. "Crazy weird teeth?"

"You'll know if you see them," she says.

He turns his squint on me. "And what makes you think I'd tell anyone anything, huh? Have I ever done that before?"

I shake my head. "Yeah. Right. Sorry. Just a reflex."

"Well, reflex your way outta here. You're hurtin' my ulcer."

"You've got an ulcer?"

"Scram!"

So we scram, all right, through a swamp of monster weeds and trash to the shaky chain-link fence.

"What is Shovel Man doing with the Vampire?" I ask. "And what do they want?"

"I think André's right—it can't be about the windshield wiper."

"Then what?"

"I have no idea." She trips on something and picks herself back up. "What is this place? It's like a big cage of junk."

"I don't know, but let's hurry, okay?" I scurry up the fence. "You've got a key to your back door on you, right?"

"Yeah. Luckily it's the same as the front door." Holly starts climbing up as I work my way down the other side, but when we're at about the same level, she stops and says, "I just thought of something."

"What?" I ask her through the fence.

"The front door's unlocked. It may not even be *shut*."

I stare at her. "But . . . he saw us leave. You don't think he'd just walk in, do you?"

"He might if he didn't buy our act. Did you see the way he was looking around the lobby?"

My skin creeps a little. "Yeah. He was pretty intense."

"And obviously no one's going to cover for us at Maynard's."

"Good point."

We start moving again, and when we're both safely on the other side, we check around, then sneak over to the back door of the Pup Parlor.

"Please don't go home," Holly whispers as she slips the key in. "Call your grandmother and tell her you're spending the night. Vera and Meg are both really heavy sleepers and there's no way I want to be here alone."

I tell her, "Okay," because besides seeing that Holly's scared, I'm also not wild about having to go home. See, I have to sneak up five flights of fire escape stairs to get into my building because I'm not *supposed* to be living with my grams. It's actually, like, a federal offense or something that I am since the Senior Highrise is "government subsidized" and for seniors *only*. So if people find out I'm living there, Grams will be kicked out and she can't exactly afford to live anywhere else. And since sneaking up the fire escape is tricky enough when nobody's on the lookout for you, I sure don't want to risk it now that somebody is.

Anyway, as we step through the Pup Parlor's back door we look around for something to defend ourselves with.

Holly grabs a broom, but all I can find is a toilet plunger. I hoist it like a softball bat and whisper, "Let's go."

We make our way past stacks of towels and pet carriers to the main part of the Pup Parlor, tiptoeing along with our eyes peeled and our ears perked. We don't see anyone, but the front door *is* open a crack.

Holly shuts and locks it, but that's not really making me feel any safer. "What if he's upstairs?" I whisper.

She looks at me all bug-eyed—like she hadn't even considered the possibility. And before I can say, "You want me to call Officer Borsch?" she's racing up the steps.

"Wait!" I whisper, but she's already halfway up. So I chase after her and once we're inside the apartment, she hoists her broom again and I do the same with the plunger, ready to knock the, you know, *intestinal stuffing* out of someone.

And then all of a sudden we hear footsteps coming down the hallway.

Holly yanks me around the corner into the kitchen, and we hold our breath and shake in our shoes as we watch a shadow creep forward across the floor.

It's a big person's shadow.

And there's something in their hand.

Something long.

Raised high.

And my heart practically explodes when I realize what it is.

I mouth, "That's a shovel!"

Now, there's no way I want to take on Shovel Man with a toilet plunger—even with a broom backing me up. So we cower back into the kitchen and I know Holly's thinking what I'm thinking: What if he's already killed Meg and Vera?

And just as I'm looking over my shoulder for a *real* weapon, like a butcher knife or something, Shovel Man pounces.

"AAAAAH!" Holly and I cry.

Only it's not Shovel Man.

It's Meg in a puffy bathrobe holding a vacuum cleaner attachment.

"What are you girls *doing?*" she gasps, holding her heart.

"Uh, we heard a noise?" I tell her.

"So did I!" She looks at Holly. "I thought you said you were going to bed. I thought you were sound asleep!"

"I was planning to but—"

She looks at me, so I tell Meg, "I got scared going home and . . . and I was hoping I could spend the night?"

Meg blinks at us both for a minute, still holding her heart. Finally she says, "Is that all right with your grandmother?"

"Can I call her?"

"You haven't?" She points to the phone in the living room. "Go! Call! Now!"

So while I call Grams and get permission and another mini-lecture about making her worry, Holly brings me a towel, a blanket, and a change of clothes, and Meg goes back to bed.

And while Holly's taking a shower first, I peek through the curtains, down to the traffic on Broadway, wondering if the Vampire and Shovel Man are out there in the Deli-Mustard Car looking for us.

And if they are, *why* they are.

It felt like we were in real trouble.

Way more than we knew.

TEN

It felt great to take a shower and get into some clean pajamas, but I still didn't sleep very well. It wasn't the couch—I'm used to couches. It was because for some reason I kept looking out the window. Kept checking Broadway for the Vampire and Shovel Man and the Deli-Mustard Car.

Which was stupid. I mean, it's not like we'd dented a Mercedes, or *stolen* something.

But still, I kept looking out the window.

Meg and Vera may go to bed early, but they're also always *up* early. Holly says they like to squeeze in a little life before the poodles and schnauzers start showing up for grooming, and I can't blame them. They work really hard, including on Saturdays, and are always busy, sometimes clear to eight at night.

But when you've been up half the night looking for vampires and shovel men and deli-mustard cars, 5:45 is a little early in the morning to rise and shine for biscuits and gravy. And since the family room runs right into the kitchen, there was really no avoiding the noise or the light or the smell.

"Just go sleep on the floor in Holly's room," Meg told

me when she saw me hide my head under a pillow. "You've got young bones, you'll be fine."

So I dragged myself into Holly's room and crashed on the rug. And I did close my eyes and try, but I couldn't get back to sleep. Maybe it was what Meg had said about my bones, or maybe it was just leftover images from Halloween, but I kept picturing myself as a skeleton on Holly's floor.

One with a stupid, laughing skull.

"You awake?" Holly whispers.

I open my eyes, and there she is, looking over the edge of the bed, her little poodle, Lucy, peeking out from under her arm. "Yeah. I can't get back to sleep."

"What a night, huh?"

"No kidding."

"You still worried about those guys finding us?"

I sit up cross-legged. "You know, André's right—even if they do see us, they won't recognize us."

"What I don't get," she says, sitting up, "is what the big deal was."

Now, for as long as I've known Meg and Vera, they've only owned one dog, and that's Lucy. Lucy rarely barks, she doesn't fuss, and the instant Holly walked through the Pup Parlor door, Lucy decided Holly was *her* girl.

Something that can make a big difference to someone who's been living homeless.

Anyhow, Lucy immediately curls up in Holly's lap and cocks her head at me like, Why are you here?

I give her a little scratch on the head and kind of start thinking out loud. "Everyone agrees that trespassing in the graveyard is not that big of a deal. I mean, we didn't hurt anything, right?"

"Right."

"And denting the roof of a rust-bucket car or bending an ancient windshield wiper . . . ?"

She strokes Lucy's fur. "Not worth tracking someone down."

I nod. *"But . . ."*

"But what?" Holly asks, because she can see that the wheels in my head are gaining some traction.

"But we weren't the only ones chased through the graveyard last night."

"El Zarape?"

"Right."

"Didn't we decide that Shovel Man had chased him from the haunted house to get those skulls back?"

I give her a little squint. "Did that ever make sense to you?"

She shakes her head. "Not really."

"Plus if the Vampire and Shovel Man are both roaming through a graveyard at night and then cruising the streets of Santa Martina *together,* they must know each other. And at least one of them must have a key to the graveyard gate."

"Right."

"So I don't think it has anything to do with recovering stolen property from the haunted house."

"Then what?"

"Well, if we've ruled out trespassing, and we've ruled out damages to the Deli Mobile, then I think they're after Billy."

"Billy? Why Billy?"

"Because he's got El Zarape's sack of skulls."

"But why would they . . ." She stops petting Lucy and stares at me as it sinks in.

"First Shovel Man's chasing El Zarape. Why? We don't know. Then the Vampire sees Billy with El Zarape's sack—he must've seen it, right?"

"Right."

"So he tells Shovel Man and now they're looking for *us*." I nod. "They *must* be after the sack."

Holly's looking a little pasty. "But . . . why?"

I eye her. "I think those skulls are real."

She scoops Lucy into a hug. "That would be very . . . disturbing. Why would someone be carrying around skulls?"

We both sit quiet for a minute, and then I say, "Whatever the reason, we need to tell Billy and Casey. It's way too early to call or go tapping on windows, so I'm thinking we should go back to the haunted house and check out the skulls they had there—just so we can compare them to the ones Billy's got. I mean, everyone else thought they looked the same, and I don't want this to be another case of my imagination running wild."

She laughs. "Right. Because we all know how dangerous *that* can be."

I laugh, too. "At least it'll be a place to start."

"Okay, let's do it."

So we make up some excuse about wanting to go for a walk, grab a couple of biscuits and bananas, and hurry downstairs before Meg or Vera starts asking questions. And we're beelining for the front door when all of a sudden both of us stop, look at each other, and, without a word, turn around and go out the back door.

I guess we were both still feeling a little shaky from our close encounter with the Deli-Car Duo.

It was almost seven, so it was light out, but it's not like the sun was blazing overhead or anything. And since the air was pretty chilly, we wound up jogging most of the way to Feere Street, just to get warm.

The street barricades were down, and as we walked to the haunted house we noticed how what had seemed spooky and creepy in the dark was pretty unscary by daylight. But it wasn't until we got to the haunted house that I realized how fake a haunted house it really was. The pointed roof and the whole second story—the dormer windows, the shutters, the shingles—it was all a façade that was now leaning against the porch in sections.

Holly just blinks at it. "It's just a regular house?"

I shake my head. "I can't believe they did all that for one night."

"You girls are up early," a man calls from under the tree where he's collecting the spears and skulls and putting them in a coffin. He's got a puffy black ponytail and is wearing a tool belt, jeans, and a T-shirt. And even though it's still nippy out, he's sweating.

"I can't believe you're tearing this down already," I tell him.

"Hey, yesterday was Halloween," he says as he wipes his brow. "Today is All Saints' Day. And I've got a deal with my lovely wife—she helps me indulge in my obsession

with Halloween, and I make it all disappear the next day."
He snickers. "And then she drags me to church to pray for
the souls of the dearly departed."

I give him a little squint. "You're serious?"

He shrugs and grins and gets back to work. "Call it a
compromise of cultures. She's from Mexico, I'm from
Hollywood. We've been married nearly twenty years, so
I guess you'd say we respect each other's beliefs."

I'm still having a little trouble wrapping my head
around this, so I say, "And you believe . . . ?"

He laughs. "That Halloween's the most righteous hol-
iday ever!"

"But not that you're worshipping the dead or the devil
or . . . or whatever?"

"No! It's just fun. It has nothing to do with worshipping anything."

Then Holly asks, "So . . . were you an actor?"

He shakes his head. "Set builder." He nods at the
façades stacked up against the house. "Loved the work,
hated the biz."

We watch him take down two more spears, and then
I tell him, "We were here last night."

He grins. "I figured that."

"The mummy totally got me."

He seems to get a big kick out of that. "You're not
alone, believe me."

"So . . . are these Hollywood props? I mean, some of
them are really realistic. Like those skulls? Those are
great."

He picks one up and jostles it in his hand like he's

trying to guess its weight. "Love these babies. They're the best money can buy."

"Can I see?"

"Sure," he says, and walks it over.

Holly and I take turns admiring it, and when we hand it back, I tell him, "It's really nice that you do all this. We had a great time last night. It was amazing."

"Why, thank you. I appreciate that."

"I'd worry about people stealing stuff if I were you. I mean, that's a really cool skull. I know a lot of kids who'd want to snag it."

"Nah. Most kids are good." He grins again and says, "The werewolf only had to come out twice last night, and that was for littering." Then he goes, "Ghrrraaaaarghhhh," and jumps at us with one hand up like a claw and the other shaking the skull.

I back up with a laugh. "Anyway, thanks for everything!"

"See you in church!" he calls as we head down the driveway, then snickers like it's the silliest joke ever.

But the instant we're back on the street I turn to Holly and I can tell she's thinking the same thing I am, and there's absolutely nothing funny about it.

We have to find Billy!

ELEVEN

We would have gone straight to Billy's house but we didn't know where he lived or even what his phone number was. Casey did, but to add to the ridiculousness of the situation, we didn't have a cell phone or any money in our pockets to use a pay phone to call Casey and ask him.

I *did* know where Casey lived, though, and although that used to be a ways out of town with his dad, it's now in town with his mother and sister.

A bad situation on all counts except one: We could walk there, no problem.

And I guess because I was so intent on getting to Casey's quick, I didn't even think that we were going to walk past the graveyard, but suddenly there we were.

"Want to take a shortcut?" Holly joked.

I smirked at her. "Very funny."

I didn't really want to go past it, but unless we were going to backtrack, there was no avoiding it. "They say people always return to the scene of the crime, you know."

"Are you talking about us?"

I laugh. "Well, here we are!"

And the truth is, I did feel kinda guilty. About more than sneaking into the graveyard or bending some dilapidated car's windshield wiper.

It was those skulls.

I didn't even *have* them, but I was still dying to get rid of them.

Then Holly says, "Looks like someone's getting buried today," and nods across the street.

Through the gate where we'd scrambled over the Deli Mobile, we can see a pickup truck parked near a big green canopy and a couple of people putting out chairs.

Holly shivers a little. "The whole thing is awful, don't you think?"

"Getting buried?"

She nods. "I'm with Marissa—I get claustrophobic just thinking about it."

"They used to install little bells, did you know that? So if you were buried alive, you could pull on a cord and ring a bell. Or a flag would go up. Something like that."

Holly shivers again, and this time it's a big one. "Can you imagine?"

Then I see that the people in the graveyard are picking something off the ground.

Planks.

Long wooden planks.

I find myself crossing the street to get a closer look.

"What are you doing?" Holly asks, chasing after me.

It comes out all breathy when I say, "Those must be the boards we ran over last night."

"You think?" We watch the men move the planks a few

feet to each side, leaving an opening in the earth. "So we ran over . . ."

She looks at me all bug-eyed, so I finish for her. "An open grave."

We let this sink in a minute, and finally Holly says, "What if those boards hadn't been there?"

"We'd have fallen in and killed ourselves?"

"Wow," she says, staring into the graveyard.

I force a laugh. "Either that or *Marissa* would have killed us!"

We watch as the workers put a couple of cross braces widthwise over the grave, then cover the hole with a big piece of AstroTurf.

"Why the fake grass?" Holly asks.

"Maybe so people don't have to see inside the hole during the service?"

"Yeah, I guess the less you have to think about it, the better."

"No kidding." I grab her. "Let's get out of here."

So we hurry away from the graveyard toward the sanity of regular neighborhoods.

Which just goes to show you how relative things can be.

After all, we were heading for the Acostas' house.

Home of Heather the Horrible.

Now, there was no way I was going to ring the Acostas' doorbell. Aside from not wanting to wake the Wicked Monster, I didn't want to wake her mother.

Candi Acosta is just like Heather, only scarier. Imagine being in a horror movie, fighting off a giant hairy arachnid mutant with all your might, not sure you'll ever be able to land your harpoon in a place that'll keep it from killing you. It's closing in on you with its rancid breath and fangs dripping with blood . . . and then in walks another hairy arachnid mutant that's ten times bigger than the first one.

That's pretty much what it feels like when Candi Acosta comes to her daughter's defense. And since chances were two out of three that a hairy arachnid mutant would answer the door, I was not *about* to knock or ring the bell.

What I did have going for me was that I'd infiltrated Heather's house during a costume party last Halloween and knew which room was hers. I also knew that her mother's bedroom was at the back end of the house, which left me with a pretty good hunch that Casey's room was the first window on the right side of the walkway.

"Ready?" Holly whispers after we'd stood on the sidewalk for a minute.

"Let's do it."

So we tippy-toe up and I do a gentle *ratta-tat-tat* on the window.

Nothing happens.

"Try again," Holly whispers after we've spent a whole minute stupidly staring at the curtain.

So I ratta-tat-tat again.

Still nothing.

So I ratta-tat-tat a little *harder,* and this time the curtain lifts.

Trouble is, the person looking out at us is not Casey.

It's the vicious little arachnid mutant monster.

I duck quick, but it's too late. Heather sees me and

instantly goes from half-asleep to full-on rage. She cusses at us through the glass, then fumbles to open her window so the whole neighborhood can hear her tirade.

Well, I'm not about to wait around for *that*, so I grab Holly and ditch it over to the window that *used* to be Heather's room, thinking that if Heather's sleeping in the first room, then Casey's got to be in Heather's old room.

We get around the house quick and right away I rap on the window loud and fast.

The curtain flies up, only instead of seeing Casey, I'm face to face with Heather again!

I jump back and cry, "Aaaah!" because it feels like there are *two* Heathers in there and something about that totally freaks me out.

She wrestles the window up about six inches and hisses, "Go away! You're trespassing! If you don't leave right now, I'm calling the cops!"

Now, she's not screeching like she was when she yelled at me through her window. It *feels* like she's yelling, but it's really just a whisper, so I know she's trying to get rid of us without waking up Casey, who must be in that room still sleeping. So I just call past her, "Casey! We need your help finding Billy!"

Slam, the window comes down and the curtain drops. And before I can pound on it or call anything through the glass, a *tornado* hits. I swear. The curtain twists and flops, goes up and down, twists some more. The top of a head bobs up, then drops back down. There's more flailing at the curtain like someone's *drowning* in there. And then finally the curtain goes still.

Holly and I just stare at it, then each other, then back at the curtain.

Nothing.

Then all of a sudden the curtain pops open and we're face to face with the world's goofiest grin.

Holly and I go, *"Billy?"*

His hair's sticking out all over the place, and he lifts the window, saying, "Sammy-keyesta and the Hollister! Tryin' to wake the dead!"

"What are you doing here?"

"Had me a sleepover!"

Heather's voice is in the background yelling, "I don't care what you say! Mom says she can't come in! Those are the rules! If you don't like it, *leave.*" There's a short silence and then she yells, "Why would I stay out of your room when your loser girlfriend beats down the window of mine?"

Billy looks over his shoulder, then whispers. "I'd ditch it if I were you. It took both of us to get her out of here and I think she's coming back."

"Look, we don't want to come in, but we really need to talk to you!"

He looks over his shoulder again. "I don't think now's a good time."

"Can you and Casey meet us somewhere? Like Hudson's?"

"When?"

"As soon as you can get there. It's important."

"Okeydokey," he says.

"Oh, and bring the . . . bring Grim and Reaper."

"My buddies!"

"Be sure to bring them, okay?"

"Okeydokey!"

I shake my head a little. "Are you always this cheerful in the morning?"

"Always!" He gives me a goofy grin. "Except when I'm not!"

"Get to Hudson's as quick as you can, okay? And tell Casey I'm sorry. I had no idea Heather had switched rooms."

Then we hustle out of there before Heather can sic Candi on us.

I never feel bad about just dropping in at Hudson's. It's sort of a home away from home. At least his porch is. It's big and airy and a great place to hang out.

But, really, it's Hudson that makes his porch a little harbor in the storm of life. He always takes the time to listen, and he treats me like I'm a friend, not some pesky kid.

I think Hudson's porch is also *Hudson's* favorite place to be because he spends a lot of time there with his boots kicked up on the rail. Usually he's reading the paper or a book, but sometimes he's just watching the world go by.

I like that Hudson still gets a real paper. Maybe it's the big sweep of newsprint as he switches pages. Or the fact that he can pull a section out and hand it to me. It's very . . . Zen—like we're sharing a moment of enlightenment.

Although he usually reads the news while I snag the funnies.

Anyway, it didn't surprise me to find Hudson on the

porch reading the paper. What *did* surprise me was how he was dressed.

"Wow, Hudson. Nice boots."

He lowers the paper and grins at me. "My Sunday best."

I eye Holly, then look back at him. "But . . . it's Saturday, isn't it?"

"Yes," he says, putting the paper aside. "But it's All Saints' Day, and I'm taking your grandmother to church."

"You are?" I go up the steps. "What is that, anyway?"

"All Saints' Day?"

"Yeah. The guy who did the haunted house said his wife's dragging him to church for All Saints' Day, too."

Hudson picks up the paper again. "Are you referring to the haunted house on Feere Street? Did you go there last night?"

"Yeah—it was awesome."

He raises an eyebrow at me. "Does your grandmother know you went all the way over there?"

"It's not *that* far."

He hands me the paper, and I see a big picture of the haunted house, with a fat streak of lightning Photoshopped in behind it, trying to make it look super scary. The headlines over it read:

HALLOWEEN HORRORS
STABBINGS, DISAPPEARANCES,
AND BEATINGS CREATE COMMUNITY FEAR

I start to read the article—*October ended the way it began—with a mysterious disappearance*—then skim through the first few paragraphs before looking up. "But none of this stuff happened at the haunted house!" I point to the Photoshopped picture. "The guy who owns it used to be a set builder in Hollywood, and he goes through all the trouble of turning his regular house into a haunted house because he thinks Halloween is *fun*." I hand the paper back to Hudson. "It's like they're trying to *create* fear with this."

Hudson thinks a minute, then nods. "You have a point. But it doesn't negate the fact that last night there were two stabbings, a beating, and yet another man's gone missing."

Holly holds her hand out for the paper. "What do you mean, 'yet another' man?"

"This is the third disappearance in a month," Hudson says, handing the paper over as he goes inside to answer his ringing phone. "No trace of any of them."

"The *third*?" Something about this gives me a weird kind of draining feeling. Like all the blood in my body is running for cover. "Holy smokes."

I must've looked as pale as I felt, because Holly stops reading and nudges my arm. "What's the matter?"

"Yesterday was the *third* disappearance."

She shakes me a little. "Yeah? And . . . ?"

"So before yesterday there were *two* people missing?"

She just stares at me.

"You know . . . *two*?"

She's still not getting it.

"Two people, two bodies, two *heads*?"

She gasps. "You're not thinking . . . ?"

I nod and for some reason I can barely breathe. "That's *exactly* what I'm thinking."

TWELVE

Hudson's phone call had been from Grams, who'd gotten a call from Meg, who was wondering what had happened to Holly and me.

Specifically Holly, who was supposed to help out in the shop.

"What time is it?" Holly asked after Hudson relayed the news.

"Half past nine."

Holly jumped up. "How'd that happen?" Then she beat it down the porch steps, calling, "Come over later! I want to know what happens."

I wave and call back, "Okay!"

The minute she's gone, Hudson eyes me and says, "What happens with what?"

I look at him, wondering where I'm going to start with this, only he's not sitting down, getting comfy, kicking his boots up—he's just standing there.

Now, this whole skull thing is not something I can explain with him *standing*. It's just not. But even when I say, "Well, it's kind of a long story," he doesn't sit down.

So I finally ask, "Uh . . . what time do you have to pick up Grams for church?"

He scratches one of his bushy white eyebrows. "I should be leaving now."

"Oh. Well, never mind, then."

"Why don't you come along?"

"I can't. Billy and Casey are meeting me here." I look down the street. "They should be here any minute."

He takes a deep breath. "Well, I can't be late." He gives me a kind of sheepish smile. "It's taken me a long time to get out of the doghouse."

I laugh because it's so true. Grams would never admit it, but she was pretty sweet on Hudson, and then he went and got love-punched by a phony *artiste* and messed the whole thing up. "Arrroooo!" I tell him, then shoo him along. "Go!"

"You sure?"

I say, "Of course!" because I'm thinking that talking to Hudson won't change anything—that I really just have to talk Billy into turning the skulls over to Officer Borsch.

A few minutes later Hudson's purring down the road in his 1960 sienna rose Cadillac—a car only Hudson Graham could pull off. And then I just sit there.

And sit there.

And *sit* there.

Well, I fidget and pace and look up and down the sidewalk a *gazillion* times, but in between all of that I just sit there.

And then finally Billy and Casey come loping up the walkway.

I jump up and start to say, What took so long? but then I see that Billy's arm is all bloody. So instead I say, "What *happened*?" and *then* I notice that he doesn't have the skulls so I say, "Oh, no! How'd they find you?" but *then* it hits me that the Vampire and Shovel Man must have somehow followed Holly and me to the Acostas' so I say, "Oh, *maaaaan*, I'm so sorry. I had no idea they were tailing us!"

Billy and Casey look at each other, then back at me like, Whoa . . . *what*? And finally Casey says, "They?"

That throws me a little. "Shovel Man and the Vampire?"

Billy says, "It wasn't the Vampire or Shovel Man."

"Then who?"

Casey snorts. "Try El Zarape."

I look at Billy. "*El Zarape* did that to you?"

"Yeah." Billy scowls. "If he'd have come up and asked, I would've just handed Grim and Reapy over. But no, he had to go and pull a switchblade."

My eyes bug out at him. "Are you serious?"

"Yeah, and you know what? That guy's older than I thought. He's like twenty-five or thirty or something."

"Are you sure it was him?"

"Yes!"

"Was he wearing a zarape?"

He gives me a puzzled look. "Are you wearing zombie stuff?"

"Oh. Good point."

"And I told him, 'Here, have them!' but he was, like, *possessed*."

"I'm telling you," Casey says, "he didn't understand you."

"He didn't speak English?" I ask.

Billy gives us an exasperated look. "He didn't speak at *all*. He just flicked that knife around! So I chucked the knuckleheads at him and dived in some bushes."

Casey gives a twinkly little smirk. "Rosebushes."

Billy checks out his bloodied arm. "I should have gone up against the knife."

I sit down on the porch and hold my head, because I'm having a little trouble fitting all this in with the Vampire and Shovel Man. I mean, why were they *all* after those skulls? Were they working together?

But . . . why would Shovel Man be chasing El Zarape through the graveyard late at night if they were working together?

Did they have a falling-out?

Did El Zarape steal the skulls from *them*?

Were *they* the ones making people disappear?

Finally I look up at Billy and Casey and say, "There was a reason I thought it was the Vampire and Shovel Man."

"Yeah?" Casey asks. "What."

So I tell them about Holly and me being spotted at the Pup Parlor and how we ditched Shovel Man through the Heavenly only to about clobber Meg with a toilet plunger. And then I explain how we figured out that they were after the skulls, and that Billy was probably in danger. And when I get to the part about going over to the haunted house to

97

check out the skulls over there, Casey asks, "So how'd they compare?"

"The best-that-money-can-buy fake skulls are lighter and plastickier, and they have *seams* on the inside." I look at Billy. "Grim and Reaper were the real deal. Those were actual human skulls."

Billy eyes Casey. "Dude, I told you."

Casey's eyebrows go flying. "You told *me*? I told *you*."

I give them both a squint. "What are you talking about? Last night you both said they were just awesome fakes."

Billy heads over to the spigot by the porch and says, "Yeah, but that was before last night."

"Last night? What happened last night?"

He turns the water on and starts washing off his arm. "Casey's house was *possessed*."

I roll my eyes. "Uh . . . Heather's living there?"

Casey snickers, but Billy's serious as he rubs off the blood. "There were *sounds* . . . ," he says all mysteriously. And since he's not, you know, elaborating, I ask, "What kind of sounds?"

"Scratching. And screeching. And rubbing."

"Rubbing?"

He shuts off the water and squeegees his arm with his hand. "Like shuffling footsteps. And the scratching was like someone trying to claw out of a room. Or a *coffin*."

Now, it's not like I don't remember the way the air felt when the skulls were out at Hudson's, but shuffling footsteps? Clawing out of a coffin? I can't help it—I laugh. "Oh, please. It was just Heather messing with you."

"You're wrong, Sammy-keyesta!" he says, and his eyes are enormous.

I turn to Casey, but he just gives me a little shrug like, You shoulda been there.

So after staring back and forth at them for a minute I finally grab the newspaper off the table on Hudson's porch and hand it over.

Casey shakes his head when he sees the picture. "That is so fake."

"What's *real* is the fact that another person in Santa Martina has disappeared. Just *poof*, nobody knows where he is. That makes a total of three people who have disappeared this month. Well, *last* month. *Three*. As in, there were *two* people missing, and now there's one more."

I wait for them to react to the stunning significance of this, but they don't say anything.

So I try again. "As in, *two* probably dead people plus one more."

Casey eyes me like he can't quite believe what I'm suggesting. "As in, two bodies with two *skulls*?" he asks.

"Exactly."

They both stare at me a minute and then Billy laughs and says, "You think *I'm* nuts, Sammy-keyesta? A body doesn't rot and leave a clean-as-a-whistle skull in less than a month! It takes years!"

"So maybe they burned the bodies! Maybe they dissolved them in acid! Maybe they threw them in the river and let a bunch of barracudas loose!"

Billy squints at me. "Barracudas?" And Casey says, "What river?"

"That's not the point! The point is, there are two people missing and nobody knows where their *skulls* are!"

"Or the rest of them," Casey points out.

"I know," I grumble. "But for some reason, Shovel Man, the Vampire, and El Zarape are all after those skulls! And why? You don't just go carrying people's heads around! Not unless you're a sicko murderer!"

So, okay. I know I'm being a little over the top, but for some reason I can't let this idea go. I mean, it just seems too coincidental. Two bodies missing, two skulls found—there had to be a connection. But I take a deep breath and say, "Look, the reason Holly and I came over so early was to warn you about Shovel Man and the Vampire being after the skulls and to tell you we thought the skulls were real. I'm sorry I woke up Heather, and I'm sorry you got ambushed by El Zarape. And maybe those skulls don't have anything to do with the missing people, but what if they do? I really think we should tell the police everything we know."

They both just look at me, and I can tell that (a) they don't think the skulls and the missing people have anything to do with each other, and (b) they're not too keen on telling all of this to the police.

"Please? Just go over to the police station with me?"

Billy scratches the back of his neck. "Is it even open on Saturdays?"

"Sure. And with everything that happened last night, Officer Borsch'll be around somewhere." I shake my head. "I hope so, 'cause I really can't see explaining this to anyone else."

Casey and Billy look at each other and shrug, and Casey says, "Probably a good idea."

The Santa Martina police station is smack-dab in the middle of downtown. It's across the street from the mall, next door to the fire station, around the corner from the library, and really near St. Mary's Church and the Salvation Army.

It's also not far from Hudson's, so before long we were pounding up the station steps, and once we were inside I went straight to the counter where a receptionist I'd never seen before smiled and asked, "May I help you?"

"Uh, yeah," I told her. "We'd like to talk to Officer Borsch. Is he here?"

"Just a moment," she says.

Now, I don't know how many moments it takes to make ten minutes, but it's got to be in the billions. And with every moment I waited, I felt more and more antsy.

Probably because I could tell that Casey and Billy did not want to be there.

"Sorry!" I kept mouthing over to them.

"It's okay," Casey kept mouthing back, but I could tell—they wanted to leave.

Finally the receptionist tells me, "Sergeant Borsch isn't presently at the station but should be arriving momentarily."

Well, since *momentarily* has *moment* in it, I figured that meant it could take half an hour. Maybe more. So I ask, "When he gets here, could you *please* let him know that Sammy's waiting for him out front?"

101

"Sammy?" she says, like, Are you sure that's your name?

"Right," I tell her. "Sammy Keyes. Please tell him as soon as he gets here. It's important."

She makes a note of it and nods, and I tell the guys, "Come on," and hightail it out of there.

Trouble is, as we're going down the steps, someone else is coming up.

Someone who's totally ticked-off and hostile.

And also the last person on earth I want to see.

THIRTEEN

At first we all just stop moving and stare. Then Officer Borsch tugs on Danny's arm and says, "Let's move it, Urbanski," and continues up the steps.

"It was *you*," Danny spits out at Casey. "You narc'd!"

Casey squints at him. "About what?" And then he sees the Preacher Man's speaker and microphone in Officer Borsch's meaty hand. "It was *you*?" He shakes his head. "I had nothing to do with you getting caught."

Danny's eyes shoot darts at me. "Then it was your snoop-happy girlfriend!"

"Shut up!" Casey says, stepping in his way, and I swear he's gonna push him. "She had nothing to do with this, either!"

"Move aside," Officer Borsch barks at Casey as he pulls Danny along by the arm. And as they pass by us Danny snarls, "Narc!" over his shoulder.

"Wow," Billy says when they're gone. "I can't believe they put him in *cuffs*."

Casey stares after them. "I can't believe he's really the one who mugged that guy. And for a cheesy speaker and a microphone?"

"He's in handcuffs," Billy murmurs. "Dippin' Dots Danny. In *handcuffs*."

I start to say, Dippin' Dots Danny? but stop myself. I may only know Danny Urbanski as a smooth-talking two-faced jerk, but the nickname paints a completely different picture. A picture that has sunshine.

And water slides.

And laughter.

All of a sudden I feel terrible. Like I made a huge mistake by calling Officer Borsch. I remind myself that Danny beat a guy up, cracked his ribs, stole his stuff, and *bragged* about it, but in the pit of my stomach I'm sick.

Sick, and also scared.

No matter how much sense it made to turn Danny in, if Casey finds out I did it, the pit of his stomach will feel sick, too.

Toward me.

"You okay?"

It's Casey, and I do know what he asked, but for some reason I just blink at him and go, "Huh?"

He takes my hand and says, "I know," which makes me feel even worse because he's obviously thinking that I'm thinking how terrible it is that Dippin' Dots Danny is now a bona fide juvenile delinquent, when what I'm really worried about is how to get out of the pickle *I'm* in. I mean, if I had told Casey about calling Officer Borsch before we'd run into Danny, that would be one thing. But now that Casey had stuck up for me?

Now that I knew Danny's nickname?

All I can think is that if Casey finds out I turned Danny in, he'll never look at me the same.

That it'll be the beginning of The End.

I kept quiet as we walked along. I wasn't even sure where we were going, and it didn't really seem to matter. Billy and Casey talked about Danny, while I frantically tried to sort out what I would not know if I hadn't called Officer Borsch or eavesdropped from the underbelly of the Urbanskis' car.

So while Billy was going on about the handcuffs, I couldn't jump in and say, Well, gee. He fractured the guy's ribs—what do you expect? because that was something I only knew because I'd called Officer Borsch.

And I couldn't suggest that Nick or Danny's other two friends knew he'd be pawning the speaker and microphone today so maybe *that's* how the police had been tipped off.

Even saying something about pawning would give me away!

I felt like I was walking through a minefield of ill-gotten information, and one false word could set off a relationship-crippling explosion.

So I was quiet.

Mum.

Worried.

Casey kept on holding my hand, and even though we'd walked for blocks, it still wasn't a lax, easy hold. It was firm. Like he'd let go of part of his past and was latching on to me . . . but was still feeling a little unsteady.

"You okay?" he asked again, and the way he said it wasn't like, Hey, how's it goin'?

It was like he could tell something was wrong, and he really *cared*.

Which made me feel even worse.

And made my hand start sweating.

I pulled away and wiped my hand on my jeans. "Sorry!"

He laughed. "You think I care?" then held on tight again.

And that's when the very thing that had me running scared the night before came to my rescue. "Look!" Billy says, pointing toward the back of the Bosley-Moore Funeral Home, and there's the Deli-Mustard Car, parked mostly out of view.

We all just stare for a minute because something about it being there is really . . . creepy.

"Good thing Marissa's not here," I finally say. "She'd be freaking out about him sucking blood out of dead people."

Casey does an exaggerated chin rub. "I thought we decided that vampires don't drink cold blood."

"Apparently they will in a pinch," Billy says with an oh-so-serious nod.

I scowl at him. "Like I said, Marissa's not here."

Billy shrugs. "So what do *you* think he's doing here?"

"Uh . . . maybe he's a funeral director?"

It's weird—the switch from talking about Danny to talking about dead people seems to have *lightened* the mood. A mischievous look crosses Billy's face as he says, "So you think he's a cadaver conductor?" and Casey

"So you think he's a cadaver conductor?" and Casey throws in, "A posthumous priest?" and Billy shoots back, "A deacon of the dead?" which makes Casey cry, "A cardinal of corpses!" and Billy come back with, "A minister of . . . memorials?"

"Stop!" I laugh. "I don't know *what* funeral directors are. I just heard my grandmother talk about them. I've never actually been inside a funeral home."

"*Parlor,* if you please," Billy says, pointing to the PARLOR AND CHAPEL sign that's right below the main BOSLEY-MOORE FUNERAL HOME sign.

"Fine. I've never been inside a funeral *parlor.*"

Casey eyes the front door, where a steady stream of people are filing in. "We could fix that, you know."

I look down at my jeans and thrashed high-tops. "Don't parlors require, you know, lace gloves and shiny shoes?"

"There's a guy in jeans," Casey says, nodding toward the entrance.

"Yeah, one."

But I *am* curious. I mean, there are lots of cars parked in the front lot, but it's not full or anything, so the only reason the Vampire's car would be parked around back is if he worked there. Or had some, you know, *business* being there. But even if he was in the mortuary business, that didn't explain why he was cruising through the cemetery at night in his Deli Mobile, or why he and Shovel Man were stalking us to get those skulls.

Obviously I wasn't going to get any answers by standing on the sidewalk, so when Casey says, "There's another guy in jeans," and starts toward the entrance, I pull him back and say, "If we're going to do this, we need to split up."

He looks at me. "And then . . . ?"

Through my mind flashes something Holly had told me about the way she dealt with things when she was homeless. "And then we attach ourselves to our own little group of adults as we go in. We look solemn, avoid eye contact, and once we're inside, we don't hang out together or act like we know each other."

Casey thinks a minute. "I can do that."

I eye Billy. "I don't know if *he* can."

"Hey!" Billy says. "I can be as solemn as the next guy. I can be *more* solemn than the next guy! No, wait! I can be as solemn as the *dead* guy."

I look at Casey and say, "That's pretty solemn," and Casey agrees. "Very solemn."

So we watch the people filing into the funeral home for a minute, and then Casey says, "It was my idea, so I guess I'm going first."

He's quick, sly, and never looks back.

"Okay," I tell Billy. "My turn."

I sidle up behind a middle-aged couple helping along an old lady. It's slow going, but I hold back a little, trying to seem like I'm just patiently walking with Grandma to a sad, sad day at the funeral parlor.

But as we're approaching the doorway, the middle-aged woman looks back at me and says, "You can go ahead."

"No, no. I'm fine," I tell her, and I back off a little until they're right up to the door.

Then in we go.

There's a little sign on a post with movable white letters that spell out CHAPEL with an arrow pointing to the left, and VIEWING with an arrow pointing to the right. And standing beside the sign is a short, pear-shaped woman wearing a dark purple dress and a dark green and purple hat. To me she looks like a giant, smiling eggplant.

"Cynthia! Roscoe!" she says to the people I'm with. "And Mrs. Kennedy! Thank you so much for coming."

There's a bunch of people milling around, blocking the entrance to the chapel, so before she can even think about saying something like, "And who is this darling ragamuffin?" I ditch it to the right.

Now, I'm trying to remind myself that the whole reason we're infiltrating a funeral parlor is to find out more about the Vampire. Stuff like, does he work there? And if he does, what does he do? Maybe it's his job to check out the gravesite for a next-day burial. Maybe he's really just a normal guy with a rundown car and unfortunate teeth.

But as I'm looking around for the Vampire, I keep getting distracted by the whole *parlor* part of the place. Seriously, there's a main room with a fireplace that's all decked out like an old Victorian living room. It has little flowered couches and oval-framed pictures on the wall and an Oriental rug under a sideboard with a silver tea service and a plate of crunchy-looking cookies. And really, it looks more like a fancy tea parlor than anything to do with death.

I try to mosey through the people like I belong, which isn't easy because I sure don't feel like I belong. The jeans I'm wearing are bad enough, but my shoes? I feel like I'm

109

wearing muddy army boots to a prom. And even though the adults don't seem to notice me, there are a few other kids, and they do. Especially this one girl with a perfect little blond bob. She's about ten and she's wearing a blue velvet dress over black tights, and her shoes are definitely shiny.

I try to ignore her as I move around, casually looking inside a room that has a little conference table, and another room that's obviously an office, and then a kind of oversized closet that has display cases of urns and a wall filled with coffin samples. They're each about six inches deep and a foot across, and there are dozens of them mounted in a giant grid on the wall. It's like coffin corners as *art*.

There are more rooms farther back, and I'm thinking about taking a quick little tour through them, but no one else is even as far back as the coffin room. Plus when I look over my shoulder, there's that girl again, glaring at me.

So I move back into the "parlor" room, and I try smiling at Little Miss Nosy Bob, but she just keeps on glaring. It crosses my mind that maybe I should snag a cookie and deliver it to her, but she's definitely not the kind of girl who'd take cookies from a stranger. So instead, I start to mosey on back to the chapel side of things. But the Oversized Eggplant is coming toward me, and when I look over my shoulder, I see that Little Miss Nosy Bob has gotten her mother's attention and is pointing right at me.

So to ditch all of them I take a quick right turn through two open French doors into another room.

Trouble is, the room happens to have a big, open rosewood coffin perched on a thick, wide pedestal, and standing looking in the coffin are Billy and Casey.

"What are you *doing*?" I whisper as I hurry up to them. "You're supposed to stay separated!"

"And who, pray tell, are you?" Billy asks, looking at me like he's never seen me before.

"Knock it off!" Then I ask, "Did you see him?"

"Who?" Billy asks.

"The Vampire!"

"No . . . but it looks like he's been here," Billy says, wiggling his eyebrows at the coffin.

So okay. I can't help it. I look. And there, laid out in a dark blue suit, is . . . some old dead guy.

I shiver, because, well, even though I don't know him, and even though he *is* old, he's also *dead*.

Plus, he looks pasty.

Sort of . . . *waxed*.

"Did they put makeup on him?" I ask, leaning in a little.

"Too much rouge, if you ask me," Billy says.

"I think we should get out of here," Casey says, looking over his shoulder. "I don't know where the Vampire is, but I did find out he's not the funeral director."

"How do you know that?"

"Because I heard someone in the chapel ask who the funeral director was and the person they pointed to was a normal-looking guy in a suit."

And that's when I see Little Miss Nosy Bob standing in the middle of the double French doors, tugging on her mother with one hand and pointing at me with the other. I let out an "Uh-oh," and Casey asks, "You know her?"

"Nope."

He looks her over. "I'm guessing her name's Trouble."

Luckily Trouble's mother is talking to the Oversized Eggplant and not focusing on her daughter, and since there's a side door, I whisper, "This way!"

So we duck through the side door and escape.

And we wind up in a weird closet-like area with three *other* doors.

"Now what?" Casey asks.

Billy goes into announcer mode. "Behind door number one we have an old man in a coffin. Behind door number two?"

"I think it's the office," I say, trying to get my bearings.

"That leaves door number three or door number four. Samantha Keyes, what is your destiny?"

I can hear Little Miss Nosy Bob out in the other room, whining, "There! They went in there!" and I know that if I don't move quick, my destiny is to be busted.

So I toss a mental coin and go through door number three.

It was definitely not my lucky day.

FOURTEEN

We find ourselves inside a sort of industrial alcove. There's a stainless-steel counter and sink to our right, cabinets on our left, and the floor is just cement.

It's not a dead end, though. There's a wide opening past the cabinets, and from the amount of light coming into the alcove, it seems like it must go to a much bigger room—one I'm hoping will lead us outside.

I can hear an odd kind of whirring, ticking, running-water sound coming from around the corner. It's like someone's taking a shower with a metronome going. I also notice a smell. It's not super strong or anything, but it does remind me of . . . I'm not sure what.

Then we peek around the corner.

I choke down an "Aaah!" and right away I know what the smell reminds me of.

Biology class.

Only here, instead of frogs, there's a human body.

Actually, there are two bodies—a dead one, and an *alive* one working on the dead one.

The alive guy is faced mostly away from us, and he's wearing lots of clothes—blue scrubs that tie in back over a regular shirt and slacks, latex gloves, a hairnet, and a surgical mask.

The dead guy, on the other hand, is face up and wearing *no* clothes.

Well, except for a little white towel across his groin.

The dead guy's on a big steel tray on a wheeled stand near a sink, and the whirring-ticking-shower sound seems to be coming from a machine on a counter near the sink. It looks like a cross between a big stainless-steel blender and a glass cooking pot. It has knobs and a gauge on the base, and the glass part is about half full of a pinkish orange liquid. There's also a long rubber tube that goes from the base, across the counter, and up to the neck of the dead guy.

"Can we *please* go back and try door number four?" I whisper, because I've seen more than enough. Besides, I don't know how we'll ever make it past the scrubs guy to the door on the other side of the room without being seen.

Billy and Casey are all for that, but just as we're turning to go, the door we'd come through starts to open.

Casey grabs me by the hand and hauls me around the corner and inside the corpse room, and out of reflex I grab Billy by the wrist and bungee him along. The next thing I know, Casey's pulled us through the partial opening of a big steel door and is shutting us inside.

It's cold inside this big steel closet.

And dark.

And the room feels like it's *purring*.

Casey hadn't closed the door all the way, and now he

starts inching it back open so we can see what's happening out in the room. The sliver of light that comes in through the crack makes it so we can see around us, too, and what I discover is that this closet is deep.

And has shelves.

Long, wide shelves that are stacked floor to ceiling on both sides, leaving an aisle down the middle.

Shelves that are almost all full.

"Are those *bodies*?" I whisper to Billy. I mean, they may be wrapped up, but from the shape and size, what else could they be?

"I'm not feelin' too good," he whispers back.

So I lean forward and whisper to Casey, "I think we'd rather be busted than stay in here!"

But Casey doesn't even answer me, and since he's watching and listening so intently to what's going on out-side, I do what he's doing.

Through the crack I can see a woman with blond hair talking with the guy in scrubs, and I can barely hear her as she asks him, "So nobody came through here?"

He shakes his head.

She starts to leave, then asks, "How is it going with Mr. Orwell?"

Scrubs pulls down his mask to speak. "Another half hour, forty-five minutes. I'll have him ready in plenty of time."

Casey and I give each other bug eyes, because there's no mistaking those teeth. "The Vampire!" we mouth at each other.

"The Vampire?" Billy asks.

I turn to Billy. "He's the guy in scrubs!"

Billy ducks down between us so he can peek out, too, and we all listen as the Vampire asks the lady, "Did they deliver the suit?"

"I have it up front," she tells him. And it looks like she's really leaving this time, only at the last minute she does a double take.

Right at us.

Suddenly she's moving fast.

Right at us!

We all duck back and move between the shelves, but she doesn't yank open the door and go, "Ah-ha!"

She does something worse.

She shoves it closed.

So there we are in the pitch black in a giant refrigerator surrounded by corpses when Billy whimpers, "Mom-my!"

Now, my diva mother would be of zero help in this situation, but I totally get what he means. I'm feeling panicked and claustrophobic, and I'm starting to shiver.

"We're not trapped," Casey whispers. "There's a release knob."

I knew he was talking about the big, flat disk on the inside of the door, but that wasn't the point. "How are we going to know when to open it?" I ask him through the pitch black. "We can't stay in here for forty-five minutes—we'll freeze to death!"

"Let's give it five minutes and then just go for it."

"Mom-my," Billy whimpers.

"Knock it off, Billy!" I tell him.

"Can I hug you?" he asks.

"Oh, good grief."

But I can tell he's actually serious, so I grope around until I find him, then give him a mondo hug. "Better?" I ask him after a minute.

"*Sí, sí*, Sammy-keyesta," he says, but it's quiet. Like he really is completely creeped out and scared.

"Look," I tell him. "Remember how cool you thought it was to have Grim and Reaper? Just pretend that—"

"This isn't helping, Sammy-keyesta."

"Sorry." I think a minute and then say, "So a fake dead body that *looks* like a real dead body is cool, but a real dead body is . . ."

"Creepy."

"Huh. I wonder why that is."

"Because one's real and one's fake!"

"So just pretend they're fake."

"But they're not fake!" he whimpers. "They're real, and I want out of here!"

"Got it." I turn to where I think Casey is and say, "I don't care if it hasn't been five minutes, and I don't care if we get caught. We're bustin' out of here."

So I grope around until I find the flat knob, and after turning it doesn't do anything, I push on it and *click*, the door unlatches.

The Vampire's back to working on the dead guy, and really, at this point, I don't care if he sees us.

That doesn't mean I wave a big red flag or anything. But after we've snuck out of the corpse cooler, I lead the guys toward the back door, tiptoeing past an emergency eyewash system, past a big trash can marked HAZARDOUS, past a mop in a pail, and a closet with bottles marked POISON.

The machine's still ticking and whirring, and maybe that makes it so the Vampire can't hear us, but in another few seconds, he's sure going to *see* us.

And then, like a miracle, he turns away from us to adjust the machine.

I abandon the tiptoeing and practically dive for the door, and when I open it, I discover a minivan and a hearse in a carport, and past them . . . daylight!

I make a break for it, with Casey and Billy right behind me. We run for blocks and blocks without stopping, and when we finally do check to see if we're being followed, we only gulp in about six breaths and then we run, run, *run* all the way to Hudson's house.

I collapse on the lawn, and then just lay there, gulping in air.

Billy and Casey bend over with their hands on their knees, and finally Billy pants out, "I am never . . . ever . . . going to be able to . . . sleep . . . again."

I look at Casey. "I can't believe you . . . dragged us into a . . . corpse cooler!"

"I didn't know what it was!" Casey pants back. "It was open, we were stuck . . ."

"Not just . . . because of the . . . cooler . . . ," Billy pants. "Because of . . . that *guy*."

"The Vampire?" I ask.

Billy nods. "His eyes."

I sit up and face him. "His eyes?" And then it hits me. "You looked back?"

Casey goes a little bug-eyed. "So he saw your face?"

Billy nods. "That dude's got wicked scary eyes."

I collapse on the lawn again. "Oh, man."

This was not good.

Not good at all.

FIFTEEN

We hadn't been at Hudson's even five minutes when Casey's phone went off. I actually like when Casey's phone rings 'cause his ringtone is the riff from "Waiting for Rain to Fall" by Darren Cole and the Troublemakers, which is "our" song, and he always gives me a little grin when he answers.

But not this time.

This time it was his mom calling, demanding that he come home right away.

Billy went with him, and since I obviously wasn't welcome at the Acostas' house, I got left behind at Hudson's. "Don't let that boy drag you through parlors of any kind," I called to Billy, and then hollered, "Thanks for the deadly date!" to Casey.

"You know I'm *mortified* about it," Casey calls back. "*Buried* in regret!"

"Don't believe him!" Billy shouts, "He took you there because he's *fatally* attracted to you!"

"*Terminally* so!" Casey shouts. Then he adds, "How else could I have survived such a *grave undertaking*?"

"At least he didn't take you to a fancy restaurant and *stiff* the waiter!"

Casey laughs. "Or run off and join the Peace *Corpse*!"

"Oh, that was bad!" I shout after him. "That was terrible."

So I'm laughing as I watch them go, but the minute they're out of sight I feel really . . . alone.

And kinda scared.

Not that the Vampire's going to find me and kill me or anything. It's more like an invisible weight. Like something is trying to crush me from the inside out.

I drag myself up to Hudson's porch and even though I'm pretty sure he's not home, I knock on the door, and then try the handle.

Locked up tight.

I really don't want to go home, but Marissa's house feels like it's way too far to walk to right now, and since Holly's working and Dot lives clear out in Sisquane and I don't have a phone to *call* anybody, I make like Hudson and sit on the porch with my feet kicked up on the rail.

I watch the world go by for a little while, but there's a whole lot of nothing going on, so I finally pick up the newspaper and look at the "Halloween Horrors" article.

Trouble is, the article reminds me of Danny, which of course reminds me of this awful secret I have from Casey, and pretty soon my brain's all muddled and stormy and doomy.

I don't know how long I sat there, but I must have been in the depths of Doomsville when Hudson clomped up the side steps, because I jerked and spazzed and jolted all at once.

He laughs. "Didn't you see me drive up?"

I scratch my head and sit up. "Uh . . . I must've been napping?"

"Napping?" He comes over and sits down in the chair beside me. "Have you been here the whole time I was gone? Didn't your friends show up?"

I blink at him as everything I'd done since he'd rolled out of his driveway flashes through my mind.

Going to the police station . . .

Running into Danny . . .

Infiltrating the funeral parlor . . .

Getting stuck in a corpse cooler . . .

Escaping the Vampire . . .

Running until I thought my lungs would burst . . .

And I don't know—the thought that it looked like I'd just been sitting there the whole time made something in me snap, and I started laughing.

Not ho-ho-ho, ha-ha-ha laughing.

Hysterical laughing.

And pretty soon I can't talk, I can't breathe, my eyes start watering, and I'm, like, *convulsing* in my seat.

Hudson puts a hand on my shoulder. "Are you all right? Sammy! Are you all right?"

I catch my breath and wipe my eyes dry. "Yeah, yeah, I'm *fine*," I tell him.

And then I start laughing all over again.

He watches me a minute, then goes inside. And when

he comes back, he's got two tall glasses of iced tea, and I've pretty much exhausted myself. "Better?" he asks, holding out a glass.

I nod, then take a deep, choppy breath and accept the tea.

"So," he says, "maybe I shouldn't have gone to church with Rita?"

"No, no, that was *fine*." I sit up a little and ask, "How is Grams, anyway?" but it comes out all goofy sounding. Like, How's the old bat, anyway?

"We had a very nice time," he says, but he's talking carefully. Like he's afraid of setting off another bout of hysteria. "We went out for coffee afterward."

"Very good!" I tell him, and now I'm sounding like some dorky schoolteacher rallying the class.

He just stares at me a minute, and I stare back as I take the world's longest sip of iced tea.

"So what's this about?" he finally asks. "Boys? School? Heather?"

The answer comes spitting out before I even know what I'm going to say.

"Death."

Then I get back to sipping my tea.

His bushy eyebrows flex way up. "What about death?"

"Why do people get laid out in a casket with satin padding and pillows and flowers everywhere? And why do people *look* at them? Why can't they just not look?" I sit up even straighter. "And what do you know about getting embalmed?"

His eyebrows are still reaching for the roof, only now his mouth is in a little *O*. Finally he says, "Did you attend a funeral recently?"

I slouch and cross my arms. "I wouldn't call it attending."

"But this is all precipitated by a . . . by a visit to a . . . ?"

I eye him. "Funeral parlor."

"And you went there because . . . ?"

I sit up again. "It's a long story, all right? It's a really long story. All I want to know right now is, what do they do when they embalm you? What does that mean?"

He takes a deep breath, gives a single nod, and settles into his chair a bit. "They replace the blood in your body with a preservative."

"Formaldehyde?"

"I believe so."

"With a machine?"

He eyes me. "Yes."

"So they drain your blood and pump you full of chemicals so you don't rot?"

"Basically, yes."

"But why? You're dead! It's over! You're eventually going to decompose anyway, right?"

Hudson is still eyeing me. "Right." Then he takes a deep breath and says, "Different cultures have different beliefs, Sammy. Some cultures believe the body will be resurrected in the afterlife."

"And what? People don't want to look like grizzle-faced ghouls when they float up to heaven?"

He chuckles. "Perhaps." Then he adds, "There was a

time when body preservation was only available to the very wealthy."

"Like pharaohs?"

"Right."

"But still. It's like people are trying to hold on to life when life is gone."

"I've always seen it as something that's done more for the living than the dead." He sips from his tea, then says, "Consider this: Embalming may go way back to ancient Egypt, but it wasn't until the Civil War that it became widely used in the United States."

I think about this a minute. "Because families . . ."

My voice just drifts off so he nods and says, ". . . wanted their fallen soldiers to be returned home. And with the distance from the battlefields and limits in transportation, getting them home was impossible without preserving the bodies. Without embalming, they'd have to be buried—probably in unmarked graves—near the battlefield."

I let all this soak in, then say, "Well, *that* seems like a good reason."

"It's really the same concept now. Funerals take time to coordinate and it takes time for loved ones to gather. And a lot of people want to say their farewells face to face. It gives them a sense of closure. Besides, most burial customs are based on a belief that the soul remains in this world for a period of time before moving on to the next, and traditionally, families have certain obligations toward the dead before their souls move on. And to *help* their souls move on." He takes a quick sip of tea and leans back. "That's what All Souls' Day is about."

"Wait—All *Souls'* Day? Didn't you say it was All *Saints'* Day?"

He laughs. "Yes. *Today* is All Saints' Day. *Tomorrow* is all Souls' Day."

I blink at him. "So you have to go back to church *again*? Why? What's the difference?"

He gives a little shrug. "Today's a holy day of obligation. You pray for people who are in heaven."

"But . . . if they're already in heaven, why do you have to pray for them? They're already inside the Pearly Gates, right? Don't you pray *to* them? Like, please help me . . . whatever?"

He laughs. "I'm sure there's a lot of that going on, too. But tomorrow—the Day of Souls—you pray for people who haven't yet ascended to heaven."

"Like, what? You put in a good word for them?"

"Right. Many people believe that collective prayers help lift a soul from its transitory state into heaven."

I scratch my head. "But why can't you just pray for saints and souls in the same visit? Why do you have to go to church two days in a row?"

He gives me a little smile. "Some people *like* to go to church, Sammy. It gives them comfort. Other people like to go to the graveyard. *That* gives them comfort." He shifts a little. "As a matter of fact, tomorrow will also be a big day at the graveyard."

"Really? Why?"

"Because we have a large Hispanic population here and people from Latin America celebrate on All Souls' Day."

"They celebrate? Like, they party?"

"That's right. They call it Day of the Dead."

"Day of the *Dead*? And that's a *celebration*?"

He laughs. "That's right. They go to the cemetery with the deceased's favorite food and drink, they decorate the grave with flowers and pictures, and they sit around telling stories about them."

"They have a picnic? At a *graveyard*?"

He grins at me. "Don't look so shocked. It's a very widespread custom, and I think it's a good one." Then he adds, "Not everyone goes to the cemetery—many build private altars in their own homes."

"Wow," I tell him. "I always think of graveyards as being sad or spooky. Having a *picnic*?"

He nods. "You know, I think you should go there tomorrow, just to see for yourself. It will seem like a completely different place to you." We're both quiet a minute, and then he says, "So, did that help at all?"

"About death?"

He nods.

"I'm not sure." I give him a little smile. "But it didn't hurt."

He waits another minute, then says, "So do you want to tell me what sparked all this? I'm guessing something upset you at the funeral parlor. Was there an open casket?"

"Yeah," I tell him, and before he can ask me anything else I get up and say, "You know, I ought to get going. Can you call Grams and let her know I'm on my way home?"

"Sure," he says with a nod, but I can tell it's not easy

for him to just let me go. He knows there's a lot more that I'm not telling him, and it bothers him that I don't want to talk about it.

And normally I *would* talk about it. Normally, I'd start to tell him a little bit and before I knew it, the whole story would come out.

But not this time.

This time I'd started, but then I'd just stopped.

I hurried away from his house, trying to ignore the fact that it bothered me, too.

SIXTEEN

I just wanted to go home.

Trouble is, as I'm walking past the mall, two things happen at almost the same time.

First I see Heather going into the mall, and before I can ditch it out of view she spots me.

Actually it's her whiny friend Monet who spots me, but she goes and grabs Heather and points me out, so bottom line, I'm spotted.

Now, I'm across a parking lot and across the street, so I just act like I haven't seen them, but then the second thing happens.

Officer Borsch pulls up alongside me in a police cruiser.

He powers down the passenger window and calls, "Sammy!"

I look ahead like I don't know him. And what's weird is that in the old days it was important that Officer Borsch didn't see me, but now it's important that I'm not seen *with* him. "Leave me alone!"

"Hey!" he calls, totally not leaving me alone. "Get in. Let's talk!"

"Go away!" I tell him, looking straight ahead. But

when I crank my eyes over toward the mall, I know the damage is already done. Heather and Monet have stopped and are looking right at us, and I know what they're thinking.

Sammy Keyes is buddy-buddy with a cop.

Sammy Keyes is the one who narc'd on Danny.

So I do the only thing I can think of to save the situation.

I jaywalk right in front of his squad car.

The first time I met Officer Borsch he wrote me up for jaywalking. He just has this thing about jaywalkers. I, on the other hand, have this thing about not going clear down to the crosswalk if it's safe to cut across the street.

Anyway, jaywalking in front of Officer Borsch is like poking a rabid dog in the eye, so I knew there was a pretty good chance that he couldn't let my "blatant disregard for the law" slide.

Which he couldn't.

Especially since as I jaywalked in front of him I pulled a belligerent face and threw my arms out at him, like, You jerk!

Yup, before I'm even at the median, his lights are flashing and his sirens are wailing, and he's doing a completely illegal U-turn to pull me over.

When I get across the street, I do a sly peek over at Heather and Monet.

They're still watching.

And this time when the Borschman pulls up to me, he doesn't try to talk to me through the window.

This time he lurches out of the car and comes *charging* at me.

I turn to face him and cross my arms like I'm really mad and tell him, "Don't look. Heather's watching and I want her to think you're ticked off."

"I *am* ticked off! You just jaywalked right in front of me!"

"Yeah, I did that to tick you off. So keep acting mad. You know, yell at me and get all red in the face and jab your finger around all over the place."

He just stares at me then says, "I don't do that when I'm mad!"

"You do, too! Now come on! Don't just stand there! Act mad! And then write me a ticket!"

His eyes start shifting around. "Where's Heather? And what does she have to do with this?"

I can tell he's about to crane his neck around so I tell him. "Don't look! She's over by the mall. She and Danny are tight, okay? They're like barbs on wire! Now *act mad*."

So *finally* he gets it, and real loud he starts going, "You think you can just thumb your nose at me? You think you can just break laws and get away with it? Well, think again!"

It's been a long time since I've seen the Borschman act this way and I can't help it—a little grin creeps across my face.

He drops his voice. "Stop that!"

"Oh, just write me up, already."

So he gets his ticket thing out of the car and pretends to scribble away, and when he rips off my copy and hands it to me he says, "Can I come by your grandmother's later?"

I snatch it from him. "Not a good idea. She doesn't know anything about what happened with Danny." Then

I tell him, "There's something I have to talk to you about, but not now, and not in front of Grams. I'll call you from a pay phone."

"Is Heather still watching?" he asks, and I know he's dying to look.

I crank my eyes way over. "Yup. Talk to you later." Then I storm off like I'm totally ticked off at him.

"Next time I'm calling your parents!" he yells after me.

"Next time I'm suing for harassment!" I yell back and keep on marching.

Since I'm now on the mall side of the street, I decide to take the winding walkway that goes around it. I love to ride it on my skateboard because it's got little hills and valleys and curves, and it goes through pine trees and oversized shrubs—it's like an amusement park where you bring your own ride.

But I don't have my skateboard, and as I walk between trees and bushes I start getting the creepy feeling that Heather could totally ambush me. I mean, she's come out of nowhere and attacked me before, and even though by now she ought to know not to mess with me, somehow I think it still hasn't quite sunk in.

Plus, even if she wasn't going to ambush me, she might be tailing me to see where I live. Heather's tried *that* before, too, and believe me, her figuring out that I live in the Senior Highrise would be disastrous.

Now, I don't want to go looking over my shoulder to see if I'm being followed. I mean, if I *do* look and she *is* there, then she'll know I knew she was watching and realize that the whole exchange with Officer Borsch was staged.

So after the next curve I do what I always seem to do when I'm trying to hide from someone—I dive behind some bushes.

It's already too late when I realize that I've picked a stupid spot. There's a straightaway ahead and if Heather *is* following me, it'll be pretty obvious that I ditched it somewhere. Plus, I'm feeling kind of ridiculous. I mean, why am I hiding in bushes?

Again.

And how paranoid am I, anyway? Like they don't have better things to do than follow me?

Well, apparently not. I'm in the bushes for all of ten seconds when I hear Monet say, "Why do you even care?"

"Look, if you can't shut up, go back!" Heather hisses.

I see them through the bushes as they scurry by, but all of a sudden Heather stops, punches her fists on her hips, and turns clear around in a slow circle. "Okay, so where is she?"

Monet eeks out, "Maybe she knew we were following her?"

"Maybe she *heard* you, you idiot!" Heather throws her hands in the air. "I can't believe this happened *again*. Where did she go?"

Monet starts looking around. "Um . . . maybe she's hiding in the bushes?"

I can practically see the light bulb go on over Heather's head, and believe me, there's definitely an Uh-oh in a thought bubble over mine.

Their backs are turned, so I pick up a softball-sized rock and hurl it over their heads and into the bushes on the other side of the walkway.

"There!" Monet cries. "Did you hear that? She's in there!" But before I can escape, the bushes where I'd hurled the rock start rustling and shaking, and a deranged-looking homeless guy comes staggering out of them.

Heather and Monet both scream and then hightail it past me, around the corner, and *out* of there. And now *they're* the ones being followed, because after yelling some pretty X-rated language the homeless guy staggers down the walkway after them.

Getting over to the Senior Highrise was pretty easy after that. Especially since I decided to use the front door. I mean, it's not like I was planning to stay inside all day, and since the manager knows I "visit" Grams regularly to bring her groceries and do her laundry and stuff like that, it's no big deal to go in the front door once in a while.

I just have to remember to *leave*.

"Hey, Mr. Garnucci!" I call over at him when I come through the door.

"Sammy!" he calls back. "Long time no see."

"Yeah, I've been busy."

"Your grandmother expecting you?"

"Yup," I tell him. "I promised I'd help her with some chores."

"Wish more kids were like you." He nods toward the elevator. "Go on up. She came home from church not too long ago."

So up I go. And while I'm riding the elevator, I'm feeling really weird. Like I'm one of those people playing about six games of chess at the same time. You know, where they make a move at one station, then go to the next and move a piece there, then go to the next, all the way down the line until they wind up back at the first game.

The difference is that people who play chess like that are really good at it. They think lots of moves ahead and store every game in some separate little corner of their brain. Me, I'm going from one board to the next with no idea what I'm doing, and no time to think about what a long-range strategy might be. I just make some random move and find myself at the next board, hoping not to get trapped in a checkmate.

Anyway, as I'm letting myself into Grams' apartment, I'm thinking that I don't want to be at home so much as I want to be *alone*.

I need time to think about my next move.

My next *moves*.

So right away I tell Grams, "I came in the front door so I could do the laundry. And then maybe I'll vacuum."

Her eyebrows stretch high. "Really?" Then she seems to rethink the wonderfulness of my offer. "You can't leave the laundry room, you know."

"I know," I tell her, because for months now some-one's been stealing clothes that have been left unattended. I wiggle my eyebrows at her. "The Nightie 'Napper."

She eyes me suspiciously. "Are you making fun of me?"

"No!"

"Because there was another incident reported just last week."

"Was it another nightgown?"

"Yes."

I give her a little grin. "Muumuus and nighties. The 'Napper's kinda kinky."

"Or very well dressed at someone else's expense," she grumbles.

"Well, don't worry. Your nightie's safe with me. I won't leave the laundry room." Then I add, "I'll bring my homework."

Now she's *really* looking at me like I've lost some marbles, but she doesn't actually say anything. She just gets some money and soap and fabric softener while I collect the bed sheets and towels and dirty clothes.

Then I haul everything down to the basement, and after I get the machines going, I scoot an old folding chair up to a small table and set out my binder and books. And while the laundry's swishing and sloshing in the machines and my homework's staring up at me, I just sit there looking out into space, trying to figure out what my next move should be.

With the skulls.

With the Vampire.

But most importantly, with Casey.

SEVENTEEN

By the time I finally hauled everything back up to the apartment, I'd decided that my first two moves were phone calls: one to Officer Borsch and one to Casey.

But how?

And when?

And what, exactly, was I going to say?

If I'd been living in a normal apartment, the how part would have been easy. I'd have taken the phone to a quiet corner while Grams was in the bathroom or bedroom and just called. But the Senior Highrise is old. And since everyone living in it is old, too, the people who own it probably figure there's no reason to do anything *new* to it. So for a phone we've got one of those old-fashioned wall jobbies. You know, with the twisty cord that anchors the handset to the wall?

It's in the kitchen, and the cord does make it over to the fridge and *almost* to the stove, but if you want to have a private conversation? Forget it.

And since I really didn't want Grams to overhear, I needed to get out of the apartment and use the pay phone next to Maynard's Market. And since I'd come in the front door of the Highrise and had to be seen leaving, it made sense to do it soon. Besides, I wanted to get it over with. I thought Officer Borsch needed to know about the skulls, and it was eating me up to have this secret from Casey. Maybe he wouldn't be able to live with what I'd done, but I couldn't live with hiding it from him.

The hard part was *what* to say. All through folding the laundry and putting it away, all through making up Grams' bed and vacuuming the apartment, I thought about what to say. Not just to Casey, but to Officer Borsch, too. And finally, after I'd loaded the dinner dishes and wiped down the kitchen counters, I took a deep breath and asked, "You need anything from Maynard's?"

Grams had been kind of quiet during dinner and wasn't making a peep now. And since she was giving me a funny look I said, "I came in the front door, remember? So I have to—"

"I know, I know," she says, waving it off, but now she's all watery-eyed.

"What's wrong? I just asked if you needed something from Maynard's."

She sniffs and shakes her head. "You've been doing chores all afternoon, and now you're asking if I need anything from the market? You've become so responsible. And you have a *boyfriend* . . ." She gives me a quivery little smile. "You're really not a little girl anymore."

Before I can say anything back Grams has opened her purse and is asking, "What would *you* like from Maynard's?" She looks up at me. "Have you outgrown Double Dynamos?"

I laugh. "Two scoops of ice cream double dipped in chocolate and rolled in yummy crunchy nuts? Who could ever outgrow that?"

She hands over some money. "Your arteries will someday, but for now, enjoy it."

I take the money and say, "Thanks," and as I'm heading out I tell her, "Don't start worrying if it takes me a while to come back, okay? I may stop in and see Holly." Then I jet down to the lobby, holler, "See ya later, Mr. G!" to Mr. Garnucci, and head over to the pay phone by Maynard's Market.

Now, when I'd been down in the laundry room, I'd gone scavenging for change. There wasn't any of Grams' laundry money left for phone calls, and even if there had been, I wouldn't have felt right about pilfering. It's pretty sad when you don't have enough change to make two phone calls, but that's the way things are, so I just do my best to deal.

I hadn't found any coins in the bill changer or the soap machine or any of the washers or dryers, but that made sense—nobody's living in the Senior Highrise because they want to, so they're not careless with cash, even change. So I'd had to look for coins that had done their version of a fire drill. You know—drop, roll, and cover?

Anyway, I'd found an old metal hanger and used it to scrape around under the washing machines, and—as the nuns at St. Mary's Church love to say—bingo! I'd found a total of nine quarters, two nickels, and a peso . . . plus a lot of really gross lint and a bunch of random trash, but whatever. The coins had cleaned up just fine.

139

Anyway for once I had plenty of money jingling around in my jeans—it was slipping the coins into the pay phone that I was having trouble with.

And then it hit me that the whole reason I was having to call Casey *now* was because I'd called Officer Borsch *before,* and here I was, about to call Officer Borsch *again.*

After pacing around the pay phone for what seemed like *forever,* I shoved in the coins and dialed, and my stupid heart started slamming around like a paddleball.

Casey picked up on the second ring.

"Hey," I said. "It's Sammy."

"Hold on."

His voice was really detached. Almost cold. And it was at least a minute before he came back on the line.

"Sorry about that."

"Everything okay?"

"Yeah, just had to get out of the house. Where are you calling from?"

"Maynard's. The pay phone outside." I give a little laugh. "I guess I had to get outside, too."

"Because?"

I pinch my eyes closed.

I'd already made a wrong move.

"Uh . . . because I didn't want Grams to hear me ask you to meet me at the graveyard tomorrow?"

"At the graveyard?"

"Yeah." I laugh because even though I'd spent a lot of time thinking it out, it *was* a weird place to ask someone to meet you. But I just went with it. "At high noon. By the main gate. Can you be there?"

"What's happening? Shoot-out at the Crypt Corral?"

I laugh again. "It's a surprise. You need to bring two bottles of water and a beach towel."

"A beach towel?"

"Yup. Can you meet me?"

He laughs. "I'll be there."

"Great."

And I'm about to say, See you there, and hang up when he asks, "Have you done anything about the skulls?"

"You mean like go back over to the police station?"

"Yeah."

"That didn't work out too well the first time we tried it. Do you think I should?"

There's a moment of quiet and then, "Don't you?"

"Maybe Billy should?"

"*Billy?* Like anyone's going to take what he says seriously?"

"So you think I should?"

"Yes!"

All of a sudden I felt way better. "Okay, then I will."

"The sooner the better, don't you think? The guy pulled a *knife* on Billy." Then he adds, "I'll go with you if you want."

I wished I could reach through the phone and hug him. "Just meet me at the graveyard tomorrow, okay?"

"With two waters and a beach towel," he says with a laugh. "Can't wait."

So I get off the phone feeling really good, and right away I pick up the receiver again and call Officer Borsch.

He also picks up on the second ring. "Borsch here."

"Hey, it's Sammy."

"Oh, good. I've been wondering what you wanted to talk to me about." And before I can say anything he adds, "I know doing the right thing has caused you trouble, and I'm sorry."

I snort. "It's like a minefield."

"Well, I'm not divulging my sources, if that's any consolation."

"It doesn't take a rocket scientist to figure it out. I was in your wedding, remember?"

"Yeah," he growls. "Not something I'll forget."

I decide to ignore his obvious dig at how I'd messed up his wedding day, and just dive in. "Well, as you know, Heather's got it in for me so I'm sure she's stirring up rumors, which for once are probably the truth. Anyway, there's something else I've got to talk to you about."

"Talk away."

So I take a deep breath, then start firing off everything that happened on Halloween. From cutting through the graveyard to running into Shovel Man and El Zarape and the Vampire, to Billy dumping the skulls out on Hudson's floor and all of that. And when all those chambers are empty and I'm reloading my brain with what came next, he says, "Go on . . ."

So I take another deep breath and ratta-tat-tat through the part about getting tailed by Shovel Man and the Vampire in the Deli-Mustard Mobile and hiding behind the brochure rack at the Heavenly and all of *that*.

"Go on," he says again.

So I tell him about ditching it out the back door of

the Heavenly and climbing the fence, and I'm in the middle of telling him about us going up the Pup Parlor stairs with a broom and a toilet plunger when he cuts in with, "Sammy, is this all really germane?"

"Huh?"

"Does the toilet plunger matter?"

"Well—"

"Was he there, or not?"

"No . . ."

"So can you *please* get to the point?"

I think a minute, then say, "Well, okay, the *point* happened the next day when El Zarape pulled a knife on Billy."

"What?"

"See? If I don't tell you the whole story, then the story doesn't make sense."

"But I don't need a whole chapter on toilet plungers if they don't matter!"

"It wasn't a chapter! It wasn't even a paragraph!"

"It was a very long run-on sentence," he mutters.

"It was not! And even if it was, that's how I think, okay?"

"In run-on sentences?"

"Yes!" Then I snap, "What are you, an English teacher or a cop?"

He sighs and says, "Go on. Tell me your story."

But now I don't feel like telling him. Now I feel stupid. Like a little kid wasting his time. So I just stand there saying nothing.

"Come on, Sammy. Just pick up where you left off."

Finally I take a deep breath and start up again, but I try

to make it like a police report instead of a story with toilet plungers. And maybe that's why when I'm finally all done he's quiet so long that I have to say, "Are you there?"

"Yes, Sammy. I'm here."

"So . . . ?"

"Let me get this straight. You think the two 'skulls' are the heads of two of the people who have gone missing."

Now, in the first place, he said *skulls* like he didn't believe they actually *were* skulls. And in the second place he said it like he was trying real hard not to let on that he thought it was the stupidest thing he'd ever heard, which was worse than if he'd come right out and laughed at me.

So I huff, "Fine. Don't believe me."

"Who said I didn't believe you?"

"Your tone of voice?"

He sighs. "Look, Sammy, I'm sorry. Normally I'd be more receptive to this, but come on. It was Halloween. You got spooked."

"The guy pulled a knife on Billy! And it he did it on All Saints' Day, not Halloween!"

He ignores that and says, "We are talking about Billy Pratt, right?"

Well, the way he said that totally ticked me off. I mean, yeah, he knew Billy from a couple of incidents at school, and, yeah, Billy has the reputation of being a goofball, but to blow off what I was saying because it involved Billy?

"He wasn't making it up, if that's what you're implying. He's all scraped up from where he dived into a rosebush to get away from the guy."

He snorts. "A rosebush. Good choice."

"Officer Borsch! You're acting like . . . you're acting like the *old* Officer Borsch."

He hesitates, then says, "What's that supposed to mean?"

"You know, back when you were the Bruiser in a Cruiser, the Crisco Kid, the—"

"Whoa, whoa. The Crisco Kid?!"

A little part of me goes, Oops, but the part of me that's ticked off is way bigger. "Yeah. You know, back when you thought I was a juvenile delinquent? Back when you didn't *listen*?"

His voice goes up a notch. "You call what I've been doing for the last twenty minutes not listening?"

"Well, okay. Back when you didn't *believe* me."

"Sammy . . ."

I wait and wait, but that's all he says. It's like he's biting his tongue so hard that it's never gonna get free to talk again.

"Forget it," I tell him. "You've got people disappearing all over the place, but if you don't want my help, fine."

He lets out a heavy sigh. "It's not that I don't want your help, it's that it's . . . illogical."

"Fine. It's illogical."

"Sammy, please."

"You don't even think the skulls were real, do you?"

"Sammy, come on. Why two skulls in a sack? Where's the rest of the bodies?"

I didn't care about the rest of the bodies. Or that it was maybe a little illogical. I was just hurt that he wasn't even considering that what I'd told him might be valuable.

145

So I wag my head like he's the stupidest guy on the planet and say, "Obviously the bodies didn't fit in the sack!"

"Sammy!"

"Never mind," I tell him. "Just never mind." Then I mutter, "Two random heads pop out of a sack and nobody cares. Whoa, where's the rest of the body? Not here? Oh, well, can't be important. Who cares that somebody pulled a knife to get them back? Who cares that two bodies are missing their heads? Who cares that two people were missing the night that two heads rolled out of the sack?"

Officer Borsch sighs. "Okay. Okay, okay, okay. I'll do a little digging. See what I can find out."

And before I can say anything, he grumbles, "Crisco Kid," and hangs up the phone.

EIGHTEEN

After I got off the phone, I went into Maynard's to get my Double Dynamo and, just my luck, Maynard's loser son TJ was working. "Oh, great," he groans when he sees me walk through the door. "Like my headache wasn't bad enough?"

I eye him. "Right back atcha, Teej." And then, because an Elvis impersonator works the counter some nights, I tell him, "I was hopin' for Elvis but instead I get the Grinch."

"Yeah? Well, what you can get is out."

"See? No heart," I tell him, and leave.

It would have been a waste of a Double Dynamo anyway because I was still upset about Officer Borsch not taking me seriously and I would've chomped through it without even tasting it.

I did think about checking in with Holly, but I was feeling really snappy, so I just went home.

It wasn't until the next morning that I switched from being miffed at the Borschman to worrying about how things would go with Casey at the graveyard.

"You're baking brownies?" Grams asks when she sees me stirring the mix.

"I'm doing a picnic lunch for me and Casey," I tell her

like it's a matter-of-fact, everyday thing. And before she can say, Oh, really, I ask, "What do you think—tuna or chicken salad sandwiches?"

"Chicken salad, definitely."

And just like that she's on board, helping me cut up leftover chicken, dicing celery, grinding in pepper, and just hanging out with me in the kitchen.

When we think it's done, we both take a taste of the chicken salad and it *is* delicious, but remembering the way Casey mixes weird combinations of food—like mac 'n' cheese and salsa—I start worrying that maybe it's kind of, you know, ordinary.

So I look in the fridge and ask Grams, "How would grapes taste in it?"

"Grapes?"

I peek out at her and can tell she's definitely not liking the idea.

"Maybe raisins?" she says. "I've had chicken salad with raisins before."

"Raisins?"

"They're just dried grapes."

"They're disgusting mummy fruit is what they are."

"*Mummy* fruit?"

"Yeah—shriveled, dry, and ugly." I dive back into the refrigerator. "There's no way my chicken salad is gonna become a sarcophagus."

Grams watches as I head for the sink with the grapes, and even though she's trying not to say anything, she just can't help herself. "What's wrong with it the way it is?"

"Nothing. I just want it to be a little . . . different."

So I quarter some grapes and put them in the chicken salad, then I make the sandwiches and gather paper plates and napkins and other picnic stuff. And after the brownies are cooked and cooled and cut up, I put everything in my backpack.

"Have fun," Grams says when it's finally time to leave.

Now, I know she's been trying super hard to trust me and not worry about me going on a picnic alone with a boy, so when she finally breaks down at the last minute and asks, "What park are you going to?" I grin at her and tell her the truth. "The bone park."

"The . . . ?"

"It's All Souls' Day, remember?"

Her eyes bug out at me through her glasses. "You're picnicking at the *graveyard*?"

"Hudson says it's a tradition in other cultures. I thought it would be interesting to check it out." I give her a quick kiss on the cheek. "Lots of chaperones, don't worry."

Then I swing on my picnic pack and sneak out of there.

Casey's already waiting at the main gate when I get to the cemetery. "Hey," I tell him, giving him a hug. He's wearing a backpack, too, so there's a little interference, but it's still nice.

I pull away and smile. "You ready?"

He laughs. "For what, I'm not sure, but yeah. Lead on."

The gate's wide open, so I grab his hand and pull him through it. "You know what All Souls' Day is?"

"Uh . . . I've heard of All *Saints'* Day. I don't really know anything about it except that it's the day after Halloween."

"Yeah, well, All Souls' Day is the day *after* the day after Halloween." I give him a bit of an evil grin. "It's also called Day of the Dead."

He grins back at me. "Is this payback for me dragging you into that corpse cooler?"

I shiver. "Don't remind me."

I lead him to an area in the new section where there are groups of people with colorful blankets and portable lawn chairs. And as we get closer, Casey says, "What *is* this? It looks like there's a party going on."

Now, even though Hudson had told me about it, it seems strange to me, too.

Very un-graveyard-like.

As we get closer we see that families are playing cards and dice games and listening to music and eating food. And every grave marker where a family is gathered has flowers and pictures around it, and a plate of food right in front of it. No one's touching the food. It's just there.

On a plate.

At the grave marker.

Waiting.

A kid runs by us with an old-fashioned pinwheel twirling and Casey whispers, "This is the weirdest thing I've ever seen."

"Weirder than someone pumping a corpse full of chemicals?"

He eyes me. "Good point."

"And this is *good* weird, don't you think?" Because I'm really liking the way all the colors and people and music make the graveyard feel. "It's so different than Halloween."

"Except for maybe the skulls," Casey says, looking at a blanket with food on it.

"What skulls?" But then I see the white, golf-ball-sized skulls on a plate on the blanket.

I guess I was staring because one of the women in the group waves hello to me. And before I even know what I'm doing, I'm moving closer to her, asking, "What *are* those?"

"Sugar skulls," she says with a smile. "You want one?"

I just blink at her. I mean, I'm a fan of sugar, but in the shape of a skull?

At a graveyard?

"You never had one?" she asks as she hands one over.

I shake my head and take it.

"Here," she says, holding one out for Casey.

So there we are, holding these candy skulls, and I'm sorry, sugar or not, there's something a little creepy about eating a head in a cemetery. But the whole family's watching, waiting for us to try them, so finally Casey and I look at each other, give a little shrug, and take a bite.

"Mmm," I say with a closed smile. "Thank you." And when my mouth is cleared a bit, I ask, "So who are you, um . . . celebrating today?"

"Guadalupe," everyone says, and then one at a time they add something. "She was my sister." "My aunt." "My cousin." "My mother." "My friend."

Then the lady who'd given us the skulls says, "She

loved sunflowers and Ricky Martin and pineapple tamales."
And the others chime in with, "Don't forget chocolate!"
"And mangoes!" "And pecan pie!" "And Kahlúa!"

And that's when I notice what's on the plate and around the grave marker:

Tamales and pie and chocolate.

And next to the plate is a vase of sunflowers.

And a bottle of Kahlúa.

I don't know why, but it kind of chokes me up. I mean, how nice is that to bring the things she liked to her gravesite? It's not like Guadalupe can have them or anything, but for all these people to get together and remember her like this?

I give them all a little smile and back away, and the only thing I can seem to get out is, "Sunflowers are the best."

I didn't want to sit near any of the families visiting graves, so I wound up leading Casey across the new section and into the old where there didn't seem to be any visitors.

"Where are we going?" he asks after I've zigzagged him through a bunch of graves.

"I don't know—who looks like they could use some company?" I smile at him. "I brought a picnic lunch."

His eyes get wide. "You did?"

"Yup."

"And you want to . . . eat it here?"

"Yup." I yank him along. "With someone who has no visitors."

We walk up to a tall stone slab that has a real weathered look to it. Gray, with black streaks running from the letters.

"'Arthur R. Jamison,'" I read. "'1881 to 1956, Graze the Lord's Pastures.'"

"Graze the Lord's Pastures," Casey murmurs. "Can you say, mooooo?"

I laugh. "Let's keep looking."

We read a bunch more grave markers as we walk deeper into the old section, and most of them have pretty normal things chiseled into them. You know—Rest in Peace, Forever Loved—that sort of thing. But then we see a simple rectangular tombstone that's sort of tilted to one side and has yellow moss growing on it.

"'Marianne Holden,'" I read, "'Silent at Last.'"

Casey looks at me. "What's *that* supposed to mean?"

I laugh. "'Thank you, Lord, for shutting her up'?"

He shakes his head. "Wow." Then he eyes me and says, "Can we not sit near Marianne Holden?"

I laugh again. "Sure."

So we wind through some more graves until Casey stops at one with two names. It's not a double-wide, either. It's one grave with one headstone and two names.

"How's that work?" I ask. "The year they died is different."

"Bunk beds? Uh . . . coffins?" Casey says.

That kicks my claustrophobia into high gear. "Not here," I tell him, and drag him along until I find a grave that has a big angel on it and a tombstone that reads, "Sophie 'Sassypants' Driscoll, 1920–1955, Brave and Sassy to the End."

I look around. It's a nice spot between two big walnut trees and has a good view down the slope. There's a bird watching us from the branch of one of the trees and the grass around the graves is tall in spots. And green. "How about we keep Sassypants company?" I ask.

"You're serious about this?"

I nod and unzip his backpack, then yank out the towel.

"Is this a tradition for your family or something?" he asks as I flap out the towel.

I swing off my backpack. "Nope. I've never done this before." Then I add, "Besides, would I be setting up camp by Sassypants Driscoll if I had family here?" But before he can say anything I mutter, "Never mind. Maybe I would."

"But . . . if you don't have relatives here and it's not a tradition or anything, why would you want to picnic in a graveyard?"

I shake my head a little, then shrug. "Maybe I'm trying to get uncreeped about death?"

"But at a graveyard?"

Inside I start to panic. Why *am* I surrounding myself with plots of dead people? Is it because I know that telling Casey about Danny is like digging my own grave?

Why didn't I just bring a shovel?

And before I even know what I'm saying my face crinkles up and I blurt out, "I don't want to be all gray on a table or all stiff in a refrigerator or all rotting in a box, okay? I don't want to even think about it! It's scary and gives me night sweats and this weird feeling that I'm falling, falling, falling and that I'll never be back. Ever! It's all over and I'm gone and the world goes on and—"

"Hey, hey, hey . . . ," he says, wrapping his arms around me. "Maybe we should talk about this somewhere else?"

"But I liked the sunflowers! And the tamales! And that people were happy remembering!"

And then I start crying. I don't know why. It's like I'm a pinched-off hose that's starting to sputter at the nozzle, and Casey putting his arms around me completely un-kinks me.

"I'm sorry," I choke out after I pull it together a little. "I don't know why I'm getting all hysterical."

"Because of yesterday?" He hugs me tighter. "I'm really sorry about dragging you into that refrigerator. I had no idea what it was."

I take a deep, choppy breath and sit down on the towel. And after looking out at all the tombstones surrounding us, I finally look up at Casey.

Look him in the eye.

"Could you sit here with me?" I ask him. "There's something I have to tell you."

It comes out all hoarse and airy, and suddenly my heart's hammering in my chest, and my mouth is all sawdusty.

Still. I know I have to do it.

It's time to tell him the truth.

NINETEEN

Casey sits on the beach towel, looks at me, and just waits.

I take another deep breath, hold it forever, and finally ask, "What would you do if you knew your sister killed someone?"

"Wait, what? Heather *killed* someone?"

"No! Sorry. This isn't coming out right."

All of a sudden his "Waiting for Rain to Fall" ringtone starts *wah-wahing*, but he mutes it quick without even looking at his phone. "Try again," he tells me.

So I take another deep breath and say, "Let's say you had a *brother* and he killed someone. What would you do? Would you turn him in?"

He doesn't answer. He just gives me a very strange look. So I blurt out, "Okay, what would you do if some random stranger killed someone—would you turn them in?"

"Uh . . . sure?" But now he's looking totally confused.

I shake my head. "Don't worry—nobody's killed anybody."

"So why are we talking about this?" He looks around. "And why here?"

"Because . . ." And then it hits me that I can't tell him

I called the police on Danny. I just can't. So I look down and say, "Never mind." And even though I have totally lost my appetite, I start unpacking the sandwiches and brownies and plates and stuff.

"What's going on?"

I shake my head. "Nothing."

He turns my face so I'm looking at him. "Sammy, tell me."

I stare at his beautiful, chocolatey eyes. His face is so open. So receptive. So . . . *concerned*. And I don't know— I just cave.

"I'm the one who told Officer Borsch about Danny."

Slowly, his hand lets go.

Slowly, his face falls.

And I can feel him pulling back.

Shutting down.

So I go into motor-mouth mode and tell him what happened. His phone goes off again in the middle of it, but he just mutes it, and when I'm all done, he sits there for the longest time staring out across the graveyard.

Finally he says, "He cracked his ribs?"

I nod.

"Maaaaaaan," he says, shaking his head. And after what seems like a hundred years of silence, he turns to me and says, "I don't even know this Danny. Who would *do* that?"

"I'm sorry," I whisper. "I wish he was still Dippin' Dots Danny, but he's not. And I wish someone else had turned him in because I don't want you thinking I'm a narc, but the truth is I'm the one who did it."

"I don't think you're a narc, okay?" He puts an arm

around me and gives me a little smile. "I think you're just braver than I am. I don't know if I could have turned him in."

I shake my head and look down. "He was never Dippin' Dots Danny to me."

He thinks about this a minute, then says, "Is that why you did that whole brother-versus-random-stranger thing?"

I nod. "Yeah, even though that didn't come out right."

"But I get what you're saying. I mean, where do you draw the line? If he was just some random dude I'd turn him in, no problem. But my brother? I'd probably try to talk to him." He eyes me. "Protect him from the consequences." We're both quiet for a long time, and finally he shakes his head and says, "And if the guy with the broken ribs was my dad instead of some obnoxious preacher dude, I'd want to *kill* the guy who beat him up."

Him saying that makes me realize that I've been halfway holding my breath for an hour, because now all of a sudden I can breathe.

He's not mad.

He gets why I did what I did.

And I'm so relieved that I almost start crying again. "I was just trying to do the right thing."

He gives me a hug. "I know. It's okay. Really." I hug him back, but then he lets go and asks, "Who else knows?"

I hesitate. "That I told the police?"

He nods.

"Holly. That's it."

"Not Marissa?"

I shake my head.

He eyes me. "Can we keep it that way?"

I blink at him and my moment of relief is suddenly swallowed up by the feeling that I'm trading one secret for another.

One trust for another.

One *betrayal* for another.

I mean, Marissa and I have been best friends since way before I met Casey, and we don't have secrets. Oh, sometimes I keep things from her for a little while, but it always comes out.

She always *makes* it come out.

And to know that I *had* to keep a secret from her? That not telling her what I knew about Danny wasn't something, you know, accidental?

I didn't know if I could do that.

Casey sees I'm having trouble with this. "Holly seems pretty zip-lipped to me. But Marissa? It'll slip out in no time."

"It's not like I *want* Marissa to know. I've actually been worried that she'll be furious with me." I eye him. "She's not exactly rational when it comes to Danny."

He laughs. "You think?"

"It's that obvious?"

He shrugs. "Come on. Sure." Then he adds, "And he knows it, so yeah, he uses that to his advantage."

We're both quiet a minute, and when his ringtone starts up again, he finally takes it out of his pocket, checks the number, and mutes it. "You want to call back?" I ask as he clicks through the call history, because obviously someone's trying hard to get ahold of him.

Instead he powers his phone down and puts it away. I can tell he's kind of upset, though, and I can't help trying to figure out who's been calling. It can't be his mom because he would have answered, and if it was his sister, he would have said, "Nah, it's just Heather." So who would be trying so hard to get ahold of him that he didn't want to tell me about?

And then it hits me.

"That was Danny?"

He hesitates, then nods. "Look, do whatever you want about Marissa. It'd be easier if people didn't find out, but whatever." He looks me in the eye. "It's not going to change anything between us, okay?" He gives me a little grin. "So . . . ? Are we *ever* gonna eat?"

I blink at him a minute, then give him a bear hug. He'd deal with Danny his own way, and I'd figure out what to do about Marissa . . . later.

For now, it was okay.

We were okay.

Somehow telling the truth, *trusting* him, had worked.

As hard as it was to believe, it had worked.

Casey loved the food—especially the grapes in the sandwich. And I don't know, maybe it was because I'd gotten all that stuff about Danny off my chest, but picnicking in the graveyard was actually fun. We talked to Sassypants and asked her questions, which of course she didn't answer, but we laid a couple of brownies by the tombstone, because, come on—who doesn't like brownies?

And then we talked about what we'd want people to

bring to our graves when we were dead and gone. I told Casey about Grams' amazing oatmeal, and how I love little champagne grapes, chocolate chip cookies packed with walnuts, and, of course, mac 'n' cheese and salsa.

He gave me a kiss and told me that all he needed was "fruity chicken salad sammiches!" which made me laugh because it was just so . . . *cute*.

So we're having an almost carefree time picnicking in the graveyard until I think I see something move. It's not anything obvious . . . it's more like a flicker in the corner of my eye. And when I turn to look, there's nothing there.

"What are you looking at?" Casey asks because my eyes are glued to the big walnut tree that's off to our left.

"I saw something," I whisper.

"A ghost?" he teases.

I stand up and head for the tree.

"Okay . . . maybe a squirrel?" he says, following me. "A bird?"

But when I get around the walnut tree, what I find isn't a squirrel or a bird or a ghost.

It's a man.

A small, *dusty*-looking man with dark eyes, oily hair, and a hoe.

I blink at him and say, "Dusty . . . I mean, *Mike*?" even though there's no doubt in my mind that it's the groundskeeper.

At first he doesn't seem to remember me. But then a spark of recognition comes into his eyes and he says, "You're Lyssie's friend."

I nod, because that's what he calls Elyssa—the little girl

who'd kept disappearing. I put out my hand. "It's Sammy, remember? And this is Casey."

"Sammy. That's right," he says, then he smiles at me. His teeth are crooked and dull, but his eyes sparkle a little. Like inside him something's been dusted off. "You helped Lyssie a lot."

I shrug that off and tell him, "She's got a big sheepdog now."

He nods. "Winnie. She'll bring her sometimes when she visits her dad." He gives me a curious look, then nods at the grave where we'd been picnicking. "You related to Sophie?"

"Sophie?" I look over my shoulder. "Oh, Sassypants!" I laugh. "No."

"Then Theodore?" he asks, nodding at another grave. I shake my head.

"Wayne?" And when I shake my head, he says, "Anna? Penelope?"

Now, Dusty Mike hasn't looked at any of the gravestones while he's been talking. He hasn't had to. It's like he's got the whole place memorized.

"No. I . . . uh . . . Actually, I don't have any relatives here. A friend told me about All Souls' Day and I thought it would be nice to come out and sit with someone who didn't have visitors."

He tilts his head a little as he looks at me, kind of stooped over and sideways. It's like he's an old raven and I'm some strange object that he can't quite figure out. "Well, that would be most any of the folks in this part of the graveyard." He hoes at some tall grass behind a head-stone. "I'm about the only one who bothers to come by."

I watch him hack away for a minute, then ask, "Do you always work on Sundays?"

He shakes his head. "I don't work here no more."

I hesitate. "Since when?"

"Since a couple months ago."

"But . . . why?"

He hacks a little harder. "They got new people."

Casey asks, "So why are you working here if you don't work here?"

Dusty shrugs and hobbles over to another grave, where he starts hoeing at a weed. "I've done it my whole life. I'm not gonna stop now." He gives Casey that side-eyed raven look. "Someone's gotta watch over them."

"Them?" I ask.

He nods, real serious-like. "There's been shenanigans." Suddenly he stops hoeing and says, "I didn't come out on Halloween and I shoulda."

Casey and I give each other a quick look and then I ask Dusty Mike, "Uh . . . why's that?"

He studies me for a minute. "Come on. I'll show you."

So we pack up quick, then hurry after Dusty Mike as he goes deeper and deeper into the old section.

TWENTY

Dusty Mike led us to an area with big trees that had thick, mossy bark that looked ready to crack right off the trunks. The paths were more like deer trails, and we couldn't even see the new section anymore. For the first time since we'd come into the graveyard I started to get a little nervous.

"Where are we going?" I finally ask.

"Right here, missy," he says, coming to a stop.

I don't see any signs of shenanigans—no smashed angels or spray-painted grave markers or even evidence of eggings.

There is just dirt.

Fresh, smoothed-over dirt.

"Is this a new grave?" I ask, but even as it comes out I know it doesn't make sense. For one thing, the headstone has moss on it. For another, all the new graves are down in the new section.

"No, missy," he says. "It's been here fifty years."

Casey looks at him. "And you didn't just hoe up weeds?"

Dusty Mike shakes his head. "Didn't touch it." He gives Casey that one-eyed look. "Someone dug it up."

My eyebrows go flying. "Dug it up? Why?"

"Must've been something valuable inside."

Casey shakes his head. "But after fifty years?"

Dusty Mike shrugs. "Relations can be strange that way." Then he adds, "People'll dig up graves for an old pocket watch."

"Are you serious?" I ask him.

"Used to be common as all get-out. And that's nothing. In the old days, folks would steal the whole body."

"What? *Why?*"

"To do experiments on." Then he adds, "But that was before modern medicine. Back when doctors had trouble findin' bodies to practice on."

I hold my head with both hands. "So they'd dig up graves?"

Mike nods. "They could pull the bodies out in no time. Especially if there was no coffin. That's why people started puttin' the heavy markers over graves. The bigger the marker, the harder it was to dig up the grave. Nowadays they're buried under a heavy liner or inside a vault, which makes them hard to get to . . . and doctors have folks donatin' their bodies to science so they don't have to steal 'em."

I let this soak in for a second, then ask him, "What's a liner?" because in my mind it's like the inside of a jacket and I can't quite put that together with *heavy.*

"Oh. It's a big cement box. Goes inside the grave, over

the coffin. Keeps the dirt from settlin' in." Dusty Mike gives us the raven look. "But there's no liners in a lot of the graves in this part. Some of 'em's shallow, too. Don't even have coffins. Just a burial cloth."

I blink at him. "They were just wrapped in a cloth and put in the ground?"

He nods. "Some religions like to go that route. Could be a matter of cost, too. What the family could afford."

I can't help staring at the fresh dirt. "But . . . you don't *know* someone dug up this grave, right?"

"Why else would it look this way?"

"Maybe a relative just cleaned off the weeds? I mean, if you were here to steal something, why close it up again and put the headstone back and make it look all even and neat and everything?"

He twists his head, first looking at me, then the grave, then me. Finally he says, "It was dug up. I can feel it." He takes a deep breath and sort of hangs on his hoe. "I told Gordon, but he won't even come up here and look. Told me I was trespassing." He shakes his head. "Me. Trespassing."

"Gordon?" I ask. "Who's Gordon?"

"The manager. You must've seen him. Big man. Likes his ball caps. Suddenly's got no use for me. But I don't see him comin' up here to tend to these graves." He lets a cackle slip out. "Afraid of ghosts, if ya ask me."

Casey nods. "That'd set you back if you worked in a graveyard."

"What he ought to do is embrace 'em. The spirits are your friends, but only if you walk *with* 'em. The minute you start runnin'? They'll chase you."

"So . . . what are you going to do about the grave?" I ask him.

He shrugs. "What's to do? It's done. The grave robbers is gone. And nobody cares. I checked the records. There's no next of kin."

"But somebody arranged to have him buried, right?"

"It's not a man," he says. "It's Ofelia Ortega. She was a nanny for the Roggazini family."

"As in Roggazini Farms?" Casey asks.

Mike nods. "Adam Senior took care of the burial. He's since passed. Him and the other Roggazinis are over in the new section."

"But"—I kind of squint at him—"how could you check the records when you don't work here anymore?"

He gives me a crooked smile as he pulls a classic-looking ring of keys out of his pocket. "Because nobody bothered to ask me for these."

"Wow, those are cool," Casey says, and he's right. The ring is the size of a bracelet, black and smooth, and the keys are old and sort of brown. There's even a skeleton key.

Dusty Mike slips them away. "Need to keep visitin' the folks in the Sunset Crypt."

"Does that place go underground?" Casey asks.

"Right," Mike says with a nod. "Fifty-two people restin' in peace down there." Then he adds. "It's got a real good feel inside. I take my lunch down there sometimes."

Well, okay. Knowing Dusty Mike likes having lunch inside an underground crypt with a bunch of dead people is really kind of creeping me out. But Ofelia's grave does look like it's been more than just, you know, gardened, so I shift

167

the conversation back to that. "If you think grave robbers dug up this grave and that Gordon guy won't even come up here to look, why don't you tell someone who can do something about it. Like maybe the police?"

"The police?" He puts some muscle into hoeing at a weed. "They don't seem to put much stock in what I tell them. Probably best if I just keep doin' what I've been doin'."

I eye him. "You mean coming over and hanging out with the . . . spirits?"

He nods, then twists his head like he's tossed his nose toward the back of the cemetery. "I live 'cross the street. I unlock the side gate and slip right in. No one notices me." He shakes his head. "Only wish I'd come over Halloween night."

Now, while we were talking, I guess Casey had turned his phone back on, because all of a sudden it *wah-wah-wahs*, and when he checks the display, he gives me a nod and answers, "What's up?" as he walks away.

Mike watches him go. "Nice of you two to visit with Sophie," he says, and just like that he's done talking and hobbles away.

A short minute later Casey's hurrying back, telling me, "Gotta go. Danny's outside Billy's house ranting." And I guess whatever's going on is pretty intense because he doesn't say a word about Dusty Mike or thank me for the picnic or say anything about calling me later. He just gives me a quick kiss and takes off.

So there I am, alone in a pretty scary part of the old

cemetery, standing beside a grave that may have been dug up by someone looking for antique pocket watches.

Or whatever.

And since squeezing around the gate we'd snuck through to get inside the graveyard on Halloween would be a lot shorter than going out the way I'd come in, that's what I decide to do.

Trouble is, Dusty Mike's hoe is propped up against the wall, and I'm worried about him seeing me break my promise.

Again.

But I'm also getting really nervous being in the grave-yard by myself.

Dusty Mike may have seemed nice when he helped me track down Elyssa, but he's definitely strange.

And more than a little creepy.

TWENTY-ONE

I decided to stop in at Holly's to talk to her about maybe keeping the whole Danny thing between us, at least for a while, but the instant I walk through the Pup Parlor door, I get attacked.

Not by a pit bull or a Rottweiler, or even a Doberman pinscher.

Nope.

By my best friend.

"Why didn't you *tell* me?" Marissa cries, flying at me. "I can't believe you followed him! And that you called the cops!"

It was just Holly and Marissa downstairs, and obviously Holly had already spilled the beans.

"Sorry," Holly tells me with a cringe. "She got it out of me."

I turn to Marissa. "Look, he broke the guy's ribs! And he stole his stuff! Danny's turned into a full-on criminal!"

"And you're what? His judge and jury?"

I squint at her. "What's the *matter* with you?"

"What's the matter with *me*? What's the matter with *you*? You don't *know* he did it. You weren't *there*. And I don't care what you heard, I don't believe it! He was probably just bragging or . . . or . . . trying to act tough. Guys have to go through, you know, rites into manhood"—her head spazzes around like it's got some jolt of current overloading it—"or whatever!"

"So you're okay with a guy who brags about beating someone up, but not okay with someone who actually does it?"

"Quit twisting my words!"

"I'm not, Marissa. I just don't get how you can stick up for him!"

"And I don't get how you can go on a *picnic* when Danny's incarcerated!'

I almost asked her how she knew about the picnic, but I figured she must've talked to Grams. So instead I cock an eyebrow at her and say, "Incarcerated? He's not incarcerated. Right now he's over at Billy's house beating down the door."

"At Billy's? Why Billy?"

"Because he's looking for Casey."

"Casey? Why Casey?"

"Because he thinks Casey turned him in."

"Why does he think that?"

"Because he saw Billy, Casey, and me coming down the police station steps."

She throws her hands into the air. "Well! There you go! The whole world knows you narc'd on him."

For all the things Marissa and I have gone through, there was never, ever a point where I couldn't see us as being friends forever and ever. But right here, right now,

I caught a glimpse. It was an awful feeling, too. Cold and shivery and scary.

Like walking on a grave.

I shake it off, grab her, and push her into a chair. "Listen, would you? Just *listen*."

She crosses her arms and looks at me like there's no way anything I have to say will make any difference.

I start talking anyway. "The reason we were coming down the police station steps is because El Zarape pulled a knife on Billy yesterday."

"What!" Holly and Marissa say at the same time.

"Exactly! Holly and I figured out that those skulls were real—"

"They're *real?*" She looks from me to Holly, and when both of us nod, her arms uncross and she says, "Wait—who said?"

"Never mind right now," I tell her. "The point is they're real and Casey and Billy were on their way over to Hudson's with them when El Zarape jumped him."

Marissa's stony stare is gone. "Seriously?"

"Yes! So we decided to report everything to the police, because what kind of wacko is running around with two real skulls? Or holding up kids at knifepoint?"

She nods like, Yeah, makes sense.

"But as we're coming out of the station, the Borschman and Danny are coming in."

"Oooh, bad timing."

"No kidding!"

"And Danny thought you were there because you'd

turned him in." Marissa's forehead goes all wrinkly. "But you *did* turn him in!"

"But the only other person who knew that was Holly! Casey and Billy had no idea! And when Danny called me a narc at the police station, Casey practically shoved him down the steps. After that I really thought I had to keep it a secret from him, but it was making me crazy. So the reason I took Casey on a picnic was to tell him the truth."

Marissa gasps. "You *told* him?"

"Yeah. And believe me, it wasn't easy."

"What did he say?"

So I tell them the whole brother-versus-random-stranger bit and what Casey said about if the Preacher Man had been his dad instead of some annoying evangelist, and when I'm all done, Marissa just blinks at me. "So he's *okay* with it?"

I nod and look down. "He was amazing about it."

She takes a deep breath, holds it for the longest time, then finally lets it out. "It's so hard to believe Danny would do something like that." Her voice is all quivery, and even though her words say one thing, I can tell she's finally starting to understand that it's true.

I squat down in front of her. "I'm really, really sorry, Marissa. He's just not the guy you think he is."

She heaves a sigh. "I have *got* to get over him."

Holly shakes her head. "How can you not be over him after this?"

"I don't know!" She covers her face with her hands and

leans her elbows on her knees. "I've liked him for so long."
She sighs again. "And I thought he liked me, too!"

Very quietly I tell her, "He plays you, Marissa. Casey
told me so."

Her head snaps up. "He did?"

I nod. "Danny knows you're nuts about him. Everyone
knows. Casey says Danny uses it to his advantage."

She covers her face again. "Oh, I feel like such an
idiot!"

"Look. Try to forget the Danny you have a crush on.
He's a figment of your imagination. Picture him kicking a
guy and stealing his stuff. Picture him bragging about it.
See the real Danny and you'll be over him."

"I don't know why I can't just *do* that. What's wrong
with me?" She looks at me all buttery-faced. "I'm sorry I
got so mad."

"Yeah," I tell her with a little laugh. "That was kinda
scary."

We're all quiet a minute and then Holly says, "So what
now? If this gets out, school's going to be brutal."

I rake my hand through my hair and sigh. "Yeah, well,
Casey's not telling anyone, and if you guys can *please* not
tell anyone, I think we could contain it."

"I have no problem with that," Holly says.

Marissa takes a deep breath. "Me, either."

I look Marissa in the eye and say, "One little slip and it's
all over."

"I can do this."

Holly nods. "Me too."

I stand up and say, "I'm sure Heather's going to be

firing off about it. I just have to remember she *doesn't* know and come up with a good defense."

We all look at each other, and even though no one says it, I know we're all thinking the same thing: Good luck with that.

My problem was that a rumor becomes the truth if you don't deny it, and how could I deny it when it *was* the truth? I decided that my only defense was an even more brutal offense, and by the time I got to school Monday morning, I knew what I'd do if Heather caused me trouble.

Which of course she did.

"There she is!" Her Royal Snideness calls from across the way. "The narc!"

She's with Monet, and there's a bunch of other people around. So instead of ignoring her like I usually do, I go toward her, and start talking loud so everyone can hear, "Nice try, Heather, but I heard *you're* the one who called the police on Danny!"

Everyone stops and stares. "Me?" she screeches, and it's almost funny to see how shocked she is that *I* would be starting a rumor about *her*.

"Yeah, you! What do you think, we're all idiots? Everyone knows what a backstabber you are! What better way to get back at Danny for dumping you?"

"What are you *talking* about?"

A crowd is forming and my heart is beating like mad, but there's no backing out now. I look at her like she's the world's biggest idiot. "You versus that hot high school girl? Who do you think's gonna win?"

"Shut up!"

I snort. "I'm not the one who needs to shut up! Apparently you're the one going around flapping her lips." I walk away and toss, "Narc," over my shoulder.

All of a sudden Holly and Marissa are next to me and Marissa's whispering, "Ohmygod! That was genius!"

Holly snickers, "She didn't know what hit her!"

And maybe I should have felt proud of myself, or at least happy that I'd dodged a bullet, but I actually felt kind of sick.

I hated that having done the right thing was somehow considered wrong.

And I hated that there didn't seem to be any other way to survive school.

TWENTY-TWO

Billy Pratt's a peacekeeper. I didn't understand that about him at first—at first I thought he was a total goofball, but underneath all his joking and silliness is a sweet guy who just wants everyone to get along.

His dad, on the other hand, apparently has no problem yelling at people, or calling the cops, because that's what Billy said happened when Danny was outside their house trying to beat his way in. Billy said Danny took off before the cops or Casey showed up, and then Casey went to find him to try to talk to him.

Trouble is, none of us had heard from Casey since.

"I've sent him, like, eight texts," Billy said when we were hanging around at lunch with Marissa and Holly talking about it. "I wonder what happened."

"It'd be nice if we could just ask his sister," I grumbled.

Well, there's no way Marissa, Holly, or I could do that, but like dowsing rods to water, our noses all turn toward Billy.

"She hates me!" he says, reading our minds.

"Everyone loves you, Billy," Marissa tells him. "And she'd love you to hate *us*, so just act like you do."

He locks eyes with Marissa for a minute, then goes, "Aw, maaaaan," and takes off.

Holly looks at Marissa, then over her shoulder at Billy, then back to Marissa. "You know what? I think he likes you."

It takes a second, for Marissa and for me, but when it clicks, it clicks hard.

At least for me.

I blink at Marissa. "I think she's right!"

"Are you guys nuts? Billy doesn't like me. Billy's just nice like that. To everyone."

Holly and I eye her and shake our heads.

"Oh, yeah?" she says. "Well, since when has he liked me, then?"

First all the things he did on Halloween flash through my mind—the way he'd grabbed her hand, the way he'd walked near her, the way he'd vampired her neck. . . . And then I think back to all the times Billy has hung out with us—how he's just *been* there, kind of waiting in the background. "Wow . . . maybe for a long time."

"Shut *up*," Marissa says, backhanding me. "Like I wouldn't have noticed?"

"Not with the way your head's been in Dannyland."

All of a sudden Dot comes hurrying up. "You guys! You guys! Guess what?"

I hadn't seen Dot since Friday afternoon when she'd decided to take her sisters trick-or-treating instead of going with us, so it could have been anything. And since she's all wide-eyed and out of breath and about to burst at the seams, I don't waste time guessing. I just say, "What?"

"Heather's in the bathroom smoking and texting and crying."

Now, the smoking and texting part was easy to believe. But crying?

"Does she know you saw her?"

Dot's head shakes like crazy. "She was in a stall."

"But you're sure it's her?"

Now she *nods* like crazy.

Holly asks, "Were Tenille and Monet there?"

Shake-shake-shake.

"So how'd you know it was her?" Marissa asks. "Did you hear her talking?"

Shake-shake-shake.

"You recognized her shoes?" I ask.

Shake-shake-shake.

And all of a sudden Marissa, Holly, and I get totally bug-eyed. "You *peeked*?" we say together.

"Over the divider," she says with a giggle.

I can't help laughing. "Payback!" because Heather and her little wannabes do that exact thing to sneer and jeer and intimidate girls who are using the stall for its, you know, intended purpose.

"Heather *hiccups* when she cries," Dot whispers all conspiratorially, and then goes into this whole hic-sob-convulsion thing that makes the rest of us just bust up.

So yeah, we were being pretty heartless, but if you knew even a fraction of what Heather's done to us, you would completely understand why.

It wasn't until after lunch that I started to get twinges of guilt.

* * *

I have science with Ms. Rothhammer, who's nice, but very strict, and the good thing is she has Heather's number. Billy's also in that class and I'm pretty sure that not-so-deep down Ms. Rothhammer thinks he's hilarious, but she never lets him hijack lesson time like he does in some classes.

Now, showing up late to Ms. Rothhammer's class is a bad idea because not only will she mark you tardy, she'll give you lunchtime detention cleaning the science lab if you do it more than once. So when Heather didn't slide in at the bell like she normally does, I thought, *Tsk-tsk,* the Tearful Texter's gonna get detention.

But then I notice that Billy's not in class, either, and since he never reported back to us after he set out to find Heather, I start wondering if maybe he found her all sobby-faced and got sucked into some of her woe-is-me drama. And *then* I start worrying. I mean, Billy's *such* a peacemaker and Heather's *such* a manipulative drama queen—was she getting him to spill stuff he shouldn't?

As far as I knew, Casey hadn't told Billy about me call-ing the cops on Danny, but I hadn't talked to Casey since he'd taken off so fast from the graveyard.

Maybe something had changed?

What *didn't* I know?

So I'm in the middle of getting the total queasies about everything all over again when Billy walks into the class-room.

"You're ten minutes late, Mr. Pratt," Ms. Rothhammer

says, interrupting her lecture on the wonders of the Krebs cycle.

"Emergency, sorry," he says, walking an admit slip up to her. Then he shows her his bandaged arm. "They say I'll live." He smiles at her. "I'm sure that's a big relief to you."

"Have a seat, Mr. Pratt," she says. It's definitely a no-nonsense command, but there's also a little smile behind it.

"Yes, ma'am!" he says, and goes straight to his desk without even glancing at me.

Now, I could see that the bandages he'd flashed her were covering the scrapes he'd gotten from diving into the rosebushes.

Scrapes that had been scabbed over at lunch.

So I started thinking that he must've made them bleed again so he could get bandages and a pass from the office, which on a normal day would have made me stifle a grin. But this wasn't a normal day, and instead I started to freak out. It had to be something serious for Billy to risk detention from Ms. Rothhammer, and I just knew it had to do with Heather.

I stole looks back at Billy three times, but he didn't seem to see me. His eyes were glued to the board, but they weren't really tracking. They were just staring.

By the time the bell finally rang I was a spastic mess and had picked up absolutely nothing about the Krebs cycle.

"Billy!" I called when I got outside.

He turned and waited for me at the bottom of the ramp.

"What happened?" I whispered.

He just shakes his head. "I know you don't want to hear this, but I'm worried about Heather. She's a wreck."

"Why is she a wreck?"

"Everyone thinks she turned in Danny. People from *high* school are sending her hate texts." He frowns. "She says you started it."

I mutter, "Man, she can dish it but she sure can't take it."

He looks at me. "So you did start it?"

"*She* started it! First thing she said when she saw me this morning was 'Narc!' I just turned the tables on her, that's all. She shouldn't start fights and then complain when she gets hurt."

He just shakes his head again and keeps walking. "Why can't you guys just get along?"

Well, I didn't think I needed to explain that to *him*. And it felt like a slap. I mean, with all the things Heather's done to me, I can't give her a little of her own medicine?

So on the one hand I was hurt that he didn't get that I was just protecting myself, but there was also this little knot in my stomach that I was having trouble ignoring.

I *didn't* feel good about what I'd done to Heather.

But why?

She'd started this war. Why did I feel bad about finally firing back?

Billy and I made it over to drama without saying much more to each other. I was really looking forward to talking to Marissa because she's also in that class, but instead I wound up witnessing this weird little non-conversation between Marissa and Billy while Mr. Chester talked.

Instead of a dialogue, it was like a *shy*alogue, where Marissa would peek over at Billy—who would smile or pull a goofy face—then she'd give a little smile back, blush, and turn away.

So obviously her mind wasn't on *my* problems, and when we got put into groups, Billy happened to be in Marissa's but I was not.

So great. I'm out in the cold with this knot in my stomach, and the more time goes by the worse I feel.

Not about Marissa ignoring me.

About what I'd done to Heather.

And then Billy zips over to me and whispers, "I just got a text from Casey. He wants you to meet him at the mall at five o'clock."

"Five o'clock? Why five o'clock? And what for?"

He shrugs and gives me a goofy Billy Pratt smile. "Dunno!" Then he zips back to his group.

Well, obviously *he's* forgotten all about Heather, but now I'm *double* knotted because I'm thinking that Casey doesn't want to meet me at the mall to, you know, meet me at the mall. He wants to meet me at the mall because he found out I started a rumor about his sister and he's *mad* at me.

When school finally lets out, I'm dying to talk to Marissa, but she jumps in with, "Billy wants to hang out with me after school. You don't mind, do you?"

Well, obviously I'm not invited to this little after-school hang, and normally that would be fine. Actually, normally I'd be *excited*.

Marissa showing interest in someone besides Danny?

Come on, I'd be ecstatic.

But I'm so tied up in knots that I can barely even get out, "That's fine."

And since Holly's working at the Humane Society after school and Dot always gets a ride from her dad, I leave school by myself feeling completely tangled up and nauseous.

And dreading five o'clock.

TWENTY-THREE

I wound up at Hudson's and right away he could tell something was bothering me. "I'm glad you're here," he says, guiding me toward the kitchen. "I've been a little worried about you since you left here Saturday."

It had only been two days, but Saturday seemed like a lifetime ago. "Yeah, that was about seeing a dead body and some skulls and a bunch of other death-related stuff. This is worse. This is about Heather."

He pulls down two glasses and starts filling them with ice. "Back to the critical things in life, huh?"

"More like annoying. And confusing."

"So what happened?"

"I gave her a little of her own medicine. It was totally in self-defense, too! But she winds up crying in the bathroom and now I feel like I did something wrong. Why should I feel bad? She started it! She always starts it!"

He pours tea on the ice, then cuts us each a piece of homemade cinnamon swirl cake. "Why don't we start at the beginning, huh?" He hands over my cake and tea. "Is the porch okay?"

"That'd be great."

Now, I know Hudson can't fix my school problems, but something about the way he listens always helps. Talking to Hudson is like soaking your feet in a river after hiking all day—it won't get rid of your blisters, but it sure makes you *feel* better.

But, wow, did I have a lot of unlacing to do to get to a place where my shoes were off and I could dip my feet in the water—I had to go clear back to Halloween night and the aftermath of the Preacher Man being beat up, and then tell him about spying on Danny Urbanski and all of that.

I did try to stick to the parts that mattered and leave out anything that had to do with the graveyard or the skulls. And even though I started to get sidetracked about seeing the Deli-Mustard Car after calling Officer Borsch, I stopped myself and fast-forwarded to Danny seeing us come down the police station steps.

Through it all Hudson didn't say a word, but now he stops me with, "Why did you go to the police station if you'd already made that 'anonymous phone call' to Officer Borsch?"

I hold on to my forehead and tell him, "We went there because of some skulls, but that's a whole other story and I'm trying to just stick to the Heather problem."

He nods, takes a bite of cake, and says, "One thing at a time. Go on."

So I tell him about picnicking at the graveyard—something that seems to really please him—and then how I'd confessed the truth to Casey, which gets a "Good for you."

And after I tell him about Casey asking me to not tell

Marissa but how Holly already had, and then about how things unfolded at school, I shake my head and finish up with, "So I guess the stuff I said to Heather kinda spread, and now Heather's getting hate texts and Casey told Billy to have me meet him at the mall at five o'clock." I look over at him. "Why am I so nervous about meeting Casey? Why do I feel so bad? Why do I feel so *guilty*?"

He's quiet for a little while, collecting little crumbs off his plate with the back of his fork. And when he finally turns to look at me, all he says is, "I think you know why."

"I do?"

He nods. "I don't blame you for what you did to Heather. But the goal isn't to become like her . . . is it?"

Like cool water across hot, angry blisters, there's my answer.

I shake my head and groan, "Maaaaan," and look down. And when I look up again, I ask, "So what do I do?"

Hudson takes a deep breath. "Ideally you'd find some way to stop the rumor and clear her, but this may just be a case of having to learn from your mistakes." He shakes his head a little. "The real tragedy here is that the issue's been so badly twisted—Danny's the one who should be on his peers' chopping block, not the person who reported him."

"I know, but that's not how it works. Junior high's a war zone, Hudson. And high school sounds like it is, too."

He nods. "I understand that. And that's why I said before that nobody can blame you for what you did." He eyes me. "Just remember—you don't want to become what you hate."

I let out a heavy sigh, then drink some tea and just sit

187

there, thinking about what I should do. I mean, I can't exactly announce at school that it was me, not Heather. That would be suicide!

Plus, there's still a part of me that thinks Heather deserves everything she's getting.

But I can tell now *that's* the part that's making me a little crazy.

That's the part tying me in knots.

I start thinking what it must be like to be Heather. She'd always been mean to me. Condescending and catty and just *vicious*. But why? When did acting that way become her M.O.? It must've happened way before she met me, because the day she started harassing me she was already a pro.

So did it start with one little thing and build from there? Did she tell herself she had to be mean in self-defense?

Is that how she turned into the Heather I know?

Hudson shakes me from my thoughts. "You have some time before you have to be at the mall. Feel like telling me about those skulls?"

"Uh . . . skulls?"

"Mm-hmm," he says with a little smile. "There was also mention of a corpse? And something about a vampire and a deli-mustard car?"

I shake my head and laugh a little. "Haven't you heard enough for one day?"

He sips his tea. "I get the feeling we're just warming up."

So after a little hemming and hawing I dive in again and

tell him the skull story from the beginning. And unlike Officer Borsch, he soaks up every word and even asks me for details and to *repeat* parts. And when I've finally got the whole thing out, he smoothes back one of his bushy eyebrows and says, "That's everything? You're sure?"

I nod, but then I remember about Ofelia Ortega's grave and Dusty Mike wishing he had been there on Halloween and all of that. And while I'm talking, I'm noticing that Hudson's eyebrows are taking a slow stretch up. So much so that by the time I get to the end of it, his eyes are wider than I've ever seen them.

"You say the dirt was smooth?" he asks. "Like someone had taken care to make the grave look nice?"

"Yeah! Which didn't make sense to me. If you're going to dig up a grave to get at something valuable, you'd just dig like mad, get it, and leave. I don't know why you'd put the dirt back and smooth it out. It was still really noticeable. And grass doesn't grow overnight!"

Hudson's eyebrows have come in for a landing, and his eyes are now twinkling. "What if the person who dug up the grave smoothed it over because they respected the person who'd been buried?"

"Then why would they dig up their grave!"

"Ah," Hudson says, standing up.

"Where are you going?"

He tosses me a twinkle. "Follow me."

Hudson's got the most amazing library I've ever seen in a house. It's floor to ceiling books, and any time I have a question he doesn't have an answer to he takes me back there and *finds* an answer.

189

But this time he didn't go for a book.

This time he went to his computer.

Hudson types with only his first fingers, but he's still quick. And before I can ask, What are you looking up, he's typed in *Day of Skulls.*

"Day of *Skulls*?" I ask.

He scans the list of websites that come up. "That's right."

"How many days of dead things are there?" I hold my head between my hands and start pacing around. "There's All Saints' Day for dead people who *have* made it to heaven, there's All Souls' Day for dead people who *haven't* made it to heaven"—I throw my hands in the air—"which is also known as Day of the Dead. . . . And now we have Day of *Skulls*?"

Then a gaspy squeak eeks out of me because all of a sudden a life-sized human skull pops up on the computer screen and it seems to be laughing at me through the ether. It's brown and spotty with dark sockets, but what's making it creepy is that it's *decorated*. It's wearing a little red and blue knit cap that has side flaps.

Side flaps!

For what?

Keeping the ear holes warm?

It's also on a bed of small, unlit white candles and flowers, and on top of the knit cap is a big headdress of flowers.

But what really pushes it into Crazy Town is that there's a burning cigarette clamped between the teeth.

I blink at the smoking skull. "Who *does* that?"

Hudson points to the caption below the picture and reads, " 'Aymara Indians revere the skulls of their relatives and believe they protect them from evil and help them attain their goals.' "

"You've got to be kidding me. They worship skulls?"

Hudson shakes his head. "I don't think it's worshipping so much as it is treasuring." He clicks to another picture, this one of a big group of people carrying decorated skulls on platters and in box lids and on pillows.

And that's when a little chill comes over me.

Not because of the skulls.

Because of what some of the men are wearing.

I point to the screen and whisper, "Zarapes!"

Hudson nods, then reads the caption. " 'People attend a ceremony on the Day of Skulls at a church in the General Cemetery of La Paz. Bolivians who keep close relatives' skulls at home flock to the cemetery chapel once a year to have the craniums blessed and to bring themselves good luck in the future. These indigenous peoples believe the skulls will protect them from evil, help them achieve goals, and even work miracles.' " He looks up at me. "Their ancestors' skulls are their good luck charms."

I sort of stagger into a chair that's to the side of his computer desk. "So you think those skulls Billy had were El Zarape's *relatives?*"

Hudson nods. "I think if you exhumed Ofelia Ortega's grave you'd find bones, but no skull."

"But . . ." I shiver. "I just can't imagine!"

He gives me a little smile. "Different cultures, Sammy, remember? If it's what you've grown up with, there's nothing strange about it."

I think about that a minute, then ask, "But why did he have *two* skulls?"

"Maybe he's reuniting his parents?"

So I think about *that* for a minute and shake my head. "But El Zarape isn't old enough to be her son. Ofelia was buried fifty years ago!"

Hudson gives a little shrug. "Well, I'm sure there's an explanation." Then he eyes the wall clock and says, "Isn't there someplace you're supposed to be?"

I look at the clock.

"Holy smokes!" I say, jumping up.

I had five minutes to get to the mall.

TWENTY-FOUR

When Casey and I meet at the mall, it's always in the center court, somewhere near the base of the tower clock that goes up between the escalators. So it wasn't like I didn't know where to find him. But if I was worried before, it was nothing compared to the way I felt when I walked through the big glass mall doors.

Casey was there by the tower clock all right, but he wasn't alone.

Heather was with him.

I almost just turned around and left. I mean, what was there to say? Maybe I'd saved our relationship from self-destruction by telling Casey the truth about calling the police on Danny, but I'd turned around and blown it to pieces by starting a rumor about his sister. Because as much as he says he can't stand her, as much as he always sticks up for *me,* Heather's his sister.

How could I have forgotten that?

So I'm about to turn around, but then I see someone marching toward Casey from the east corridor.

Someone who's got three other angry-looking guys with him.

Danny Urbanski.

Now, I don't like the way this is looking. And since I've learned that a skateboard can substitute as a weapon in a pinch, I hurry over to Casey and Heather just as Danny and his crew arrive.

Danny doesn't look like he's planning to share any Dippin' Dots, if you know what I mean. His face is hard, and his eyes are angry, and there's no doubt about it—he's there for revenge.

Casey glances from me to Danny to Heather, and I can tell from the look on his face that this is not something he was expecting.

I have half a second to wonder if Heather set Casey up—if she found out from Billy that I was meeting Casey and decided to ambush us. But it's *Heather* Danny's eyes are locked on as he spits out, "You backstabber. You promised you wouldn't tell."

"I *didn't* tell!" she says. "I swear, I didn't!"

The air around us seems to vanish. It's like a big silent whooshing ghost flying away. There's nothing to breathe. Nothing to carry sound. Nothing to separate all of us from each other.

Movement seems to slow way down, too, while we stare at each other and hold our breath and try to process. And in this slow-motion vacuum, there's only one thing, one thought making noise, and it's a *pounding* noise, echoing through my brain.

Heather knew.

All of a sudden my head feels really light. Like it's floating off my shoulders while the rest of me is cemented to the floor. I do hear sounds—people talking, the escalator clacking along, mall music—but it's like they're on the opposite side of a thick glass panel.

In a different world.

A different dimension.

I know what I have to do. There is zero doubt in my mind about what I have to do. But before I can, Casey looks from Heather to me in this slow-motion way, and before I can say, It wasn't Heather, it was me, Casey steps between Danny and Heather and says, "It wasn't Heather," then he turns to look at me.

My heart suddenly feels like it's filled with lead.

Like it can't pump.

And doesn't even want to try.

Through my mind flash all the reasons I'd kept my guard up for so long about Casey. Heather was his *sister*. Candi was his *mother*. They were linked.

Genetically.

Emotionally.

Eternally.

And as much as he may have wanted to, in the end he could never really choose me over his family because blood is strange, powerful stuff. And while my heart just sits like lead in my chest, Casey turns away from me to face Danny.

Here goes, I tell myself.

Then Casey says, "It was me."

My ears go, *What?* and I feel completely thrown, but Heather pounces on it. "See!?" she screeches, looking at Danny and pointing at Casey. "I *told* you it had to be him!"

Casey looks at his sister like he can't believe *his* ears, and there's no doubt about it—he's just been sucker punched.

In that instant the invisible barrier shatters, air comes whooshing in, and my heart gets back to work. "He did *not* do it!" I cry, stepping forward. "And neither did Heather." Casey looks at me like, No! Don't! but before he can stop me I lock eyes with Danny and say, "I did!"

After a second that seems like an eternity a voice behind me calls, "No, she didn't, *I* did!" and when I turn around, there's Holly.

"You don't have to do that!" I whisper.

"What do I care?" she says through her teeth. "He already doesn't like me."

And that's when I see Billy. And Marissa. And other kids from school. And older kids, too. Lots of them.

"What is everyone doing here?"

Holly's looking very intense. "Word got out," she whispers back to me.

"You?" Danny says, sneering as he moves toward Holly. "Actually, that makes sense. You probably spent a lot of time under bridges with lunatics like that."

"Shut up!" another voice cries, and when we turn around, there's Marissa. "And it *wasn't* Holly," she says, stepping forward. "It was me!"

Danny laughs his forced, stupid laugh. "Oh, right."

But Marissa's eyes are on fire and for the first time in all the years I've known her she is not backing down. She gets right in his face and says, "You beat a guy up, you steal his stuff, you *break his ribs,* and then you treat *us* like we've

196

done something wrong? *You're* the jerk. *You're* the criminal. *You're* the lowlife! What *happened* to you?"

Danny just stands there like he's been tazed. Maybe because Marissa was the one person he's always had power over. Maybe because he can see that the spell is finally, *finally* broken. Or maybe it's because what she said hit some Dippin' Dot hidden somewhere deep inside him.

Whatever the reason, he just stands there staring at her, his mouth going up and down a little, but no words coming out.

Marissa stares him down and in a very calm, measured way she says, "I did it, Danny. Me. So whatcha gonna do about it? Break my ribs?"

Nick and Danny's other friends have closed in, and now Nick says, "Dude, you broke his ribs?" and one of his other friends kind of snorts and says, "I wouldn't break *her* ribs, man. She's hot."

"Shut up," Danny says over his shoulder.

But Danny's now got bigger problems than Marissa. There's a guy working his way through the crowd going, "Hey, where's the lowlife who beat up Reverend Pritchard?"

Everyone sort of moves aside, because this guy's *big*. Not fat. Not even that tall. Just *big*.

Like he's carrying a lot of power on his bones.

Now, while Big Boy is muscling through the crowd I notice that two security guards are running down the escalator. They're big, too, but in a different way. And even though there's a lot of jiggling going on around *their* bones, these mall cops are obviously on a mission to break up this party before the cork pops.

"Disperse! Now!" one of them shouts while the other one's talking into his walkie-talkie. "Anyone hits anyone, I'll see you get arrested!"

Big Boy's in Danny's face now, and you can see a little lightbulb go on over his head. "Hey, I know you," he says to Danny. "You've got Hatter second period."

Danny gulps, because in that one little sentence is a world of future hurt.

Big Boy nods and smiles, and as the mall cops close in he starts to put distance between him and Danny. "See you between classes, punk."

Suddenly everyone's putting distance between themselves and Danny. Nick & Co. are backing up like they just found out Danny's contagious, the crowd that had gathered is breaking up, Heather's jetting out the main doors, and our group sort of drifts toward the west corridor, leaving Danny standing alone under the clock.

When we're far enough away, I ask Casey, "Are you mad at me?"

He shakes his head, then looks over his shoulder at the doors where Heather had escaped. "I can't believe she threw me under the bus like that."

I slip my hand inside his. "I think she was desperate, which was my fault." I look up at him. "I'm really, *really* sorry for what I did. I was trying to protect myself but . . . it was just wrong."

He takes a deep breath and says, "Look, you tried to make it right," but what he can't seem to shake is Heather. "She threw me under the bus!" he says, and his voice is hoarse. Like the words are heavy and hard to get out.

"I was sticking up for her and she threw me under the bus!" He looks at me and it kills me to see the hurt in his eyes. "My own sister."

And since I really don't know what to say, I do the only thing I can think to do.

I wrap an arm around him and hold on tight.

If Heather hadn't been Casey's sister, and if Danny hadn't been Casey's and Billy's friend and Marissa's big crush, things might have felt different. But as the five of us walked through the mall and out a side entrance the mood was pretty dark.

Like someone had died.

We hung out for a little while on a grassy area near the winding walkway, but none of us really knew what to say, so we were just kind of glum.

And then Billy pops off with, "Man, we're more like zombies now than we were on Halloween," which makes us all chuckle.

"Hey," I tell them, "that reminds me—I've actually got news about El Zarape."

Everyone perks up. "You do?"

"You're not even gonna believe it." I look at Marissa. "And you're going to freak out."

Marissa crosses her arms. "You're calling me a sissy? After what I did in there?"

I eye her. "This'll take a different kind of guts."

Holly squirms a little. "So . . . ? Tell us!"

So I start with the Day of the Dead picnic and have Casey help me explain about the families with their sugar

199

skulls and sunflowers and Kahlúa and stuff, and then we move on to Dusty Mike and the grave of Ofelia Ortega. And *then* I fill them in on what I'd learned at Hudson's about the Day of Skulls.

Now, Marissa was trying to act nonchalant when we were telling about the Day of the Dead picnic. Like, yeah, so? You ate some sugar skulls. Big deal.

But when I got to the part about digging up a grave to take out the skull, well, she couldn't pretend anymore—she squealed, and she latched on to Billy, and cried, "Ew-ew-ew-ew-ew!" as she squirmed from bottom to top.

Even Holly was having a little trouble with it. "He dug up the grave, took out the skull, and left the rest behind?"

Billy snaps his fingers. "The Headless Horseman! You know that story, right? He's a decapitated ghost who rides around with a flaming pumpkin head?" Billy's so excited he starts bouncing up and down. "It was Icabob Crane. He wanted his head back!"

"But El Zarape had a head," Holly says. "And wasn't *Ichabod* the guy the Headless Horseman *chased*?"

Billy stops bouncing. "Whatever! Someone stole his head and he wanted it back!"

Holly gives him a puzzled look. "I thought his head got shot off with a cannonball."

Billy heaves a sigh and gives her a pout. "Look, he wants his head back, okay?"

Holly laughs. "Okay! Agreed! Sorry."

Now, while Billy and Holly have been talking about the Headless Horseman, Casey's been quiet. And I figure he's still brooding about his sister, but then he says, "It's kinda creepy to think we were passing around the heads of El Zarape's parents. No wonder he wanted them back."

The jangle of Billy's phone interrupts us. He digs it out of his jeans pocket, gives a puzzled look at the caller I.D., flips it open, and says, "Ya-lo?"

We all wait and watch as his eyes get bigger and he says, "Yes . . . uh-huh . . . all right. . . . *Now?* . . . Yes, sir. . . . Okay . . ." And then right before it seems like he's going to hang up, he says, "Uh . . . sir? If you don't mind my asking? How did you get my number?" Then he gives a nervous little laugh and says, "Oh, right. I forgot about that," and gets off the phone.

We all look at him like, *Well* . . . ?

He gets up and says, "On your feet, zombies. We've been summoned to the parking garage."

We all stand up and Holly asks, "By . . . ?"

Billy starts walking. "The police."

TWENTY-FIVE

To make a very long story short, Billy and I were in some major hot water at school earlier this year that revolved around Billy's cell phone. And since the investigating cop was Officer Borsch, my brain didn't have much trouble connecting those dots.

"That was Officer Borsch?" I asked as we followed Billy across the grass.

"He said sergeant, but yeah."

"What's he want?"

"He said for us to meet in the northwest corner of the south parking structure, second level." He hesitates. "Or maybe it was the southwest corner of the north?" He shakes his head. "No. It was the northwest of the south."

"You're sure?" I ask him.

"Yeah."

"But . . . *all* of us? He knows we're with you?"

Billy nods. "He saw us from the street. He said he didn't think we'd appreciate him coming up to us."

"Wait," Holly says. "The *south* parking structure? Aren't we going the wrong way?"

We all stop, think, then do a one-eighty. And as we're

marching along I remember my last conversation with Officer Borsch and an "Uh-oh" slips out of me.

Marissa looks at me. "You think we're in trouble?"

I shake my head. "It's not like we did anything wrong." I rethink that a second. "Well, not really, anyway."

"So why the uh-oh?" Marissa asks.

"Well . . . it probably wasn't a good idea to call him Crisco Kid to his face."

"Crisco Kid!" the four of them cry.

"Yeah." I heave a sigh. "I hope this isn't payback."

It took us a little while to figure out which northwest corner Officer Borsch was talking about, seeing how the parking ramps wind around and around and the place does have a few nooks and crannies. Plus we got in a little argument about whether what we thought was north really was north or more east. But eventually we did spot him parked sideways across four spaces in a remote alcove near a stairwell.

He gets out of his squad car and says, "Is out here okay?"

I look around. "Like there's any choice?"

"Well," he says, "you could pile in."

We all look at each other, and Billy cries, "I call shotgun!"

"Billy, no, wait!" I call after him. "There are five of us! We have backpacks and Casey and I have skateboards!"

"Just leave 'em outside!"

"Then why get inside?"

"'Cause it's a paddy wagon!" He's already by the passenger door. "Marissa!" he calls. "Share shotgun!"

"Not a good idea!" I tell him, but somehow he gets his way and we wind up making a ridiculous pile of stuff on the ground before getting into the car.

"So," Officer Borsch says when the doors are closed, "I had a talk with that vampire of yours."

My eyebrows go flying. "You did?"

"Yes." He makes a *tsssssk* sound sucking on a tooth, then says, "I met with him at the Bosley-Moore Funeral Home and got some very interesting information."

We all wait while he looks around at us, saying nothing.

Finally I flip my hands up and say, "Such as . . . ?"

"Such as, he and his longtime golfing buddy Gordon Wales—who also happens to be the manager of the cemetery—were driving by the cemetery on Halloween and noticed that the office floodlight was off. They went in to investigate and discovered that the office manager was already there because kids had been spotted causing mischief. The three of them split up to try and catch the culprits, but the kids got away."

Marissa eeks out, "So he's not a vampire?"

Officer Borsch pinches his beady eyes closed and takes a deep breath. "No, Marissa. His name is Sharif Baz. His friends call him Shark, not Vampire."

Billy snorts and grumbles, "I didn't think sharks had friends—just things they like to bite."

Officer Borsch gives him an annoyed look.

"Well, dude!" Billy says. "Besides those teeth, he's got the meanest eyes on anyone I've ever seen!"

Talk about shark attacks. Calling Officer Borsch *dude*

was like dangling a cut-up leg in the water. Suddenly it's like we're trapped in a tank and Officer Borsch is after blood. His head jerks toward Billy and he snaps, "Maybe that's because some punk kids battered his classic 1963 Chevy Impala. Maybe those same punk kids showed up at his place of work and compromised his ability to uphold privacy laws. Maybe *they're* the ones who've been knocking over tombstones at the cemetery."

"Whoa, wait, what?" I cry. "We didn't knock over any tombstones!"

He turns his beady eyes on me.

"We didn't!"

He looks around at the others, slurps on a tooth for a second, then says, "Sometimes when we're with our friends having fun, we do things we know we shouldn't. We give in to peer pressure. But it's still no excuse. Desecrating a grave is a very serious offense."

All of us say, "We didn't push over any tombstones!"

"Well, somebody did."

"Officer Borsch! There are a lot of somebodies in this world besides us!" Then I add, "Maybe it was El Zarape! Maybe he was ticked off because it was taking too long to find Ofelia Ortega's grave and he needed to dig it up so he could steal her skull."

First Officer Borsch just stares at me. Then his little eyes pinch down so far that I feel like I'm looking at a big, pasty Borsch-faced pie. Finally he says, *"What?"*

So I have to go and explain everything about *that* all over again, and when I'm done, he just shakes his head and says, "I've never heard of such a thing."

"Well, that doesn't mean it's not true," I tell him like I totally believe it, even though it still sounds crazy to me.

He scratches his temple. "Regardless, the office manager saw a pack of kids running through the graveyard, so it wasn't this El Zarape character."

Casey's phone buzzes, and he shows me the text, which is from his mother: *Get home NOW.* "I've been summoned home," he says to Officer Borsch. "Can I leave?"

Officer Borsch waves him off. "Yeah, go."

At this point all of us want out of the tank, so Marissa says, "I really should go, too," and Billy chimes in with, "Yeah, me too!" while Holly opens her door without even asking.

But since I'm in the middle of the backseat I'm the last one to reach a door, and before I can scramble out, Officer Borsch says, "You got a minute, Sammy?"

"Uh . . ."

"You want me to wait?" Holly asks, but I just shake my head and tell her, "Thanks for what you did at the mall." Then I holler at Marissa, who's walking off with Billy, "You were amazing, McKenze!"

She laughs and waves, and pretty soon it's just me and the Borschman.

"Want to sit up front?" he asks.

"Nah, I'm good."

He pulls a little face and says, "My neck might appreciate it."

"Oh. Well, how about this?" and I slide over to the far side of the backseat.

He lets out a puffy-cheeked sigh. "What I was saying about peer pressure before?"

"What about it?"

"I understand that it's a powerful force."

"Wait—you still think we knocked over tombstones?"

One of his shoulders goes up like, yeah, maybe.

"Officer Borsch!"

"Look. It's what got your friend Danny into trouble, all right?"

"Is that what he said?"

"I didn't want to say that in front of your friends, especially that boyfriend of yours. But it's important to me that you get this: Peer pressure can make good people do bad things."

"Hey, it's not like Danny—" And then an enormous lightbulb clicks on in my head. "Ohmygod—Heather wasn't just there afterward? She was *part* of it?"

"Look, don't run wild with this. I shouldn't tell you any of this, all right? My point here is that I understand what peer pressure can drive kids to, and if you pushed over those tombstones, you'll feel a lot better if you—"

"We didn't push over any tombstones!"

He studies me. "You swear?"

"Officer Borsch! Yes! I swear!"

He lets out another puffy-cheeked breath. "Well, then, I wonder who did. And I wonder why the cemetery didn't file a report."

"Maybe you should ask the office manager. And while you're at it, ask him to show you Ofelia Ortega's grave."

He shakes his head. "I don't know, Sammy. Someone digging up a grave to retrieve a skull? That seems so far-fetched."

I roll my eyes. "So does finding two skulls in a sack. But they came from *somewhere*. Would you just ask about it when you're there?" And I don't know if it's the billion things that have happened in the last few days numbing my brain or what, but I've suddenly just had enough. Plus, I'm starving. So I say, "Look, can I go? I've got a mountain of homework and I . . . I need to get home."

"Yeah, sure, fine," he says like he's got a billion things jumbling up *his* head.

So I get out and hurry home. I wasn't really worried about Grams being worried, because I'd asked Hudson to tell her I'd be late as I flew out his door, but I was still glad to see her watching the evening news instead of sitting in the kitchen, eating by herself.

"Hi!" I whisper as I put down my skateboard and backpack. "Dinner smells delicious!"

"I'm glad you're home." She waves me into the living room. "There's still no trace of those three men."

"Really," I say über-seriously. "No ransom notes?"

She shakes her head.

"No trail of blood?"

She shakes her head some more.

"No sinkhole on Main Street?"

She turns and looks at me. "You're making fun of me?"

I plop down beside her on the couch. "Only a little."

"Hrmph," she says in her classic Grams way.

"All right, all right. So tell me about them. Maybe they're all members of the Secret Order of Wife Ditchers?"

She hrmphs again, then says, "Not likely. One's a wealthy businessman, one's a suspected drug dealer, and one's a doctor. There seems to be no connection."

"Well, have they looked into the SOWD?"

Grams sighs. "Samantha. Honestly. Three men have gone missing and all you can do is joke about it?"

"You're wasting time worrying about a drug dealer?"

"A *suspected* drug dealer. Maybe he's been set up." She looks at me. "Innocent until proven guilty, remember?"

I sit there with her a minute, then say, "So maybe they're all part of a drug ring? One bankrolls it, one makes it, and one deals it?"

She looks at me like I've lost my very last marble. "You have such a wild imagination."

"Maybe 'cause I'm starving?"

She laughs and shuts off the TV. "So let's eat."

Grams had made Parmesan salmon with green beans and wild rice and it *was* delicious. And as we ate I was actually thinking that maybe it was time to fill her in on the whole Danny–Heather–Preacher Man thing, but then the phone rings.

"I should probably get that," Grams says, standing up. "It might be your mother."

But it wasn't my mother.

It was my mother's boyfriend's ex's son.

Well, it was my mother's *boyfriend's* son, too, but since the boyfriend thought it was fine to leave his son in the middle of a psycho minefield at his ex's house, he didn't count.

Not as far as I was concerned, anyway.

"Hey, Casey," I said, after Grams handed off the phone. "Everything okay?"

"Not exactly." His voice is barely a whisper. "I've only got a second. Mom's confiscating my phone, so don't call it. I'm deleting your number out of the call history."

"But why is—"

"Can you meet me tomorrow after school?"

"Sure."

"But not at the mall. It has to be someplace we won't run into Heather or any of her friends."

"How about the library?"

"No. Too public."

My mind races through some possibilities, but what pops out of my mouth is, "How about the graveyard?"

"Perfect," he says. "See you there." Then he gets off the phone.

TWENTY-SIX

Grams, of course, wanted to know what was going on at the graveyard, so I ended up telling her the whole Danny-Heather drama after all. It took forever, too, because Grams always wants to know the *details* of the details.

I did manage to steer clear of El Zarape and the skulls and the other stuff that happened on Halloween—not just because I thought she'd have a total heart attack over it, but also because I had homework to do and I was so worn out from talking about Heather and Danny that I just didn't want to open that can of worms.

Or, you know, coffin of maggots.

Anyway, I was completely beat by the time I hit the couch, so I should have slept great, but instead my mind spent the whole night trying to escape things. First a squad car's chasing me with its lights flashing and I can't figure out why it's after me until I look down and see that I have a can of Crisco shortening in my hand. Then I hear "Stop, thief!" and there's TJ pointing at me from outside of Maynard's Market.

I drop the can and run through streets and alleys trying to escape, and when I finally check behind me, a big laughing *skull* is after me. It's lit up like a jack-o'-lantern, and it's flying toward me so fast that white smoke is streaming out of its sockets.

At first it seems like a demonic head cannonballing through the darkness, but then I see that it's being carried by someone on horseback.

Someone wearing a black cloak.

Someone with no head.

"Ahhhh!" I cry as the horse thunders closer, and then I realize that the skull is a giant *sugar* skull, and that the flames inside it are melting the eye sockets and the nose hole. It's bubbling, bubbling, bubbling, turning black and melting, dripping onto the arm and setting the cloak on fire.

The horse rears back and shakes the rider off and bones from underneath the cloak go flying everywhere. And then somehow *I'm* on the horse wearing the black cloak carrying my *own* head.

Sections of sidewalk start flipping up in front of me, turning into tombstones, and we go over them like we're in a steeplechase. I try to stop the horse, but it's strong and heavy. Plus it's hard to stop a horse when you're carrying your own head.

So it just keeps galloping, its hooves kicking down the sidewalk tombstones, breaking them, cracking them, knocking them flat.

And then I can't see anything anymore because my head's turned sideways, buried in the arm of the cloak.

It's dark.

And it's hot.

So hot I can't breathe.

So hot my eyeballs feel like they are going to ignite.

Somewhere in the folds of my mind a voice says, "Good heavens," and then, with a great big gasp of air, I jolt awake and Grams is standing over the couch holding my cat, Dorito. She shakes her head. "I do not understand how you can sleep with a cat on your face."

It takes me a few gasps to connect to reality. "What time is it?"

"Time to get up, I'm afraid."

So I pull myself together, eat a quick breakfast, grab my skateboard, and head for school. The ride over's kind of creepy, though, because I'm seeing the sections of sidewalk as hidden tombstones, and somewhere in my mind a giant, melting sugar skull is still chasing me.

I was more than a little worried about being at school. Maybe *I'm* living in the dark ages, without a cell phone or computer, but the rest of the world is text and message crazy and I had no idea what the fallout from the mall showdown was going to be.

Turns out, it was a really quiet day. Maybe that was because Heather was absent, or maybe it was because nothing had actually *happened* at the mall and most of the school didn't know or care who Danny Urbanski was, anyway.

The only kinda weird thing that happened was that Tenille came up to us at lunch and said, "Uh, I want you to know I'm not hanging out with Heather anymore."

It was just Dot, Holly, and me at the table because Marissa and Billy had gone to get something to drink. Dot was all, "Good for you!" but Holly and I weren't buying it. "Is this another one of your tricks?" I asked.

"No, I'm just done with her."

"So where is she today?" Holly asks.

Tenille pulls a face. "Her mom took her shopping."

"Shopping?" I snort. "Poor baby."

"Yeah, really, huh?" Tenille says, and she grins at me.

Now, if she had wanted to eat lunch with us or if she had started casually asking questions about things Heather would have wanted answers to, I would have known this was just a setup. But after standing there for an awkward minute she says, "Well, I just wanted you to know I'm not the enemy anymore," and leaves.

So that was the only weird thing that happened. The frustrating thing was that I never got a chance to ask Marissa about Billy, and I really wanted to. I mean, come on. One day she's crying over Danny, and the next she can't seem to tear herself away from Billy? Maybe Billy's liked her for a while, but I'd never heard her say she liked him.

And the truth is, I was a little worried about Billy. He may be a clown on the outside, but on the inside that boy's a marshmallow and I sure didn't want him to accidentally get burned.

Or even charred.

But I couldn't find Marissa before school, and at break and lunch Billy was around. And since the only class I have with her is sixth period and Billy is also in that class, there was never any time. And then after school Marissa took off with Billy without even saying bye or asking what I was doing.

So whatever.

I just gave up and headed for the graveyard.

Our school lets out before the high school does, but since the high school is a lot closer to the cemetery than the junior high is, I didn't have to wait all that long for Casey to show up.

"Hey," he says when he sees me, then dumps his skateboard and backpack and gives me a mondo hug.

"So what happened?" I ask when he lets go. "And why did your mom take your phone?"

"Heather happened." He collects his stuff and looks up and down the street.

"You mean she told your mother a bunch of lies and blamed you for everything?"

He nods. "Pretty much."

Now, the way he's looking around is kind of uptight. Guilty, even. And that's when it hits me. "Your mom said you're not allowed to see me?"

He pulls a face. "*Forbidden* is actually the word she used." He rolls his eyes. "Over and over and over."

I study him a minute, then grab his hand and drag him through the open gates. "Come on. Sassypants won't tell."

So we walk up the road and follow it as it curves to the left past the cemetery office. Then we leave the road and cut through the old section to the place we'd had our picnic. I plop down my stuff and say, "Hey, Sassypants, we're back. Did you like those brownies?" because they're gone.

Casey grins at me for a minute, then dumps his stuff and sits beside me. "So is this our new spot?"

I shrug and look over at the tombstone. "What do you say, Sassypants? You mind if you're our new spot?" I wait a minute, then turn to Casey. "She doesn't seem to mind."

He smiles and shakes his head. "So what's this say about us, huh? That our new spot is the graveyard?"

"Um . . . that we're not afraid of ghosts?" I laugh. "Your mom and your sister, maybe, but ghosts? Nah."

He lifts my chin and gives me a kiss and then just grins at me. "You are totally worth it."

"It?"

"Everything." He looks out across the graveyard and heaves a sigh. "I don't know what I'm going to do. They're crazy. They're both crazy."

"So tell me what happened."

"Well, Heather twisted the whole thing around so she was the victim and you and I destroyed her life. I tried to explain what really happened, but Mom wouldn't listen and Heather kept yelling and crying and making it sound like I'd come straight out of hell to terrorize her." He shakes his head. "Mom totally fell for it and started acting just like Heather!"

"Can you talk to your dad?"

"I tried! But he was like, 'Son, you've got to work this out with them. There's nothing I can do from here,' and I'm like, 'Yes there is! You can talk to Mom and tell her she needs to listen to my side!' and he's all, 'I could never get her to listen to *me*, why do you think I can get her to listen to *you*?'"

"Well, did you tell him what happened? And did you tell him how bad things are with Heather? You know, how she's really going off the rails?"

"It's like he didn't want to hear. Or believe. Or, you know, *deal*. The last thing he told me was 'It's her house, you need to play by her rules.'"

I shake my head. "I've been telling you—my mom's a terrible influence."

"Yeah, well, I think my mom's got some weird issues. It's like she thinks your mom stole my dad."

"But your parents were divorced before my mom even met your dad."

"I know, but I swear my mom's jealous. You should hear her talk about your mom—she *hates* her. And she's heard complete poison from Heather about you, so she hated you way before you and I got together. But now it's *insane*." He shakes his head. "The stupid thing is, Heather and my mom used to be at each other's throats all the time, but now they've got, like, synchronized claws."

I let this soak in for a minute. "So what are you going to do?"

"I don't know. I wish my dad would come back."

"You think he might?"

He grumbles, "No," then flicks a little twig and says, "And my mom says if I see you, she'll kick me out of the house."

"She'll kick you out of the house? Where are you supposed to go?"

He gives a halfhearted shrug. "To L.A., I guess."

"To live with your dad? Would he be okay with that?"

"Not exactly!"

I shake my head and say, "I almost can't believe this," because for the past year my biggest worry has been that I'll get caught living in Grams' apartment and wind up having to move to L.A. to live with my soap-star mother. And now Casey's kind of in the same boat, only instead of living with someone rock-solid like Grams and worrying about the rest of the world, it's the two psychos in his house that are the problem.

He gives me a little smile. "I know. Ironic, isn't it?"

"You can say that again." We're both quiet a minute, and finally I ask, "So . . . what are we going to do?"

He gives a little shrug. "Spend a lot of time in the graveyard?"

"But—"

"Well, Heather would never look for me here"—he grins—"and you're pretty good at ditching her. . . . And my mom works until five, so as long as I'm home by then at least we'll be able to see each other. Even if it is at the graveyard."

"I'm sure we can think of someplace else."

He looks around. "Actually, I'm starting to like it here." He gives me a little smile. "And I like that you talk to Sassypants. Something about that is very . . . cool."

"You hear that, Sassypants?" I call toward the tombstone. "We're gonna haunt you. Daily!"

Casey digs into his pockets. "Here," he says, handing me a scrap of paper. "I don't know how long it'll be before my mom figures out that she *wants* me to have my phone so she can boss me from the comfort of her office, but this is the number of a pay phone at school. I could work something out with Billy, where I call his cell and he tells you to call me?"

"So it's okay that Billy knows?"

He thinks a minute. "As long as Heather doesn't."

Now, we probably would have spent a lot more time figuring out a strategy, but Casey points to the new section, where a police car is slowly making its way toward the cemetery office.

"That's probably the Borschman," I tell him. "He said he was going to take a police report about those knocked-over tombstones."

"What did he want to talk to you about after we left?"

I give a little shrug. "Peer pressure."

His eyebrows go up. "He thinks we're a bad influence?"

"Wellllll," I tell him, "you *did* sort of lead us into the graveyard on Halloween, and you *did* suggest we infiltrate a funeral parlor, and those *are* the reasons we got interrogated by a cop in the northwest corner of the south parking structure, second level."

"Whoa," he laughs. "I *am* a bad influence!"

I laugh, too, then shrug and say, "I think Officer Borsch just doesn't want to see me get into trouble."

Casey thinks a minute, then says, "Is he like a father figure?"

"No!"

But then I think about some of the things he's said to me.

And how he asked me to be in his wedding.

And I start feeling bad that I'd said no like that.

"Uh . . . maybe it's more that I'm like a daughter figure? Which is plenty weird enough. I used to *hate* the guy."

He laughs. "I can totally see that."

"But underneath it, he's a good person."

We're quiet a minute, then he asks, "You really don't know anything about your dad?"

I shrug. "He could be a serial killer for all I know."

Now, I'd never even *thought* that before, so hearing it come out of my mouth was kind of scary.

Like, wow.

Maybe he was.

"Hey, you want to walk around?" I ask him, because all of a sudden I'm feeling very antsy. "We could spy on the Borschman."

He grins at me. "You want to lurk around the grave-yard and spy on people like that Dusty Mike guy and you call *me* a bad influence?"

I laugh, but the thought of Dusty Mike makes me wonder if he *is* lurking behind a tree again, spying on us. And as we're walking along I can't help it—I start checking behind things.

"Are we really going to spy on the Borschman?" Casey asks.

"We don't have to. I just felt like walking around."

"Fine by me."

So we wander around the old section, holding hands and reading tombstones. And as we make our way up the hillside and past the Garden of Repose, I sort of relax and just enjoy being with Casey.

Now, a week ago I would have said that roaming through a graveyard reading tombstones was a weird thing to do, but it's actually a really nice way to spend time. And it's interesting. The only times I got a little sad was when we'd find the grave of a baby. Some hadn't lived long enough to get a name. Just OUR DARLING BABY and then a single date. For some it was like every day was precious. The tombstone would have the name and the day the baby died and then something like 3 MO'S, 28 D'S.

"Hey, check this out," Casey says. "Marla ran off with another man, you think?"

So I read the headstone, which had two names—Clarence and Marla, and next to Clarence there are the birth and death dates, but next to Marla there's just the birth date and the "19" part of the death date. It's like they had the tombstone made *anticipating* her death, only she decided, Forget that! and found herself another man.

I laugh. "Or maybe she decided she didn't want to spend eternity with him after all."

Then we come upon this hulking shrine of a tombstone that says FATHER and underneath it the guy's name, country of origin, city of death, birth date, death date, and then the years, months, and *days* he lived, plus a sentimental epitaph.

But the grave right next to him has a flat marker in the same stone as the FATHER shrine, but all it says is MOTHER.

There isn't even a *name*.

"Nice," I say with a snort.

Casey compares the two. "Yeah, that's a little skewed, huh?"

"Unbelievable."

We walk along some more and then Casey asks, "So what would you want on your tombstone?"

I laugh. "Oh, you're asking the hard questions now." And I'm thinking about it as we make our way around a big cement angel, but then I see something on the ground ahead of us and stop short. "Is that . . . ?"

My eyes are kind of bugged out and Casey laughs and says, "Yes, Sherlock, that's a hoe."

We move toward it, but before I can say anything about how Dusty Mike would not just leave his hoe lying on the ground like that, Casey yanks me behind a big granite grave marker and puts a finger against his lips. "Shhhh!"

And that's when I hear it, too.

Voices.

TWENTY-SEVEN

Dusty Mike's hoe is ahead of us and on the left. The voices are coming from in front of us and to the right. And even though I can't see anyone yet, I recognize one of the voices.

"The Borschman," Casey whispers with a grin.

We see him come into view about fifty feet to the right of the Sunset Crypt, and even though he's avoiding the hill the crypt is on, he's huffing and puffing like mad. "That's Gordon the Shovel Man with him, but I have no idea who that third guy is," I whisper back.

"Ricky the Rake Man?" Casey teases.

I grin at him. "Very funny."

But as they keep walking up the rise, I start to get worried because they're getting closer and closer to us. "Where are they going?"

I tuck farther behind the tombstone so I've barely got an eyeball wrapped around the right side of it, and Casey does the same with an eyeball wrapped around the left. But we have our backpacks and our skateboards and keeping all of it hidden is making things really *crowded*.

And then the third guy points and says, "There it is,"

and *that's* when I finally notice that in front of us and a little to our right is a pushed-over tombstone.

It's not lying flat like a fallen domino.

It's more half over, like an uprooted tree.

In a flash things go from a kind of fun Hide-and-Spy to a heart-pounding Get-Found-and-Die because I know that if we're spotted this close to that pushed-over tombstone we'll never be able to convince them we didn't do it.

"This may not look like much to you," Gordon's telling Officer Borsch, but we've got to take the whole thing out, level the location, get cement up here, and re-set it."

"It's a *ton* of work," the third guy says.

Gordon nods. "Teddy knows. He reset the ones from the first round and they weren't nearly this size."

It flashes through my mind that Teddy's a good name for the guy, because with his short brown beard and bushy hair he looks kind of like a bear.

Plus he's wearing hiking boots and jeans like he belongs in the great outdoors.

Anyway, Teddy says, "I'm dreading this one."

Officer Borsch walks around it, taking pictures and kind of analyzing the situation as he asks, "You say the first tombstones were pushed over a week ago Thursday?"

Gordon hesitates, then shakes his head. "It wasn't last Thursday—that was the day before Halloween. And it wasn't the Thursday before that. It was the Thursday before *that*."

"So two weeks ago Thursday?"

"Whatever you want to call it." He thinks a minute. "It was the sixteenth."

"And which direction did the kids come through that first time? Was the gate open, do you know? Or did they climb the fence?"

"Again, Courtney's the one to ask. I only got here at the tail end of things."

"Both times?"

He nods. "I didn't see the kids the first time, but I sure saw the headstones the next morning. And I sure saw them on Halloween."

"Could this one have been done at the same time and you just didn't notice it until now?"

Gordon shakes his head. "Look at the dirt. Dark and fresh."

"Why didn't you call the police?"

"In my experience, it's better to keep these things quiet. Reporting it, having it in the paper or on the TV, just makes the situation worse. It gives kids ideas. Pretty soon I've got copycats causing me more work."

Teddy chimes in with, "But now they've been through *twice,* and it'd be nice to stop them from coming again."

Gordon nods. "Exactly."

Officer Borsch puts his camera in a pocket and makes some quick notes on a pad, then asks, "When will Courtney be back?"

"Not until tomorrow. We give her flexible hours because she's got a kid, and being a single mom's not easy."

"Right," the Borschman grunts. He turns to Teddy. "Did you witness any of this?"

"I wasn't here those nights. Just found the tombstones knocked over."

Officer Borsch nods, then asks Gordon, "So what can you tell me about Ofelia Ortega's grave?"

"Who?"

"Ofelia Ortega. It was reported that her grave was dug up."

There's a moment of silence and then Gordon says, "Your source on this must be Michael Poe and I'm sorry, but Mike Poe is a nutcase." Then he adds, "A *disgruntled* nutcase now that we've let him go."

"Why was he fired?"

Gordon shakes his head. "He was scaring off visitors. He worked here a long time, and *I* was used to him, but the newer staff?"

Teddy Bear kind of huffs and says, "He weirded me out big-time."

"But it was Courtney, especially. He would appear out of nowhere and scare the hell out of her. I had several talks with him because she's organizing our records and I can't afford to lose her, but he lives in a different dimension."

"How long has she worked here?"

"Six months. Maybe it was having a woman around, I don't know. She said he would talk in riddles around her. Almost like incantations."

"Like spells?"

"Well, I never heard them, but he wouldn't dare pull that stuff with me around. Teddy heard, though."

Teddy Bear nods. "Yeah. It was weird stuff. Didn't make any sense but was majorly creepy. The guy's definitely not right."

"He's a Luddite, too," Gordon says, "so it's not like I was getting a lot of help out of him, anyway."

"A Luddite?" Officer Borsch asks.

"You know—a guy who doesn't believe in progress? He wouldn't touch any of the equipment. He wouldn't use the backhoe to dig graves, couldn't even get him to use a Weedwacker. Said he could do it all with a hoe and a shovel."

Now, while Officer Borsch is soaking this in, I hear *grrrrr-ruff-ruff-ruff, grrrrr-ruff-ruff-ruff* way off in the distance.

Just like I had on Halloween.

"Did you hear that?" I mouth to Casey.

He looks at me like, Hear what? but I drop it because Officer Borsch is talking again. "Do you mind showing me the grave, anyway?" he asks Gordon. "I promised I'd at least take a look."

Gordon scuffs at the ground with his shoe. "I'd have to go through the records and see where it is. Why don't you come back tomorrow and ask Courtney to look it up for you." Then he adds, "But when it comes to wild tales about graves being robbed, you might want to consider the source . . . and the motive. We do know how to run this place without Mike Poe, regardless of what he may like to think."

"Uh, it's getting kind of late," Teddy says. "Do you want me to start on that grave, or wait for tomorrow?"

"Burial's not until Thursday so tomorrow morning's fine," Gordon tells him. "Why don't you just call it a day?" Then he says to Officer Borsch, "Hey, I appreciate your coming out. I hope you track down those kids. Courtney thinks it's the same bunch. They were in costume on Halloween so all I can tell you is that there were five or six of 'em and they looked like they were somewhere between thirteen and sixteen. But Courtney'll be able to do better than that."

So the three of them go back in the direction of the office, and the second they're far enough away, Casey says, "What time is it?"

Not having a cell phone, I do wear a watch. "Quarter to five," I tell him.

"I've got to get home!"

"You want to go out the back gate?"

"The one we came through on Halloween?"

I nod. "It'll be a lot faster, and there's no way I want to risk Officer Borsch seeing us."

He's all for that, but when we get to the gate I can tell he's worrying about us being spotted together. "You go first," he says.

"You're the one in a hurry. It's fine. I'll just wait right here for a few minutes before I leave."

"There's no way." He nudges his nose across the street. "You remember how Hoe Man Mike said he lived right across the street? Well, I'm not leaving you in here or anywhere near here alone." He grabs my skateboard and backpack. "Go through and I'll hand you your stuff."

I grin at him as I squeeze through. "Hoe Man Mike?"

He grins back. "Guess you're rubbing off on me." Then he kisses me through the gate and says, "Meet me tomorrow at Sassypants Station?"

I laugh. "Sassypants Station?"

He grins and passes me my things. "Yeah."

"I'll be there!"

So I hurry across Stowell, and I'm trucking along through neighborhoods, trying to get home as quick as possible, when I spot a little girl with her mother coming toward me on the sidewalk. They're about half a block away, but what gives them away is the mountain of fur walking beside them.

"Elyssa!" I call with a wave.

"Sammy!" she squeals, and starts running.

It's a good thing her mother's holding the leash, because their sheepdog, Winnie, is yanking hard to chase after Elyssa.

When we meet up, I give Elyssa a hug and say, "Hi, Mrs. Keltner!" then sink my hands into the woolly monster's fur and give her a tousle. "Wow," I laugh. "She's gotten so big!"

Mrs. Keltner groans. "Don't I know! And she's not even a year." She gives me a one-armed hug, too, and says, "How have you been? It's been a while."

I nod. "Fine." Then I tell her, "I've actually thought about you guys a lot lately."

"Oh?"

"I've . . . I've run into Mike Poe a couple of times."

Mrs. Keltner's eyes light up. "How is he? The last few times we've been there he hasn't come out to see us."

I look down. "He doesn't work there anymore."

"What? Why not? Is he all right?"

I shrug. "From what I understand, he got fired."

"Fired?" She blinks like mad. "Why?"

"Apparently he was making people uncomfortable."

"Mike was?" Elyssa asks. "But he's the graveyard's guardian angel." She looks up at her mother. "Right, Mom?"

Mrs. Keltner strokes her daughter's hair. "That's right, sweetheart."

Elyssa looks at her all wide-eyed. "You can't fire a guardian angel . . . can you, Mom?"

Mrs. Keltner and I both just stare at her a second, and then Mrs. Keltner wraps an arm around her and says, "No. No, you can't."

I smile at Elyssa and tell her, "When I saw him, he said he still goes there to watch over things, even though he's not officially working there."

Mrs. Keltner drops her voice and asks me, "Do you know anything more? The cemetery is that man's life. It's his *family*. I feel horrible that he's been fired."

I sort of shrug and shake my head and bite my tongue, because it seems like anything extra I have to say will only make her feel worse.

"Well, anyway," she says brightly. "It was great seeing *you*. Come by the house anytime."

"Okay!" I tell her, then give Elyssa another hug. "See ya!"

230

Now, I was kinda late getting home, so I pushed extra hard to make up some time. But the whole way home what Elyssa and her mom had said about Dusty Mike was wrestling around with what everyone else seemed to think about him.

Who was right?

Was he the cemetery's guardian angel?

Or a nutcase who should be avoided.

I also kept picturing his hoe. Something about seeing it just lying there in the graveyard bothered me.

It was like *he* was just lying there in the graveyard.

I tried to shake off that thought and forget about him. I mean, maybe it was lying there because he'd gotten sick of being unappreciated and had thrown in the towel.

Or, you know, the *hoe*.

Anyway, as much as I hurried, I was still definitely late getting home. So instead of making excuses, I just came in and said, "I know I'm late and I'm sorry and it won't happen again."

Grams smiles at me from inside the open bathroom. "I hope that's the first lie you've told today."

Well, I'm more than a little surprised by *that,* but then I notice something else. "Lipstick?" I ask her. "Where are you going?"

"To dinner and a movie," she says all prim and proper like. "If that's all right with you."

"With Hudson?"

"That's right."

"Then it's *fine* with me."

"You'll have to fend for yourself for dinner."

"Ramen does sound good."

She sprays her hair, then gives me a little frown. "You can do better than that."

"Ramen and homework?" I say with a grin. "Just getting in shape for college."

"College!" she says, blinking at me. "You're not even in high school!"

"But I've heard all you can afford to eat when you go to college is ramen noodles."

"Who's talking about college?" She's seriously blinking now. "How can you even be *thinking* about college?"

I shrug. "They talk about it at school all the time."

"Who does?"

"Teachers, counselors . . ."

"Well, don't listen to them!"

I laugh. "Now that's a first."

Her face crinkles up and she says, "And stop it, would you, please? Just stop growing up!"

I go in and hug her. And then while she finishes getting ready, I get busy in the kitchen making my chicken-flavored ramen. When it's done cooking, I set myself up with soup and homework at the kitchen table, and the rest of the time Grams is there, I feel pretty good.

But after she leaves?

All of a sudden I have the worst time concentrating.

It's not because of everything that's happened, either.

It's because I'm home alone.

Now, what's scary about being home alone is not that someone might break in and mug me.

Please.

I live in an old farts' home.

No, what's scary about it is that I'm free to break *out*.

I can go anywhere and do anything and Grams would never know.

And as much as I need to do my homework, there *is* actually someplace I'd like to go. Just for a minute. Just to check.

But I'm also a little scared to do it, so I try to get back to my homework and forget about going anywhere. Trouble is, the more I try not to think about it, the more I *do* think about it.

Pretty soon I'm up and pacing around, thinking about it.

So I finally pick up the phone and call Holly.

"Hey," she says when she's on the line. "What's up?"

"Can you get away?" I ask her. "I need to check on something and I don't want to go by myself."

She hesitates. "Skateboard or no skateboard?"

"Skateboard."

"Time?"

"Now. It'll probably take half an hour."

She hesitates, then says, "So I should count on an hour?"

I laugh. "Meet me at Maynard's in five minutes?"

"I'll be there."

We hang up and then I scramble around getting ready.

I put on a dark sweatshirt and a ball cap.

I put a flashlight in my pocket.

I grab my skateboard and my softball bat.

Then I take a deep breath and slip out of the apartment, even though I know . . .

This is a bad idea.

TWENTY-EIGHT

I explained everything to Holly on the way over to the cemetery, and once we got to the gate where Casey and I had said goodbye, we checked to make sure no one was watching, then ducked inside.

Dusty Mike's hoe was not leaning against the wall.

"You want to park the skateboards here?" Holly whispers.

"Good idea," I whisper back.

So we put them along the inside of the wall and start moving through the graveyard.

"Déjà vu, huh?" Holly whispers.

"Oh, this is much worse," I whisper back. "And darker."

"No kidding. Why don't you turn on the flashlight?"

To me a flashlight is only for when you're desperate. When it's on, your eyes adjust to having light so if you have to switch it off you're pretty much blind. It's also like a little beacon telling other people that you're there.

But since it *is* really dark and I *am* feeling pretty spooked, I click it on.

"You're jumpy," Holly whispers after we've walked a ways, 'cause I'm flashing it around all over the place.

"I know! I'm just all . . . I don't know what to think!"

"You mean about whether Dusty Mike's a serial killer or a guardian angel?"

I whip around to face her. "Who said anything about him being a serial killer?"

She blocks the light from her eyes. "I thought that's what you were thinking. You know—because those three people have disappeared?"

Thinking about this makes my heart hammer even harder. "Do Meg and Vera know where you are?"

"*I* didn't know where we were going. I just told them you needed some help and I'd be home in about an hour."

"And they let you go? What were they *thinking*? It's nighttime! People are disappearing all over town! And I'm notorious for doing questionable stuff." Then I whimper. "I should have left a note for Grams!"

Obviously I'm having a little breakdown, so Holly tries to be brave, saying, "Let's just do what we came to do and get out of here."

"Right." So I try to be brave, too. I tell myself to take deep breaths. I try to keep a steady beam coming out of the flashlight. But in my head I'm wish-wish-wishing for a second softball bat, and every nerve in my body is quivering.

"We're close," I finally say. "It was right . . ."

And there it still is.

In the exact same place.

Dusty Mike's hoe.

All of sudden there's a rustling sound that makes my heart jump into my throat. "What was that?"

Holly snaps up the softball bat as I flash the light around the base of the nearby tree. "I don't know," she whispers.

Then we hear it again.

"Up there!" Holly whispers, and when I flash the light into the branches above, I see Dusty Mike up in the tree, ready to pounce.

"AAAAAGH!" I cry, jumping back.

Only it's not actually Dusty Mike.

It's an owl.

And it *bombs* us.

We dive down and the owl swoops right over Holly's head, then vanishes into the night.

"That thing's *huge*," Holly gasps.

I scramble back to my feet and yank her up by the hand. "Let's get out of here!"

Fear is like a runaway train. Once you lose control of it you just have to hold on and hope you don't totally derail and fly off a cliff. And Holly and I were definitely riding a runaway train. We ran and stumbled and fell and scrambled to get out of the graveyard as fast as we could. By the time we'd made it to the gate we were both out of breath and shaking.

"Wow," Holly says after we've collected our skateboards and squeezed out. "That was crazy."

We don't waste any time escaping up to Stowell Road, but by the time we're waiting at the light, the train's leveled off and coasting to a shaky rumble.

"So what now?" Holly asks.

"I don't know. It's just a hoe, right?"

She eyes me. "Meg always tells me to listen to my gut."

I think about that a minute. "My gut tells me something's happened to Dusty Mike."

"But if he's a serial killer, that's a good thing, right?"

"But if he's a guardian angel, it's not."

She nods. "So what are you going to do?"

"I really don't know." I look back down Nightingale. "He lives somewhere right across the street. I guess we could go door to door."

"Like, trick-or-treat for Michael Poe?"

I snort. "Yeah. Something like that." But then I get another idea. A *quicker* idea. "We could check mailboxes?"

"For mail addressed to him?"

"Yeah. If there's mail in the box, he hasn't been home today, right?"

"Well, at least not since it was delivered."

"Right. But it would also mean he wasn't expecting to be gone."

"Or that maybe he just didn't get around to taking in his mail? And if there's no mail in the box we still won't know whose house it is or where he lives."

She's right but I still like the idea. "At least it might give us a clue."

Holly's not so sure. "Isn't it a federal offense to tamper with mail?"

"We won't be tampering . . . we'll just be *looking*."

She checks her watch. "Okay. But we've got to be quick."

The houses all around the cemetery are like most of the houses in the old part of Santa Martina—small and either really cute or really run down, and most of them have a one-car, detached garage set back from the sidewalk. But the mailboxes are all up by the street, which makes it easy and quick for Holly and me to look inside them.

Now, in the first mailbox I do notice that there's a piece of paper taped inside the door, but since there's no mail in the box I don't pay any attention to it. But after checking a few boxes, I realize that there are little papers taped inside *every* mailbox door. So finally I shine the flashlight on one to see what these little pieces of paper are about.

"It's names!" I gasp.

"Names?"

"Of who gets mail here!"

We hurry to the next box, and the next, and sure enough every door has a little cheat sheet for the mailman, all in the same handwriting. Sometimes it's a list of last names, sometimes it's just one.

What we also discover is that we don't really have to worry about people thinking we're tampering with their mail, because it's so late in the day that every one of the boxes is empty.

And then all of a sudden there's one that's not, and staring up at me from inside the door is only one name: POE.

"This is it!" I whisper, and my heart starts hammering as I pull out his mail and flip through it. There's a gas bill, a Coupon King envelope, and a flat cardboard mailer, all addressed to Michael Poe.

I put the mail back, close the box, and look at the number on the front of the mailbox—736-B.

"Where's the B?" Holly whispers. "It's a house, not an apartment."

Now, I know from experience that *B* usually means that the garage has been converted into a place to live. So I whisper, "Come on," and lead her to the driveway.

It's bright enough from the nearby streetlight to see the little garage behind a low fence with a gate at the end of the driveway, and that the swing-up garage door has been plastered over.

"My guess is, that's B," I tell her.

We sneak down the driveway and see that what used to be the side of the garage now has a front door and two windows, and that it's got a big stick-on *B* on the doorframe.

"Sure doesn't look like anyone's home," Holly whispers, and she's right—there's no light shining out from anywhere.

"You want to ring and run?" I whisper back. "Just to see?"

"We could knock and say hello."

If I'd been alone I'd have probably just done a ding-dong-ditch, but I had Holly, a softball bat, and a skateboard, which together made me brave enough to go through the gate and knock on the door.

Nobody answered, so I knocked again.

And again.

Then I put my ear up to the door to see if I could hear a television or, you know, somebody snoring.

Finally Holly whispers, "Nobody's home, Sammy. Let's go."

So we head out, riding toward home pretty fast because it's already been almost an hour. And even though riding my skateboard usually helps clear my mind, my brain is still a muddled mess when we reach the intersection of Broadway and Main.

My gut, though, has a definite opinion.

Holly sees me thinking and pants, "Maybe he just went to visit relatives."

I shake my head. "Something's wrong."

"Are you going to call Officer Borsch?"

"He already thinks I'm nuts because of the skulls, and the guys at the cemetery made Mike sound like a real creeper." I know she's antsy to get home, so I just tell her, "Whatever. I'm really glad you went with me, thanks."

She nods. "I'll see you at school, okay?"

So she heads across Broadway while I go across Main, and then I sneak up the fire escape and into the apartment. And I do try to get cracking on my homework, but I can't concentrate. It's like my brain keeps walking slowly across a teeter-totter.

Up, up, up.

Over, over, over.

Down, down, down.

Then I turn around and do it again.

Up, up, up.

Over, over, over.

Down, down, down.

I can't seem to decide if Dusty Mike is a guardian angel or a lurking devil. I mean, I'd never spent as much time with him as I had on the day we'd followed him to Ofelia

Ortega's grave. Before, I'd kind of accepted that he was a little different, but that day I *had* felt the creeps.

What kind of person eats lunch in a crypt with dead people?

But then there was Elyssa and Mrs. Keltner's reaction to him being fired and how I used to believe, like they did, that Dusty Mike was a little strange but *kind*.

So maybe they just hadn't spent enough time with him.

Maybe he'd never told them about eating lunch in the Sunset Crypt.

But what also kept scrambling through my head was how often I had misjudged people . . . and how often they'd misjudged me. Like how Officer Borsch had thought I was a juvenile delinquent . . . but I wasn't. And how I'd thought Officer Borsch was a big blustery *jerk* . . . but he wasn't.

Well, okay, big and blustery yes, but not a jerk.

And then there was Shovel Man and the Vampire—two people we'd been sure were trick-or-treater haters. People who'd *seemed* like bad guys. But then seeing things from the other side of the table—or, actually, *tombstone*—they—well, at least Gordon—seemed reasonable.

Plus there were things Dusty Mike had said about Gordon that just didn't seem like the truth anymore. Like how Gordon was afraid of the old section. He sure didn't seem that way to me. We'd watched him walk right through it with Officer Borsch.

So maybe he'd just stayed away from the old section to avoid running into Dusty Mike.

Maybe it was as simple as that.

I'd also been wrong about El Zarape. I'd thought he

was a desperate trick-or-treater—someone kinda like us—but he turned out to be a skull robber who had no problem pulling a knife on a kid.

Added to all of that was the fact that everyone had jumped to conclusions about us, too. People at the cemetery thought we were tombstone-tipping troublemakers, but we'd had nothing to do with it!

So was Dusty Mike like us zombies? Strange looking and misjudged by people?

Or had *he* maybe pushed over the tombstones himself to get his old job back? Maybe this was a case of him faking vandalism so he could say, See? You need me here. This wouldn't have happened if I'd been here.

So maybe El Zarape had nothing to do with Ofelia Ortega's grave. I mean, come on—digging up a grave to take out the skull?

But then . . . what was El Zarape doing, running around the graveyard with two skulls?

Plus the office manager said she'd seen kids knock over the tombstones, which eliminated Dusty Mike.

So I really didn't know what to think. And by the time Grams got home from the movies, my brain was fried and my homework was still not done, and there was really only one thing I could think to do.

Pack it in and go to bed.

TWENTY-NINE

Heather was back at school the next day strutting around in a pair of distressed black jeans that had metal studs in the shape of a dragon going up one leg.

"Wow," Dot whispered. "Those must've cost a fortune."

Holly just shook her head. "I don't know how she does it."

Heather was getting a lot of attention for the jeans, but she still didn't seem happy. Oh, she'd smile and nod and agree that they were the coolest jeans ever, but when she wasn't holding court she looked all . . . furrowed.

I had nothing to say to her and that's exactly what I tried to do. But on my way into history she was waiting at the classroom door and hissed, "You're gonna wish you were dead."

"Cool jeans," I told her, and took my seat.

Still, I knew I had to be careful, and not just for my own sake. Maybe a sane person would be thanking Casey for defending them in front of Danny, but Heather was queen of Psycho City, so instead she'd do whatever she could to get Casey in trouble, even kicked out of the house.

And then at lunch I forgot about Heather because Marissa and Billy walked up holding hands.

"All right," I said, grabbing Marissa and yanking her to the side.

"What?"

"Since when did you start liking Billy?"

"I've always liked Billy!"

"No! I mean, liking-liking. When did you start *liking* Billy? When you found out he liked *you*? That's no reason to like someone!"

"I *do* like Billy. This has been, like, the funnest two days of my life!"

"But is this a rebound thing? Because if it is, you have to be careful. Billy's all funny on the outside, but inside he's a marshmallow."

"Would you stop worrying?" She frowns at me. "You'd think you'd be excited for me. You'd think you'd be happy I was over Danny. You'd think you'd be saying, Yay Marissa!"

I close my eyes and take a deep breath. "Sorry. You're right. I'm sorry."

So we left it at that and she went back to Billy and that's pretty much all I saw of her for the rest of the day.

Now, all day I'd been trying to keep Dusty Mike out of my mind, but he'd been there, sort of haunting me. And by the time school let out, I'd decided I needed to check some things before I met Casey at the graveyard. So when the dismissal bell rang, I didn't even wait for Marissa to tell me she was going to hang out with Billy. I just grabbed my skateboard and flew over to Nightingale as fast as I could.

The first thing I did was open Dusty Mike's mailbox.

There were now five pieces of mail in it—the three from yesterday plus an electric bill and a subscription postcard for *Horticulture* magazine.

I put it all back in the box, closed the door, and went to his converted garage.

The curtains were drawn, I couldn't hear any noise coming from inside, and when nobody answered the door, I checked the knob.

It was locked.

So I went up to the front door of the main house and rang the bell, and when a woman with a sleeping baby on her shoulder answered and whispered, "Yes?" I whispered back, "I'm wondering if you know where your neighbor is. The one who lives in the converted garage?"

"Mike?"

"Yeah."

She shakes her head. "He's pretty quiet. We don't say much but hi to each other."

"So you don't know if he has relatives or friends or . . . people he visits out of town?"

She shakes her head. "He works at the cemetery. That's about all I know."

I thank her and turn to go, but she asks, "Why all the questions? Is something wrong?"

"I'm not sure," I tell her, but in my gut I *am* sure—something bad's happened to Dusty Mike. So I get out of there, cross the street, squeeze myself and my stuff through the cemetery gate, and hurry over to the place Holly and I had been the night before.

Sure enough, Dusty Mike's hoe is still lying there.

Same place, same angle, same everything.

So I go back to the gate, squeeze out of the graveyard, then haul down Stowell on my skateboard until I get to a gas station where I know there's a pay phone. I pop in some leftover change from my laundry room scavenging and call Officer Borsch's cell phone. And when he answers, "Borsch here," I say, "Hey, it's me. Sorry to call *again*, but to make a long story short—which I know you like me to do—I think something bad's happened to Dusty Mike."

"Who?"

"Michael Poe."

A slow, heavy sigh comes over the line. Like he's just too tired to deal with me or my overactive imagination.

"Officer Borsch, look. I know that Gordon guy thinks he's a loon, and maybe he is, but Dusty Mike hasn't picked up his mail in two days, he doesn't answer his door, his neighbor hasn't seen him, and his hoe has been lying on the same grave in the exact same way for two days."

"His *hoe* has."

The way he says *hoe* is so huffy and slow that my mind flashes to an image of him in a Santa hat with so little jolly left in his big ol' belly that he can't even finish a ho-ho-ho.

"Yes! It's just lying there! In the graveyard! For days! Which I know sounds stupid, but I've never seen him without it!"

He heaves another sigh. "And how often have you seen him, Sammy?"

In my head I count quick and get all the way up to maybe six. In almost a year. "Lots!" I tell him, but he's right—it's not like I've seen him that often.

Or know anything about him.

"Officer Borsch, listen to me. Something's wrong. I can just tell."

"Sammy, this sort of thing happens all the time. People report someone missing and it turns out they're at a friend's house. Or they went away for the weekend. Or they're taking a nap. No one's reported him missing and—"

"*I'm* reporting him missing!"

He sighs again. "No *family* member has reported him missing. No co-worker."

"He was fired!"

"Nobody who *knows* him."

"Well, what if he doesn't have family? What if *I'm* the only person who cares?"

There's a moment of silence and then, "Why *do* you care, Sammy? From what I've heard, Michael Poe is a pretty strange character."

"Why do I care?" Something in my head snaps. "The same reason *you* should care! He looked after Elyssa last year when nobody knew she was running away from home to visit her dad's grave! And since her dad was a cop and you saw him get killed—"

"Okay, okay!" he says, shutting me up. Then he grumbles, "It would have helped a lot more if he'd called the department and told us a young girl kept appearing at the graveyard without supervision."

"But that's not how he is. He's just kind of in the shadows, watching out for people."

"So I've heard," he growls. "A real stalker type."

"How can you say that! You don't know anything about him!"

"I've been told plenty by the office manager and the cemetery workers."

I take a deep breath. "Officer Borsch, he may be strange, but he's nice and he cares, and it's really starting to bug me that nobody seems to care about *him*."

He's quiet a minute, then says, "Look, I can't do anything official for forty-eight hours."

"What about unofficially?"

"Sammy, do you have any idea what I'm going through here? I am buried in investigations."

"What if Dusty Mike's the fourth person to go missing?"

"It isn't even in the same ballpark!" he snaps.

"You don't have to get mad."

"Sorry," he grunts.

We're quiet a minute before I say, "I take it those other cases aren't going well?"

"We're getting nowhere fast," he growls. "They all just vanished. No trace. No ransom. No body . . ."

"Sounds like Dusty Mike to me. No trace, no ransom, no body . . ."

"Oh, Sammy, please," he says like he's rubbing out a migraine. "Just because *you* don't know where he is doesn't mean he's missing."

"I'm telling you, Officer Borsch, something's not right."

"And I'm telling you, Sammy, he's not missing until someone who *knows* him reports that he's been missing for forty-eight hours."

"What if no one ever reports him missing and he never comes back? Does that mean he's not missing?"

He hesitates, then growls, "Look, Sammy, I've got *real* work to do," and hangs up without even saying goodbye.

I stand there for a minute staring at the phone, then I slam it on the cradle and ride toward the cemetery to meet Casey.

Now, from where I am, using the main cemetery entrance is way quicker than going back to the sneak-through gate. Easier, too. And since there's an actual road, I just cruise up the driveway on my skateboard, go through the open gates, and keep on riding.

The road leads right to the cemetery office, so at first I feel a little like someone's going to come out and bust me for riding a skateboard through the cemetery. But I tell myself they drive *cars* through, so what's a skateboard going to hurt?

And maybe I should also have been worrying about someone seeing me and thinking I was one of the Tombstone Tippers, but I'm by myself, not with a bunch of other kids, and besides, I'm not really thinking about tombstones or Halloween.

I'm thinking about Dusty Mike.

And just as I'm getting ready to turn with the road as it goes to the left, I get a brilliant idea. I check my watch, and since I'm still running a little ahead of when Casey would be able to get to Sassypants Station, I hop off my skate-board and carry it up to the cemetery office.

The sign on the door says OPEN, so I turn the knob and go inside. . . .

And right away I wish I hadn't.

THIRTY

Hudson says that if you act like you've done something wrong, people will assume that you have. So when I walk through the cemetery office door and find myself face to face with the ruby-haired woman we'd seen on Halloween, I try real hard to act like I've never seen her before in my life.

Even though her van had practically run us over.

Even though she'd watched us slide down the Vampire's car.

Even though we'd seen her calling the cops on us.

I remind myself that I'd been dressed as a zombie on Halloween and that there's no way she'll recognize me. Still, the office is small and cluttered and she's staring at me, so right away I feel claustrophobic and panicky.

"May I help you?"

She has a beautiful smile—sparkly and warm—and I suddenly feel worse about any trouble I caused. Especially since it's obvious that she's in the eye of a big junk storm. There are files and papers and boxes and catalogs and boots and jackets and a leaning tower of ancient computer parts and printers and just *junk* all around her, but her desk is really tidy. It's got only a big desk calendar over it, a phone to her left, and a pencil jar and a small vase of flowers to her right.

I blink at her and out of my mouth comes a real intelligent, "Uh . . ."

What was I going to ask?

She laughs. "Or maybe you took a wrong turn?"

There are lots of chairs crammed into this office. Two in front of the desk, two off to the side, and one near another door that's straight across from the door I'd come through.

Oh. And then there's the one she's sitting in.

So I guess my brain figures it's okay to let my shaky knees take a little break, 'cause before I even know what I'm doing, I'm sinking onto the edge of a chair in front of her desk, holding my skateboard across my lap. "Uh, no. I, um . . . I'm actually wondering if you have files on people who work . . . or *worked* here."

Her smile fades a little. "Files on . . . Why would you be interested in that?"

"Because . . . um . . ." And then my mouth just starts motoring. "You know how at schools they make you fill out an emergency contact form where you have to put down who to call in case something happens? Like, if I fall and break an arm, they know who my doctor is and who to track down and say, Hey, this idiot daughter of yours was riding her skateboard down a ramp and fell and broke her arm. You know . . . that kind of thing?"

She grins at me. "Sure."

"So is there something like that at places where people work?"

Just then the door on the other side of the office opens and Teddy Bear walks in saying, "Hey, Courtney—" and then he sees me. "Oh, hi. You her sitter for tonight?"

I shake my head and look at Ruby Red, who laughs and says to him, "Give me five, would you?"

And that's when the weirdest thing happens.

I hear that pack of dogs again.

Grrrrr-ruff-ruff-ruff, grrrrr-ruff-ruff-ruff.

Only this time the dogs go from being somewhere out there in the distance to being *loud*.

And *tinny*.

Before I can finish blinking, ol' Teddy Bear's swept his cell phone out of his pocket and is going out the back door saying, "What's up?"

Half of my brain feels stun-gunned, and the other half is zapping around trying to wake up the first half. But it's like there's a force field between the two halves and nothing's getting through.

"So yes, we have personnel records," Ruby Red is saying, "but it's against the law for me to share them with you."

"Huh? Oh."

"Who were you wanting to know about?"

Half of my brain's screaming, Get up! Leave! but apparently my mouth's wired to the other half, because it says, "Michael Poe." Then real fast, I add, "I know he's a little strange and all that, but he's been really nice to a friend of mine and we're worried about him because he hasn't been home in two days."

She stares at me a minute, then says, "I wouldn't worry about Mike Poe. I'd worry more about your friend."

"My friend? Why?"

She cocks her head a little. "I wouldn't let my kid anywhere near him."

I just sit there, perched on the edge of the chair, and finally the lightning-storm half of my brain starts to break through to the stunned half. "So I should ask the police to look into his . . . what did you call them? Personnel records?"

"The police?"

"Well, you'd show it to them, right? So they could try and track him down?"

She stares at me a minute, then says, "Well sure. But I just can't imagine a young girl like you would have any concern over a strange man like Michael Poe."

I stand up and tell her, "I just want to know he's all right."

"Well, here," she says, twisting around in her chair and opening a filing cabinet. "Let me make sure we even have contact records on him. He was hired so long ago . . . I don't know what the policy was back then."

So I wait while she paws through files, and that's when I notice that her calendar has BURIAL written in red in certain boxes, with a time and a name underneath.

Something about that gives me the shivers. Her calendar goes from July to December—half a year laid out in front of her. And in the blink of an eye you can see what sort of month Death had.

He was really busy in September.

There are, like, eight BURIALS.

Not so busy in October—there were only two.

But already November had two written on it, and it wasn't even a week old.

"Here we go." She pulls a file halfway out, then thumbs through it and shakes her head. "All we've got is a mailing address and his phone number." She gives me a sorry-honey look and says, "And I don't think anyone here's going to be able to tell you much, either. He's a loner, and, sweetheart, honestly, you should stay away from him."

"So no one here's seen him the last two days?"

She shakes her head. "He was let go, you know." I nod, so she adds, "There was a reason for that."

I tell her thanks and start to leave, but stop. "Maybe *you* could call his number? As a favor?"

She hesitates, then shrugs and says, "Sure, I can do that." And after checking the file again she picks up the phone on her desk and punches in the number. And I'm watching her wait as the line rings, expecting her to tell me there's no answer, when suddenly her face clicks into action and she says, "Michael? . . . Yes, this is Courtney, I'm sorry to bother you, but there's a girl here who's concerned because she hasn't seen you in a couple of days. . . . Uh-huh . . . Uh-huh . . . I'm not sure, let me ask." She covers the mouthpiece and asks me, "What's your name?"

"Sammy."

"Sammy?"

I nod. "And my friend's name is Elyssa. He calls her Lyssie."

"It's Sammy and Lyssie," she says into the phone.

I put out my hand and whisper, "Can I talk to him?"

"Sammy wants to talk to you, is that okay?" But as she

listens her eyes get bigger and bigger, and then she says, "I'll relay that," and drops the phone on the base like it's contaminated.

"What did he say?"

"To put it in polite terms, he wants all of us to leave him alone." She shakes her head. "It's sweet of you to be concerned, but honestly, he's not someone you should be associating with." She looks up at me. "And obviously he's fine."

I take a deep breath and say, "Well, thanks," then head out the door.

Now, I was feeling kind of stupid. Stupid and a little bit mad. I mean, why had I wasted so much time thinking about Dusty Mike? Why had I been so worried? I really *didn't* know him, and it was pretty clear from what he'd told Courtney that he didn't care if Elyssa and I were worried about him.

Since I was now late meeting Casey, I decided to make a beeline into the old section by taking a shortcut across the pavement that went around the office. I'd never paid any attention to the office area part of the cemetery before, but now I saw that it was way bigger than just the office—it was a whole little complex. Next to the office was an open storage unit that had canopies and AstroTurf and casket gurneys inside it. And behind that was a wide paved area and two big garages. The garage doors were all open, and I could see a riding mower, a flat trailer, and some sort of oversized Tonka truck thing with a boom and a winch coming out of it.

So that was all a little surprising, but what made me do

a double take was something completely unexpected. There, in the big breezeway area between the office building and the garages, parked in the middle of two pickup trucks, a silver van, and a golf cart, was the Deli-Mustard Car.

I look around quick for the Vampire, and I can feel my heart speed up and my hands start to get clammy. He *had* seen me—at least the back of me—without my zombie disguise when we'd escaped the funeral parlor. And since I'm wearing the same shoes and jeans and sweatshirt I'd had on then, the last thing I want is to come face to face with him.

Since the nearest place to really get out of view is behind the Sunset Crypt, I cut up to it as fast as I can, then catch my breath and make sure nobody's watching.

I can't see the cars anymore because the garages are in the way, and I also don't see the Vampire anywhere. So I head out, moving toward Sassypants' grave, but staying behind as many of the big monuments as I can.

Casey's already at our spot. "Hey," I pant as I dump my backpack and skateboard and give him a hug. "Sorry I'm late!"

"I was starting to think you weren't coming."

I kind of roll my eyes. "I *was* early, but then I got sidetracked."

"Sidetrack Sammy," he says with a grin.

"Yeah, that's me." So we sit down and I tell him about running into Elyssa and going back to the graveyard with Holly and getting dive-bombed by an owl and checking Dusty Mike's mail and Officer Borsch hanging up on me and all of that. Then I take a deep breath and say, "But that wasn't the sidetrack. The *sidetrack* was going into the cemetery office."

"Why'd you go there?"

So I tell him about the personnel records and meeting Ruby Red and Teddy Bear's dog-pack ringtone and Dusty Mike wanting to be left alone, and about having to cut up to the Sunset Crypt because of the Deli-Mustard Car.

"Wait. So the Vampire's here? Now?"

"Somewhere! Or at least his car is. And since he saw you *and* me at the funeral home, I do *not* want him to see us."

He wraps an arm around my waist and scoots me in close, and for some reason he's grinning. "Copy that, Sidetrack."

"I'm serious!"

He gives me a kiss. "I am, too."

I shake my head and sigh. "This whole thing is so confusing. And I feel so . . . jumbled. Like I can't tell right from wrong anymore. Or good from bad. Or something. It's like what *sounds* and *seems* reasonable feels . . . off." I look right at him. "Why would a man not take in his mail, not answer the door, and yet answer the phone?"

Casey shrugs. "Maybe he's in lockdown? Depressed? Not getting out?" He eyes me. "Maybe he saw it was you?"

"What's he got against me? Besides, there's no peephole in the door, and the curtains were closed and didn't move. I watched. Plus it was dark. No light anywhere."

"Maybe he went out?"

"If he went out, he wasn't locking himself in, right?

If he went out, he would have taken his mail in when he got back, right?"

He gives a yeah-that-makes-sense shrug, and after we both look out over the graveyard a minute he says, "So maybe she didn't really call."

My head snaps to face him. "You mean she pretended to call? Why would she do that?"

He eyes me. "Why *would* she call? She's the reason he got fired, right? Because he was stalking her or whatever?"

"They didn't say *that*."

"Well, lurking around, being a creeper . . . same thing."

I blink at him. "But . . ."

"*I* wouldn't make that call. Not if I got someone fired. I'd let the police do it."

"But . . ."

"But she didn't know you knew that about her, right? So she could *pretend* to make that call, no problem."

"But . . ."

He waits, and when I don't actually *say* anything, he grins and says, "You're sure cute when you're baffled."

I laugh and punch him in the arm. "Shut up!" But right away my mind clicks back to Dusty Mike and Ruby Red. "I did ask to talk to him, but she turned it around."

"Turned it around? How?"

"She said Mike wanted to know my name, so I told her, and after she relayed it she said he said he wanted to be left alone."

He gives me a little smile. "Convenient. And now she knows your name."

I just sit there, blinking.
It seems so out there.
So unbelievable.
But still.
Something about it *feels* right.

THIRTY-ONE

Casey and I did talk a little about school and Heather and his mom, but that got interrupted when I saw a silver van drive from over by the office toward the main cemetery gate. "There she goes," I said, pointing down the rise. "Too bad there's not a way to find out if she actually called Dusty Mike." Then I throw in, "And where's the Vampire? And what's he *doing* here?"

"The Borschman said they're friends, right? Him and Shovel Man?"

"Yeah, but what are they doing? Having a game of poker in the shed?"

A little while later we got our answer.

"Hey look!" Casey says, pointing at the golf cart that's come out from behind the office. "You think that's them?"

I stand up and squint, trying to see better. "Wish I had my binoculars." But as the golf cart gets closer I can see that there are definitely two people in it and that the passenger has longish black hair. "I think you're right!"

"You want to move closer?"

"Sure!"

So we gather our stuff and scurry down through the

old section, going from one big monument to the next to avoid being seen. Ahead of us, the golf cart turns off the main road and onto a smaller one, then bumps up onto the grass. It zooms cross-country, right over the graves, and when it stops, we hide behind a big grave marker and watch as the passenger jumps off and grabs something from the back of the cart.

I nod. "That's definitely the Vampire."

"What's he got? A flag?"

Sure enough, it's a little black pennant flag on a tall skinny post, which he sticks in the ground. Then he hops back on the golf cart and they drive over a bunch more graves before stopping again.

Off hops the Vampire.

In goes another flag.

We watch them do this seven more times, and finally they stop for good. I have no idea what these black flags are for, but Casey grins at me and says, "Graveyard golfing."

"What?"

"Nine flags? Nine holes?"

"So the holes are the built-in flower vases?"

"Seems like."

Sure enough, Shovel Man and the Vampire both grab clubs, put down balls, and tee off.

"Unbelievable!"

Casey grins at me again. "But fun."

A white truck appears from behind the office and cruises along the main road until it gets close to the graveyard golf course, where it stops and idles. "See you tomorrow!" a voice shouts.

"Later, Teddy!" Shovel Man hollers back.

"Enjoy the concert!"

"Will do! Thanks again!"

"No problemo!"

So Teddy Bear takes off and Shovel Man and the Vampire keep golfing, and after a few minutes I look at Casey and say, "Are you thinking what I'm thinking?"

"That you can see how Dusty Mike did not fit in with the rest of the people working here?"

"That is *not* what I'm thinking."

"But you can, right?"

"So you're okay with people riding golf carts over graves and golfing in the graveyard? You don't think it's a little disrespectful?"

He shrugs. "Come on, Sammy. There's no one else here. Besides, if you buried people for a living—if you *embalmed* them—you'd need to have a way to lighten things up." He looks at me. "So what were you thinking that I wasn't thinking?"

I eye him. "That everyone's out of the office."

It takes him a minute. "You're kidding."

I shake my head.

He hesitates. "Is this payback for infiltrating the funeral home?"

"Parlor," I say with a grin, then grab his hand and pull.

"You're serious."

"It's probably locked."

"But why?"

I pull him along. "Check call history? Find the file on Dusty Mike?"

We keep one eye on the graveyard golfers as we hurry through the old side toward the office, taking a little detour to park our backpacks and skateboards behind the Sunset Crypt.

"Is this really that important?" Casey asks as we're closing in on the garages. "If I get busted for breaking and entering—and busted with *you*—I'm gonna be in a world of hurt."

"We won't break, okay? And it's probably locked, so we won't even be entering." We take a second to check to make sure the coast is clear, then move along the parking area between the garages and the office. The garage doors are all still open, and there doesn't seem to be anyone around. "Helloooo," I call, "Anyone here?"

We pass by the Deli-Mustard Car and I kinda cringe when I see that the wiper is still bent.

"Is there a back door?" Casey whispers.

"Right there," I tell him, and it's actually wide open.

"Helloooo?" I call again, leaning in through the doorway, only it's not the back door to the office—it's a door to a break room, complete with a little TV, a microwave, a water cooler, and two beat-up couches.

Nobody's taking a break in it, though, and straight across from me is what must be the back door to the office.

"I can't believe they leave everything wide open like this," Casey whispers.

I take one last look down the breezeway and tell Casey, "You stand guard and I'll go in."

"What's our signal?"

"How about 'Someone's coming!'"

He laughs. "Sounds good."

"And if you have to bail, I'll meet you back up at the Sunset Crypt."

"I won't bail."

I smile at him, then zip across the break room, grab the doorknob, and turn.

And just like that I'm inside the office.

I give Casey the thumbs-up, then leave the door open and go straight to the file cabinet. But after three minutes of pawing through it, I still haven't found the file on Dusty Mike.

"Anything?" Casey calls.

"No!" So I look another minute, then give up and start checking out the phone. It's an ancient desk console, though, with a lot of buttons and I can't find anyplace that shows call history.

Plus the longer I'm in there the more amped I get and the less I seem able to *think*.

"How we doing?" Casey calls.

"Terrible! I can't figure out this phone."

A second later he gives me a heart attack, 'cause he's standing right there. "Let me see."

So I step aside and let him have at it. The desk calendar has phone numbers and notes and stuff written on it in pencil, so I scan it for anything that might have to do with Dusty Mike. But the red BURIALs keep distracting me. And then I notice that they're in sort of an L-shape. Down two, over one. Down two, over one. Like the way a horse moves in chess. Which makes my mind flash through that dream

I'd had about the Headless Horseman and the sidewalk sections popping up as tombstones.

"I can't figure it out," Casey is saying, which shakes me off my horse. And then I hear a motor running outside.

"They're back!" I gasp.

We look at each other with bug eyes, then as quick as I can I pull the back office door closed and escape with Casey out the front.

We sneak around the buildings and over to the old section, where we hide out behind a big granite monument and catch our breath. "That was close!" Casey whispers. We wait another minute, and since no one seems to be looking for us, we make our way up to the Sunset Crypt.

"At least I didn't drag you into a corpse cooler, right?" I ask when we've collected our stuff, but the truth is I'm feeling pretty stupid. I'd almost gotten us in huge trouble, and for what?

"Are you sure you were looking in the right file drawer?"

"Positive. There were a lot of folders, so maybe I missed it, but I don't think so."

"So maybe she was faking the whole thing. Maybe that was her way of getting you to stop worrying about a guy she thinks is a creeper." And before I can say, Or maybe she just didn't want me to call the police, he gives me a sweet smackeroo on the lips and says, "You are big trouble, you know that? If this keeps up, I'm going to be kicked out of the house by the end of the week!"

I look at my watch and gasp. "You're late!"

"I know!"

So we run to the gate on Nightingale, and this time he doesn't argue when I tell him to go first. "Meet me tomorrow?" he asks through the bars.

I laugh. "If you think your nerves can take it!"

"I'll be there!"

I watch him go, and then, before I head home, I cross the street and check Dusty Mike's mailbox.

The mail's still there.

I also knock on his door.

Still no answer.

On my ride home I try to make sense of the noise in my brain, but I can't seem to stop the static. There is one sound that chimes through, though, and that's Teddy Bear's ringtone. I was sure I'd heard it when we'd been racing across the graveyard on Halloween night. No one else had, though, so . . . had I just imagined it? Or maybe it *had* been a real pack of dogs like I'd thought on Halloween.

No, I told myself, it couldn't have been real dogs. Where had they been? Where had they gone? What had shut them up?

And *no*, I told myself, I didn't imagine it.

But if it *had* been Teddy Bear's phone ringing, where had he been? He told Officer Borsch he wasn't there on Halloween, so did someone else have his phone?

Did someone else have that same ringtone?

In the still night air, sounds could really carry, but . . . how far?

And from where?

"I'm so glad you're home," Grams says the instant I've slipped through the door. "I had a conversation with your mother today."

"Uh-oh."

She pats the couch, inviting me to sit beside her. "She thinks you meeting Casey in the graveyard is a bad idea."

"You told her?"

"Well, she is your mother and she's entitled to know." Then she adds, "And I'm not so sure I like the idea, either. A graveyard is just not a healthy place for young people to spend so much time."

I plop down on the couch. "Well, great. Just great. You think you might have talked to *me* first? 'Cause Mom's for sure told Casey's dad and he's probably discussing it with Crazy Candi as we speak! Which means that Casey will get kicked out of the house!"

"That makes no sense. Why would Candi do that?"

"Because she's forbidden Casey to see me, and if he does, he's kicked out of the house."

She blinks at me through her glasses. "So why is he seeing you?"

"Because his mother's irrational, crazy, and jealous! Just like his sister! You know that!" I hold my head. "I can't believe you *told* her!"

"Well, I'm sorry, but she *is* your mother. And a picnic is one thing. But every day after school?"

"It's only been two days!"

"Do you have plans for tomorrow?"

I look down and let out a big puffy-cheeked sigh.

She nods. "We need to establish some guidelines. Some limits. And what about homework? How are you doing in school?"

"Wait—what happened to you thinking I was so responsible? So grown-up? Where did that go?"

It's her turn to look down.

"Grams, she may think she can be a parent from Hollywood, but guess what? She can't." I put my hand on her knee. "What do *you* think?"

She sighs. "I think young people should not meet in a graveyard."

Now, a week ago I would have said, I agree! It's weird! But it didn't seem weird to me anymore. It seemed . . . nice. So instead I tell her, "It's not like we have some morbid obsession with death. We only meet there because Casey doesn't think Heather will ever see us there."

"I think you're too young to be this serious about a boy."

I take a deep breath. "You need to trust me, okay?"

She looks me right in the eye. "I need to set down some ground rules."

"Fine. But I can't call him and he can't call me unless it's from a pay phone because of his mother. And we don't go to the same school. And his mother says he has to be home by five. And we can't meet at the mall or the library or somewhere normal because Heather is out there roaming wild. So what does that leave?"

She puts a hand to her forehead and nods. "The graveyard, after school."

"Exactly."

"Can we at least choose some days?"

"You mean like Mondays, Wednesdays, and Fridays?"

She shakes her head. "I don't know. The whole thing just seems wrong. If he's living under his mother's roof, he should be abiding by his mother's rules."

"Even if she's psycho?"

"If she's truly psycho, he shouldn't be living with her at all."

"Bingo."

"But in the meantime . . ."

"In the meantime what?"

"You need to abide by Candi's rules." She takes a deep breath. "Just like you need to abide by my rules while you're living here."

"So . . . are you saying your rule is Candi's rule? That I'm not allowed to see him?"

"I don't know! Yes!" She waves her hands frantically at the sides of her head. "I just don't feel right undermining another parent's authority."

She didn't want to discuss it anymore after that, and it put a huge damper on anything else we might have talked about during dinner. And after dishes she took a book and a glass of water and said, "I'm exhausted," and pretty much locked herself in her room.

A book and bed sounded really good to me, too, but I was way behind on my homework, and my binder and papers were a mess.

So I emptied my backpack and all the rumpled papers and got things separated and organized. Then I started catching up my school calendar. I wrote the assigned homework in regular lead pencil, the projects in blue pencil, and the tests in red.

Now, normally when I catch up my calendar I have this big feeling of relief, because instead of my schoolwork being like a big stressball in my brain, it becomes a beast I can see.

Can *tackle*.

But this time writing the word *test* felt like the word *burial* on Courtney's calendar. It wasn't just that I was so far behind in my classes that facing tests felt a little like facing death. It was that it got me thinking about everything that had happened. And maybe my brain was just trying to avoid death by homework, I don't know, but it kept picturing the word *burial* on Courtney's calendar, and I found myself writing it on mine. Under the homework that was due tomorrow, under the test I had in language, there was now a red BURIAL.

I didn't like the thought that there was a burial tomorrow. I could picture the Vampire embalming the body in the back room of the Bosley-Moore Funeral Home. I could picture the coffin. I could picture all the people gathered around the grave. It was like seeing the future, and something about it felt like *my* future.

I tried to shake off the heebie-jeebies of that thought. It wasn't *my* burial tomorrow. It was somebody else's. Someone who was already dead.

And I tried to get back to updating my school assignments, but instead I found myself writing *burial* in my November 1st box. And before you know it, I'm flipping back to October and duplicating the L-shape I had seen on

Courtney's calendar. I wrote *burial* on the 2nd, then went down two and over one and wrote *burial* on the 17th.

Then I just sat there, not knowing why I was writing *burial* all over my calendar.

Maybe I *did* have a morbid obsession with death.

So I shake it off again and get back to organizing my papers. But then in my head I can hear Gordon telling Officer Borsch that October 16th was the day the tombstones were knocked over the first time.

How did he remember it was the 16th?

I went back to the calendar and drew a tombstone on the 16th *and* one on Halloween, because that was the other day someone knocked over a tombstone.

And that's when I realize that both squares with tombstones are next to squares with red BURIALs.

My skin tries to crawl. It's like a baby shiver, wanting to be big but just not having enough, you know, *muscle.* But it does feel like there's something to this, so I just sit there, staring at my calendar, flipping back and forth between October and November.

Had anything bad happened in the graveyard the night before October 2nd?

Was something bad going to happen tonight?

And then, like ink being sprayed onto my brain, I can see the opening sentence of the "Halloween Horrors" article in the newspaper: *October ended the way it began—with a mysterious disappearance.*

All of a sudden my shiver's got muscle.

Big-time muscle.

And as I sit there staring at my calendar, little bits and

pieces from the past week snap together in my head. Pretty soon my lips are dry, my hands turn sweaty, and there's one loud thought pounding through my head.

What better place to hide a chicken than a chicken coop?

THIRTY-TWO

I sat there with my heart banging and my mind racing, and finally I got up and put my ear to Grams' door. It was only a little past eight-thirty, but I could hear her in there, snoring.

So I went to the kitchen, and as quietly as I could I dialed Officer Borsch.

It rolled straight over to voice mail.

"It's Sammy," I whispered. "I think Dusty Mike is dead. . . . Where are you? I really wish you were there. . . . Anyway, if you get this, I'll be at the graveyard. I think they're going to hide his body tonight."

I hang up, then tiptoe back over to Grams' door, and when I hear she's still snoring, I grab a flashlight and my softball bat, put on my dark blue sweatshirt and my baseball cap, and start for the door.

But I'm scared.

I'm actually more scared than I've ever been.

So I turn around and make another phone call.

"Marissa?" I whisper when she answers the phone. "I need you to do me a big favor."

"Why are you whispering?"

"Just listen. Please just listen."

"What's wrong?"

"I need you to call Billy and have him call Casey."

"Why don't *you* just call Casey?"

"Marissa, please. I can't explain. This is very important, okay? Call Billy and have him tell Casey to meet me at the Sunset Crypt as soon as he can."

"The Sunset Crypt? In the *graveyard? Now?*"

"It's a long story, and I've got no time."

"Are you in trouble? What's going on?"

"Look, I've got to go. I'm counting on you to get the message to him. Do it *now.*"

Then I hang up the phone.

Before I leave the apartment, I set up the couch to make it look like I'm in bed and turn out the lights. Then I grab my skateboard and get down to Broadway as fast as I can.

Before I'm even across the street, though, I hear someone calling, "Sammy!" and when I turn around, I see that it's Holly, totally jayriding Broadway *and* Main on her skateboard to catch up to me. "Marissa called," she pants. "She says she's sure you're getting yourself into some sort of danger." She eyes the bat in my hand. "That you're going to the graveyard."

I nod.

"Why didn't you call me?"

Now, the truth is I'm *way* relieved to have her riding beside me, but what comes out of my mouth is, "Because I already dragged you out there once. And really, you should just turn back. I asked Marissa to have Casey meet me because he's up to speed on everything."

"So get *me* up to speed. What happened? What's going on?"

"It's really long and complicated and it sounds nuts."

"Like I care? Tell me!"

I glance at her. "What it comes down to is that a graveyard is the perfect place to hide a body. No one would ever think to look there."

"What do you mean?"

"Say someone hides a body in a grave *before* they lower the casket in . . . who would know? They dig graves a day or two before a burial, then they cover it up with boards so people don't fall in. Then the day of the burial they put a big lowering contraption over the hole that covers it up, and then they lower the casket into the grave."

"Are you saying someone could bury a *second* body in the grave the night before?"

"Exactly. They'd barely have to cover it up. The casket gets lowered right on top. No one would ever know."

"So who do you think is doing this?"

"Ted and Courtney."

"*Who?*"

"Ted works at the cemetery and digs graves. He's the one who fixed the pushed-over tombstones, but I think he also *knocked* them over."

"Why would he do that?"

"Because they needed some excuse as to why they were there after hours."

"They being Ted and Courtney?"

"Yeah."

"And Courtney is . . . ?"

"Remember that red-haired lady in the van who almost ran us over on Halloween? Her."

"What does she have to do with this?"

"She's the office manager."

"The office manager!"

"Right. Remember how she was on the cell phone when she almost ran the light? And then we saw her parked on that side street and we thought she was calling the cops on us? She wasn't calling the cops. She was calling Ted. And you know where he was?"

"Where?"

"Under those boards we ran over."

"In that grave?"

"Right. Today I found out that his ringtone sounds like a pack of angry dogs."

"So he was right there? Under us? *Burying* someone?"

"Courtney must've been calling, giving him updates. And I'm guessing that when she almost ran the light she was frantically telling him that Gordon and the Vampire had shown up and to *cover* up. Gordon said they went in to investigate why the floodlight was off and that Courtney told them she was there because she'd seen kids in the graveyard. *Again.*"

Holly's catching on quick. "So then she parked on that side street where she could see when Gordon and the Vampire left, and let Ted know the coast was clear."

"Exactly. And us being there just made things easy for her. Like there we were, proof that there were kids messing in the graveyard."

"So Ted goes and pushes over a tombstone."

"That's my guess. He's the one who led Gordon and Officer Borsch to it. He might even have done it after he found out the police were coming. They must've thought they needed a distraction, or insurance, or something to point to and say, See?"

"But how'd you find out that Courtney works at the cemetery?"

So I tell her about what had happened in the cemetery office and about the desk calendar and making the connection between the burial dates and the days people had gone missing. "You can't keep a dead body around for very long—it starts to stink! And the window of opportunity is pretty short if you have to do it the night before a burial. And since there's a burial scheduled for tomorrow, I've got to go there tonight."

We ride along for a minute and then she asks, "Do you think they've killed Dusty Mike?"

I nod. "I think he must have overheard them, or seen something. I think they're going to hide his body in the grave tonight. He's been missing for almost three days."

"So they've got to be pretty desperate to get rid of the body."

"Right. I think Ted bought Gordon and the Vampire some kind of concert tickets for tonight so they wouldn't get interrupted again."

We ride along fast for a little while and then Holly says, "Shouldn't we be calling the police instead of trying to take murderers on alone?"

"I left a message with Officer Borsch."

"You left a *message*? Ever heard of calling 911?"

"How would I explain this? How would I explain this in *time*? It sounds so crazy! And I'm not planning to take them on—I just want to go and see if there's anyone there."

"And if there is?"

"I'll figure that out then. Look, even if I could get the police to show up, I don't think it would help nail them. I think Courtney's the lookout and Ted does the burying. So if she sees the cops coming, she's either going to pull the plug or tell him to hide. If we're just watching from the old side, she'll never know we're there." Then I add, "Besides, what if I'm wrong?"

When we get to Nightingale, I check Dusty Mike's mailbox again, even though I know the mail's still going to be there.

Even though I know I'm too late.

And I really do feel like crying as I cross back over to the gate. It's just all so frustrating and sad. "Maybe you can't fire a guardian angel," I mutter, "but I guess you can kill one."

"What's that?" Holly asks.

I shake my head. "Never mind. Let's just get in there." But at the last minute I stop and tell Holly, "You don't have to come, you know. You can go home. Or wait right here."

"Are you nuts?"

"I'm just saying . . . I know this isn't safe and I shouldn't drag you into it."

"Tough," she says, squeezing through the gate.

She starts to park her skateboard by the wall like we had the last time but I stop her. "Bring it."

"Why?"

I look her in the eye. "It makes a good weapon."

"Wow," she says, and looks at her board like she's never fully appreciated it before.

"It makes a good bed tray, too, in a pinch."

"I'll have to try that," she says with a grin.

But that was the only joking we did. After that we were heart-whacking serious, going around tombstones and hurrying toward the Sunset Crypt. There was some moonlight, which helped, and I was glad for it because I really didn't want to shine the flashlight.

"Hey," Holly says, "aren't we near where his hoe was?"

She's right, and when I see it still lying on the ground, I hand her my softball bat and pick it up.

"Nice," she says, thinking what I'm thinking—that it would make a great weapon.

Once we get up to the Sunset Crypt we spend a couple of minutes catching our breath, and then I start to get antsy. "You can't see it from here, but there's a breezeway between the office and the garages. It's where they park cars."

"So you want to go see if there's a van parked there?"

I nod. "But Casey is supposed to meet me here. Can you wait while I look?"

"No. We should stick together."

"I promise I'll be right back."

"No!"

So we stand there with a hoe, a bat, and two skateboards, *waiting,* until I finally can't take it anymore. "Look, if the van's not there, then we're here for nothing! Either we're too late, or we're too early, or I'm just completely out of my mind about this double-burial thing!"

"I don't think you're out of your mind," Holly says. "I think you're right." She eyes me. "And I think we need some *patience.* It's only nine-fifteen."

I look at her. "Do Meg and Vera know where you are?"

"No. They'd both already called it a night." She shrugs. "And I stuffed my bed."

I laugh. "I stuffed the couch!"

"We're terrible," she says, but she's grinning.

"I think this is what Officer Borsch meant about friends getting each other to do things they shouldn't. In the last week I've cut through the graveyard, infiltrated a funeral home, ditched my grandmother twice, rifled through an office, and tampered with mail. And I took a friend along for every single one!"

"Or they took you along."

I let out a sigh. "It's not like we broke anyone's ribs, though, right?"

"Yet," Holly says.

And then I see a silver van pull up to the main gate. "Look!" I gasp, pointing.

We watch as Ted gets out of the passenger side and

opens the gate and then waits for the van to drive through before closing it. And once he's back inside, the headlights go off and the van pulls forward, disappearing behind the office.

"What are we going to do?" Holly whispers.

Just then there's a noise behind us, and when we whip around, there's Casey.

And Billy.

And Marissa.

"You're *all* here?" I gasp.

"This better be important," Marissa says, her eyes darting all over the place.

"You probably shouldn't have come," I tell her.

"So what's going on?" Casey asks.

The floodlight by the office switches off, and since I'm pretty sure we're running out of time I fire through the whole story as quick as I can.

When I'm done, Marissa's eyes are totally bugged out. "So they're *murderers*? And you're planning to take them down with a *hoe*?"

"Shh!" Casey whispers, then points down toward the road where Ted's cutting across graves on the new side, a short shovel on his shoulder.

Casey whips off the backpack he's carrying and pulls out binoculars. And after he's got his focus tight he mutters, "He looks like Smokey the Bear with that shovel."

"But where's the body?" Holly asks.

I nod. "It's probably in the van."

Now, I'm holding his hoe, and the thought of Dusty

Mike dead in the van is making me really upset. And I don't want to sit there just watching. I want to *do* something.

Pound someone.

So when Marissa says, "Don't you think we should call the cops?" I say, "Yeah, I think we should."

Trouble is, the only one of us who has a phone is Billy, and when we turn to him, he goes all crinkly-faced. "It's in my charger!"

I look around at all of them and take a deep breath. "I guess we'll have to use the office phone."

Then I huddle them up and tell them what I'm thinking.

THIRTY-THREE

Casey takes one last look at Ted through the binoculars. "He's moving a plank over . . . he's getting inside . . ."

"A *grave?*" Marissa whispers. "How will he get out?"

"Apparently he has experience," Casey says, putting away the binoculars. "At least we know where he is, but we'd better hurry. I have a feeling this won't take him very long."

I figured the van would be hidden between the buildings, and I had a pretty good hunch Courtney wouldn't be in it. If her job was to keep an eye out for unexpected company, she'd be watching from the office, where she could see the road in both directions.

Besides, the floodlight had been switched off, and that seemed like something that would be done from inside the office.

Now, since Holly and I have a hoe, two skateboards, *and* a bat, I give my skateboard to Billy, who's got nothing but jittery nerves. "If you hold it like this," I tell him, grabbing it by the axles like a shield, "it'll protect you." Then I switch to holding it like a bat. "Like this, and it'll do some serious damage."

"Against a gun?" he eeks.

There's not much I can say to that, so I just hand Marissa my softball bat. Marissa may be skittery, but she's a slugger on the softball field, and if anything needs slamming with a bat, Marissa's the one you want holding it.

Which leaves Casey with his skateboard, Holly with hers, and me with Dusty Mike's hoe.

"Ready?"

Billy answers by putting a hand out. "Zombies to the rescue?" he says in a shaky voice. And even though I'm sure it's too late to actually *rescue* anyone, we all put our hands on his. "Zombies to the rescue."

Then we slip through the darkness between tombstones and trees until we get down to the breezeway. "There it is," I whisper, pointing out the van, which is parked facing us.

My heart's slamming in my chest as we sneak across the breezeway. It's dark, so we can't see if anyone's sitting in the van, and even though I *think* Killer Courtney is in the office, I don't know that. But the horn doesn't honk and the car doesn't zoom off or anything as we approach, and when we're near enough, we can see that there's nobody in the driver's seat.

We can also see that the lock buttons are up.

I take a deep breath, grab the slider handle, and pull.

The interior lights come blazing on and inside is . . . nothing.

No backseats.

No body.

Nothing.

It's just a big empty van.

"Close it!" Marissa whispers, but right before I do, I see the curve of a smooth black piece of metal on the floor between the front two seats. It looks vaguely familiar but I can't place it until I lean forward and see the keys. "Look," I gasp, grabbing it off the floor. "Dusty Mike's keys!"

"Close the door!" Marissa whispers, and she's sounding really frantic.

So I close the door, and now I'm *mad* because now I've got proof—Courtney *is* a liar.

And a killer.

I slip the key ring over my hand like a bracelet, pick up the hoe like a bat, and head for the break room door. Dusty Mike is dead because of these creeps, and it's making me so mad I can barely think.

"Where are you going?" Marissa whispers, then she sees the look on my face and backs out of my way.

"She's stormin' the castle," Casey says, "Let's go."

The break room door's locked, but it kicks in easy.

The back door to the office does, too.

And then all of a sudden, there we are, face to bug-eyed face with Killer Courtney.

She makes a break for the front door, but she's barely got it open when Casey slams it closed with a foot. And when she starts punching the buttons on her cell phone, I give it an up-cut with the hoe handle and send it flying. "Where is he?"

She backs away from us into the corner, and starts hurling random stuff at us. Books, boxes, work boots . . . anything she can get her hands on.

But the skateboards work great as blockers, and while

Billy, Casey, and Holly are knocking things down I manage to get in and jab Courtney in the stomach with the hoe handle and shove her against a stack of boxes.

"Where is he!"

She grabs the hoe and tries to push it aside. "I don't know what you're talking about!"

I lean in harder and jiggle the keys on my wrist. "Oh, really?"

She obviously hadn't seen the keys before, because all of a sudden she goes completely quiet, and her face loses its color. Still, I'm in a bad spot and I know it, because without a body, what proof do I have?

A ring of keys?

I try not to let her see my doubt. "I know you're going to bury him tonight," I tell her. "I know Teddy Boy's in the grave now, digging it a little deeper so you can slip Mike in before tomorrow's burial."

"You're those brats from Halloween," she gasps. "I'll have you arrested!" Then she twists to the side and dives for the desk phone.

But Marissa's all over that, bringing down the softball bat like an anvil.

Which totally smashes the phone.

We all look at Marissa like, Whoa! And she cringes back. "Sorry."

"Find her cell phone," I tell Billy. "And call the police." Then I turn to Courtney and say, "This is your last chance. Where's Mike?"

"I don't know what you're talking about," she warbles.

"Fine. You saw what she did to the phone? I'm happy

to do that to you with this." I flip the hoe so the blade is now facing her. "Recognize this?" Her face twitches, so I say, "Yeah, I thought so. Mike was a good person. He looked out for the people here. And *you*"—I swing the hoe and send her flower vase smashing against the wall—"are nothing but a lowlife"—I swing the hoe again, sending her pencil jar flying—"*killer*."

"I didn't kill anybody!" she quivers.

"They why do you have his keys? Why were they—" And then, just like that, it hits me.

I'd walked right by Dusty Mike.

I'd been doing it for *days*.

"He's in the crypt?" I gasp.

Her face says it all.

"Oh my God!" I blink at her. "You just shoved him in there and left him to die?"

"I had nothing to do with it!"

Billy's found the phone and has dialed 911. "Yes, hello, right. We have a situation here? There's crazy people burying people at the graveyard?"

"Billy!" we all snap.

"Sorry! Sorry!" He hands the phone to Holly. "You do it!"

So Holly takes the phone out to the break room while Courtney looks at me and whimpers, "Ted's going to be back any minute."

"Sit down!" I tell her and she actually does. Then while Casey goes to the front window and Billy goes out to the breezeway to stand guard, I yank the pull-ropes out of the window blinds and Marissa and I tie Courtney's hands and feet to the chair. Then for good measure I take a dirty old sock that had fallen out of a work boot she'd thrown at us and stuff it into her mouth. "Suck on that, angel killer."

"Nothing yet," Casey says from behind his binoculars. "If we get over there quick, maybe we could trap him inside until the cops get here."

"Like stand on the planks?" I ask.

"That's what I'm thinking."

"Hey!" Billy calls through the break room. "There's a golf cart with keys in the ignition."

Casey and I look at each other. "Let's go!"

Holly's still trying to explain things to the emergency operator as the five of us pile onto the golf cart. And I guess I was distracted by what she was saying or else I would have said that somebody, *anybody* besides Billy should drive. But since I was distracted, and since Marissa called, "Shotgun!" somehow Billy got the wheel.

And he drove just like you'd expect Billy Pratt to drive. We about fell off to the left, about fell off to the right, got whiplashed and bounced around, and the whole time poor Holly's pleading with the emergency operator to take her seriously.

Billy did get us there quick, though, and just in time, too, 'cause Ted's half out of the grave when we roll up. And since none of us exactly wanted to *touch* him, Billy just guns it, driving the cart right at him.

"What the hell!" Ted shouts as he falls back in, and we all pile off quick and move the boards so they close off the grave.

"Hey!" he shouts through the planks. "What are you doing! Let me out!"

"That's what Michael Poe's been crying for the last three days!" I shout back at him.

One of the boards starts to move so we all jump on top, which makes him squeal like a stuck pig and threaten to kill us.

"Can you guys stand on the boards until the cops get here?" I ask them. "I need to go open the crypt."

"I'll go with you," Casey says.

"I'll stay and walk the plank!" Billy cries.

"We should probably stay, too," Holly says to Marissa.

So we start to take off, but just then a cell phone rings.

It's not the *grrrrr-ruff-ruff-ruff, grrrrr-ruff-ruff-ruff* ringtone. It's musical bells.

Courtney's phone.

Holly grins at the caller ID and slides it open. "Ted?"

"Those brats from Halloween have me trapped in the grave!"

"What do you want me to do?" Holly asks sweetly.

"Run them over! Get me out of here!"

"Not likely," Holly singsongs. "See, I'm tied up in the office with a dirty sock in my mouth. Oh, and those brats have my phone. Which they used to call the police."

He lights off some really ripe language, then beats the planks with his shovel. But there's no way he'll get out with the three of them standing on the boards.

"You guys got this?" Casey asks.

"Oh, yeah," Billy says, "I'm a master at walking the plank!"

So Casey and I hop in the golf cart and go flying across the graveyard and get as close as we can to the Sunset Crypt. Then we race up the hill to the front of it and stand on the shiny black threshold.

DISTURB NOT THE SLEEP OF DEATH.

There's a locked metal gate in front of a door that looks like it's made out of black marble. I try each key in the gate lock and it's the skeleton key that turns it.

The gate creaks open, and then I fumble through the keys again until I find the one that unlocks the door.

Casey holds me back. "This isn't going to be pretty."

"I know," I tell him, and all of a sudden I'm a mess. I can't breathe, my heart's galloping around, and my eyes are stinging with tears. "I wish I'd figured it out earlier."

"Maybe we should wait for the police?"

I shake my head and pull the flashlight out of my pocket, then we move inside and start down the marble steps.

The air goes from cool to cold pretty quickly, and as we make our way down I see that the walls are made up of rectangles.

And that the rectangles have beautiful brass plaques on them.

"So people are buried right in the walls?"

Casey nods. "I think those are the actual crypts."

"Like coffins?"

He nods.

We keep going down, step by step, and discover that there are places to sit. Little alcoves. Little benches. And marble stands with statues. I also notice puddles of wax. Like candles burned completely down.

"Mike?" I call, even though I know it's hopeless. No one could survive in here for three days. "Mike?"

We come to the floor of the crypt. I flash the light around and see that it's just a little rectangular room with brass plaques from floor to ceiling.

And then I notice a blanket in a corner. It looks like nothing *but* a blanket, but when we get closer, I see a tuft of black hair sticking out. "Is that him?" I whisper, because I can't believe there's really a *person* inside.

Casey kneels down and moves the blanket, and my eyes flood with tears, because, yes, it's Dusty Mike.

A pack of matches falls out of his hand as Casey pulls on the blanket.

It's almost like he's handing them to me, saying, Here—I can't use these anymore. But through my haze of tears something hits me.

"He's not stiff."

It barely comes out a whisper.

"What?" Casey asks.

"He's not stiff," I say louder. "His hand opened up!"

Casey realizes what I mean and puts his fingers on Dusty Mike's neck.

I hold my breath and wait until I can't stand it anymore. "Anything?"

His head bobs up and down. Just a little at first and then harder. "Yes! It's really faint, but there's a pulse."

"Let's get him out of here!"

But as I swoop down to grab his feet, the light shines on the two plaques he'd been curled up next to.

LANDON M. POE.

ANNA BELLE POE.

"Oh my God," I whimper as my eyes flood with tears. "Everyone thought he was a nutcase—he was just having lunch with his parents."

"Come on, Sammy, get his feet," Casey says as he scoops his arms under Dusty Mike's shoulders. "I'll go first."

So I hold the flashlight with my mouth, and we struggle him up the steps, one by one. And we're about halfway up, turning a corner, when we hear someone barking, "Sammy! Sammy, where are you?"

"In here!" I shout past the flashlight. "Call an ambulance!"

Of course it comes out sounding like, "Wa-wa! Wa-wa-wawawa!" but the next thing you know Officer Borsch is in the crypt, helping Casey carry Dusty Mike.

"Is he alive?" Officer Borsch asks when we're outside.

"Barely," I tell him. "We need an ambulance."

Officer Borsch has his weapons belt on over a button-down shirt and slacks. It looks ridiculous, but I'm just glad he's able to snatch his radio off his belt and call for help.

"They're on the way," he says when he switches off. "They should be here fast." He picks up Dusty Mike under the arms again and says, "Let's get him down to the road."

So Casey and Officer Borsch carry him while I shine the light and ask, "Did you arrest the other two?"

"The other two?"

"Yeah! Ted's trapped in the grave and Courtney's tied up in the office."

"They're *what*?"

"Didn't Holly and Marissa explain?"

"They were talking a mile a minute and I couldn't understand anything they were saying. I just wanted to make sure you were all right."

"So are other cops arresting them?"

"What other cops?"

"We called 911!"

"So why aren't they here?"

"Don't ask *me*. It's *your* department!"

He shakes his head. "Sammy, I got your message and you sounded . . . scared. In all the wild messes you've gotten yourself into I don't think I've ever heard you sound scared. So I just wanted to find you. I really have no idea what's going on here."

"Well, you might want to call for backup," I tell him, "'cause we've got serial killers trapped in the graveyard."

"You've got *what*?"

The ambulance is already coming through the gate, so I flash my light on and off at them to let them know where we are. "It's a long story," I tell him. Then I grin and say, "With lots of sidetracks."

He gives a rare smile back, and in his face I see something soft. Almost sweet. "That's all right," he says, and I swear there's a little catch in his voice. "I want to hear every word."

THIRTY-FOUR

Courtney was so glad to get the filthy sock out of her mouth that right away she started talking. She swore she hadn't killed anybody or touched any of the bodies—that it had been all Ted and that he was forcing her to help him, threatening that if she didn't she would lose her daughter.

The daughter she'd apparently snatched from her ex when she and Ted had fled from Wisconsin on embezzlement charges.

And when they hauled Ted out of the grave and over to a police car and he heard Courtney flapping her lips, he blew a fuse. "You backstabbing liar! You took half of everything!"

So they started screaming at each other, and it came out that they weren't the killers—that they'd "taken delivery" on bodies and made them disappear.

At twenty thousand dollars a pop.

So Officer Borsch tried to find out who *had* been killing people, and that's when the fighting stopped and they both demanded lawyers.

I knew sorting things out would take a long time, and at this point I was worried about two things: (a) whether

Dusty Mike was still alive and (b) how dead I was going to be when I got home.

We were *all* worried about being grounded for the rest of our lives, but somehow we each managed to sneak back home without being missed.

Even Marissa.

And the next day, instead of meeting Casey at the graveyard after school, I went to the hospital to visit Dusty Mike. I brought his hoe, and since he was sleeping I just sat next to him for a while, watching the heart monitor bleep.

I went back on Friday and found him awake. "Hi, Mike," I said softly. "How are you feeling?"

He just nodded. "They told me what you did," he said hoarsely. Then he opened his hand and tried to smile. "Thank you."

His hand opening reminded me of being in the crypt.

Of the matches falling out.

Of the feeling that he was passing something over.

Not matches, not life . . . some sort of *gift*.

Something I still didn't quite understand.

So I took his hand and smiled back and what came out of my mouth was, "Tell me about your parents. I want to know all about Landon and Anna Belle Poe."

He gives me a very weak version of the dusty raven look, then says, "They were gentle. And kind. And they taught me to feel the spirits."

And with a little prodding he told me all about how his dad had been a grave digger and his mom had kept house and watched after him, their only child. He talked about how his mom sang like an angel and how his dad could

297

whistle bird calls, and that the two of them would sing and whistle while they washed the dinner dishes together.

He also explained that he'd suspected for some time that something was wrong at the graveyard—and that he had a bad feeling about Ted. He told me how he'd been caught eavesdropping on Ted and Courtney discussing a payoff and how Ted had chased him down, taken his keys, and forced him into the crypt.

"Good thing I had matches for the candles, and the blanket I keep down there." He closed his eyes. "I dreamed I died."

"I'm glad you didn't," I told him softly. "The graveyard needs you."

He gave a small smile, but his eyes stayed closed so I left to let him get some sleep. But I came back later with Elyssa and Mrs. Keltner and just stood to the side as they talked. And when it was time to go, Mrs. Keltner invited him to come over for dinner when he was back on his feet and feeling better, and he said he'd like to.

Then on my way out I ran into Gordon and the Vampire in the hallway.

"Wait," Gordon said, "don't run off."

I turned around. "I'm sorry, okay? I'm sorry we cut through the graveyard on Halloween, I'm sorry we messed up your windshield wiper and dented your roof, I'm sorry we snooped through the funeral parlor and violated the dead guy's privacy—we thought you were bad guys, okay? But we didn't vandalize anything. We were just trying to figure out about the skulls, but it turns out you weren't after them at all."

298

"Skulls?" the Vampire says. "What skulls?"

I shake my head. "Never mind. The point is, we did some things we shouldn't have, but nothing, you know, malicious." Then I look right at Gordon and tell him, "But how could you have fired Mike? He knew something was going on at the graveyard—that's why he was eavesdropping on Ted and Courtney. He's worked there his whole life—his *dad* worked there *his* whole life—and you *fire* the guy?"

Gordon looks down. "I'm here to make that right."

So I felt good about all of *that,* and then on Tuesday Officer Borsch tracked me down on my way home from school and told me that they'd brought in special equipment—infrared or X-ray or I don't know what—that allowed them to see through the ground, past the coffin and the body that was *supposed* to be there, clear to the body hidden underneath.

"They're there, Sammy. And I'm sure they're the people we've been looking for. We'll need to exhume the graves and recover the bodies, but first they're examining all the graves that have been filled since those two started working there." He eyes me as he sucks on a tooth, then says, "I also had them examine Ofelia Ortega's grave."

"You did?"

He grunts, which I know in Borsch-speak means yes.

"And?"

"And Ofelia Ortega's bones are all laid neatly together except for the skull. It's gone."

I slap him across the arm. "See!"

"I know, I know—I shoulda listened." He shakes his

head. "But come on, Sammy. Even after reading about it online, it's still unbelievable."

"Yeah, but they probably think it's unbelievable that we pump people full of chemicals."

We're both quiet a minute, and then I ask, "So what are you going to do about it?"

He sighs. "I don't know. He's long gone by now. I called the Roggazini ranch to get some information on Ofelia Ortega, but the answers I got were pretty sketchy. My guess is she was an illegal who died suddenly. The Roggazinis probably didn't know anything about her roots, greased some hands to get the paperwork through and avoid any legal hassles, and had her buried here." He shrugs. "So where's the actual crime? In this country it's illegal to desecrate a body, but she shouldn't have been buried here. She should have been returned home where apparently digging up your relatives' skulls is something done out of respect and honor." He takes a deep breath. "So what am I going to do? Nothing. I've got my hands full with this double-burial nonsense."

"How are you doing on arresting the actual killer?"

He frowns. "The feds have taken over."

"The feds?"

"Turns out we're dealing with organized crime. Our three missing people seem to be part of a much bigger story." He gives me a stern look and says, "Organized crime, Sammy." He shakes his head. "Why did I think I could take a night off and go to dinner and a movie with Deb?"

I laugh. "Tell her I'm sorry!"

He frowns. "You have a way of messin' up our dates, you know."

"It won't happen again."

"In my wildest dreams," he grumbles, but under all the gruff he's smiling. Then he says, "One more thing."

"Yeah?"

"Danny Urbanski's hearing was yesterday."

"And?"

"And that young man is fortunate he's not three months older. If he was fifteen instead of fourteen, things would not have gone so easy for him. I can honestly say, though, that he's showing remorse. I've never seen a grown boy do so much crying."

"So what's going to happen to him?"

"The court set him up with probation and community service, and his parents will be paying for Reverend Pritchard's medical expenses." He raises an eyebrow. "Reverend Pritchard also requested 'a discourse about the Lord' with him. Of course the courts couldn't order that, but Danny's parents have agreed."

"Wow."

"Yeah. We'll see how that goes."

So after that the only thing that was still really *un*settled was Casey and me. Not *us*, but how to deal with his mom's rules about us. We had been talking pay phone to pay phone at school, but other than that, I hadn't seen him since the showdown at the Crypt Corral.

Grams totally stuck by her guns about it, too, but being a local news junkie, she did eventually piece together that the "minors who unearthed the serial killer's dumping ground" included Casey and me. I played everything *way* down, but it caused some sort of shift in her. I couldn't tell what it was, exactly. At first I thought she was mad, or worried in hindsight, but I really couldn't tell. She was just . . . quiet. I'd catch her staring at me as I was doing my homework, and when I'd ask her, "What?" she'd just shake her head and go back to reading her book or fixing dinner or whatever.

But then last night she picked up the phone and dialed a number like she was on a mission and nobody better get in her way. And when someone on the other end answered, she said, "Candi? . . . Yes, this is Rita Keyes, Samantha's grandmother? I'd like to invite you and Heather and Casey to join Samantha and me on a picnic tomorrow. . . ."

I look at her with huge bug eyes and she gives me one of her prim old lady looks and puts a hand up like, Don't mess with me!

"Mmm-hm," she says after a short pause. "Well, I was hoping we could start over. Get to know each other a little bit." There's another short pause and then all of a sudden Grams pulls the phone away from her ear, so even *I* can hear Candi screeching on the other end. Then the line goes dead and Grams stares at the phone a second before hanging it up.

"That went well," I tell her with a grin.

"The *language*," Grams gasps, and slowly she goes from pale to flushed. "How dare she!"

"Welcome to my world," I tell her.

She storms around the kitchen for a little while, then

pops a fist on her hip and says, "If you want to break her house rules, you go right ahead!"

"Thank you!" The next day was Saturday so I might have just had Billy relay a message to Casey to meet me for a picnic at Sassypants Station, but all of a sudden I get a flash of a different idea.

A *better* idea.

I want Grams to be there, too.

Her and Hudson and the zombies!

So I call Holly and tell her, and at the last minute I tell her to invite Meg and Vera, too. And then I call Marissa and tell her to bring Mikey, and I call Billy—because I've finally got his number—and tell him about the picnic and to get Casey to come.

And while I'm at it, I call Officer Borsch and tell him to bring Deb and Dusty Mike and Elyssa and Mrs. Keltner.

"At the graveyard?" he asks. "You want to picnic at the graveyard?"

"High noon tomorrow! Bring a blanket and a side dish. Be there!"

So the next day Grams and I pack the biggest picnic lunch you've ever seen, plus I bring my whole sack of left-over Halloween candy. Then I make Grams put on her red high-tops and we get Hudson to give us a lift in his sienna rose Cadillac.

"I like the look," he tells Grams when he sees her shoes and jeans.

"You're next," I tell him.

So everyone shows up and Dusty Mike leads us to a perfect spot near the Garden of Repose where we put down the blankets and spread out lunch. And pretty soon we're telling stories and eating and laughing our heads off.

In a graveyard.

So even though death still scares me, even though I don't know if I want to be buried or cremated or dropped in the sea, even though I have no idea if there's a heaven or a hell or a purgatory that you can get prayed out of, I do know that somehow when I'm in the graveyard with my family and friends, I feel happy.

Peaceful.

It's a place where I appreciate *life*.

So maybe it's as simple as that.

Maybe it's not about how you're buried or where you're buried or who prays for you or what you believe.

Maybe the way to rest in peace is to find some peace in life.

Wendelin Van Draanen spent many years as a classroom teacher and is now a full-time writer. She is the author of many award-winning books, including the Sammy Keyes mysteries, *Flipped, Swear to Howdy, Runaway, Confessions of a Serial Kisser,* and *The Running Dream.*

Ms. Van Draanen lives with her husband, two sons, and two dogs in California. Her hobbies include the "three R's": reading, running, and rock 'n' roll.